INVASION

Also by K.F. Breene

Darkness Series

Into the Darkness, Novella 1 – FREE

Braving the Elements, Novella 2

On a Razor's Edge, Novella 3

Demons, Novella 4

The Council, Novella 5

Shadow Watcher, Novella 6

Jonas, Novella 7

Charles, Novella 8

Warrior Chronicles

Chosen, Book 1

Hunted, Book 2

Shadow Lands, Book 3

Invasion, Book 4

INVASION

BY K.F. BREENE

Contact info:
www.kfbreene.com
Facebook: www.facebook.com/authorKF
Twitter: @KFBreene

CHAPTER 1

PANICKED BREATH LEFT Jezzia's mouth in puffs of white. The rough surface scratched her bare arm as she huddled against the wall. She closed her eyes for a moment, steeling her resolve, before bending slightly to peer around the corner. Darkness crouched in the empty space of the town's square, beckoning to her.

Heart in her throat, she ran, lengthening her stride on light feet. The tatters of her ruined dress flew out behind her. She wouldn't last long like this. Not in what she was wearing. But she had no choice. Master wanted an heir, and she had been chosen to bear it. It was either run now and risk death, or brave life locked in a gilded cage.

Her palms slapped the side of a ruined building. It had been burnt three years ago when the Graygual had invaded. She slipped into a shadow. Falling still, she listened.

Leaves softly clattered in the breeze like dancing skeletons. Somewhere a baby cried.

Or was that a woman? It was hard to say. Lately, one

could be heard as often as the other.

She wiped a tear from her cheek. Taking a deep breath, gritting her teeth so they wouldn't chatter, she eased along the wall as quietly as she could. A smattering of laughter sounded distantly to her right. Then, closer, she heard the siren of death: "She went toward the horses!"

Fear stole her breath and dumped adrenaline into her body. She ran. Blindly, unable to think. Tree branches *thwapped* her in the face. She waved her hands in defense, ducking too late. A root caught her foot, making her stumble. Her forehead bounced off the hard dirt as she fell. Up ahead, not twenty paces, a horse neighed.

Salvation!

Small stones scraped her bare knees. She pushed herself to her feet and ran on, moisture in her eyes blurring the edges of the yawning barn door in the moonlight.

"I see her!"

"No," Jezzia cried.

Terror ripped the sobs from her chest as she ran into the barn. Her body smacked into a padded chest and stomach, partially concealed by shadows. She bounced off, eyes going wide as she stumbled backward.

"What have we here?"

Jezzia's back hit wood, stopping her.

"A runaway, eh? You know what happens to runaways..." A large man stepped closer to her, a sneer coating his dirty face. In the faint light from a nearby lantern, she could make out the stains down his shirt front. Blackness gaped between a few yellowed teeth. Lust sparked in his eyes as his gaze roamed.

Tears running down her face, she covered herself as her mind furiously searched for a way out.

"She went into the barn," someone shouted.

"Wish I could keep ya." The man's voice grated. "But they'll torture me for that. A small feel won't hurt, though. Something to remember on cold nights."

His hand reached out to her. She squeezed her eyes shut against the grope she knew was coming but couldn't block it out no matter how often it happened.

The stable master grunted, then coughed. Wetness sprayed across her face. She flinched as the voice outside yelled, "Raton, bring her out. You know you can't have her."

"Woman."

Confused, Jezzia opened her eyes to the strange, musical voice.

The soft light fell across a face as handsome as his gaze was terrifying. Stormy gray eyes, hard and desolate, assessed her. His light hair, soiled and greasy, fell around his chiseled face in a disheveled wave. A foreign style of clothing, equally soiled, adorned a lithe but muscular body.

"Are you hurt?" he asked.

She looked down at the lifeless body of the stable master. She fingered her face and saw the glimmer of crimson across her fingertips.

The shadows behind the handsome man moved. Coalesced into an arm and shoulder, and then another face. Other men, then a woman, stepped out of the darkness like ghosts. Gleaming swords and knives caught and threw the light. Despite their dirty and scruffy appearance, they'd kept their weapons clean.

Jezzia grabbed at the fragments of her dress and pulled them tighter around her.

"Raton, you barking fool," came the voice. "Is Master's prize in there? Don't make me come look for myself. You know what'll happen if you get caught handling his possessions..."

The stranger's eyes narrowed as he glanced toward the front of the barn. His head tilted a fraction, before he looked toward the back. Within the deep shadows, metal clinked and chimed as leather groaned. More than one person was saddling horses, Jezzia could tell, but she couldn't see anyone in the darkness. She couldn't hear any footsteps.

They'd been waiting in the deep shadows, whoever these people were. The stable master could not have known. His death had been inevitable.

"Killing a Graygual will mean being hunted," Jezzia whispered as three people, two men and a woman, walked to the sides of the barn doors. The curvy woman smirked. Her lips moved, as if she were talking, but the sound didn't carry to Jezzia. The man in front of her chuckled. His smile seemed predatory.

"Burn it all!" Hard footsteps approached the barn. "I know she's in there, and I'm going to take great pride in—"

As soon as the chest of her pursuer reached the entrance, the stranger beside the barn door reacted. His limbs moved so fast Jezzia couldn't keep track of him. The Graygual grunted once, before crumpling to the ground. Another of the strangers stepped forward to help the first, dragging the body inside. Liquid spilled onto the barn floor before the body was thrown to the side in a splash of limbs.

"How many were chasing you?"

Jezzia blinked stupidly at the man in front of her. No matter how many people she'd seen murdered in cold blood, it still shocked her. Worse was the screaming, though. The begging for their lives.

Jezzia shuddered and dragged her mind from the memories. "I don't know. Usually they'd only send one or two after a runaway. There isn't far we can go. But I'm..." She tried to harden her voice. She hated the quiver. "Master had special plans for me. He'll bed anyone pretty and young, but I'm…"

She couldn't bring herself to say it out loud. And then she didn't have to.

"They think it's a great honor to be chosen for breeding." The woman beside the barn door grimaced while staring out. "They'll send more to fetch you. At least three, I would bet. They won't want you wandering off and dying from the cold. Such a kind people."

"Kind, indeed," the man who had helped carry the body said. "A quick death is too good for them."

"What should we do, Kallon?" the woman asked.

The handsome man—Kallon—stared at Jezzia for a silent beat. What he was looking for, she couldn't say. He turned his head toward the barn door, as if in thought. The others waited silently.

Finally, he said, "We can't take back the town; there are too many. I can't risk losing anyone. But we can take down the officer and anyone guarding him."

"Agreed." The woman nodded to emphasize her comment.

"It won't do much good if no one completes the job," the other man said. "They'll just move in someone else to take over."

Kallon's stormy gaze hit Jezzia again. "Are there many left who can fight?"

"Wh-what do you mean?" she stuttered.

"If we cut out the officer and those closest to him, it

will leave a hole. The other Graygual stationed in this city are weak, not much better than rats. They are not skilled. If we take out the officers, do you have towns-people who can fight? We can help mend this town, but we cannot cure it. We do not have the time even if we had the numbers."

Jezzia shook her head. "We have no one to fight the mind power. We tried—so many died trying. My father—"

"Is there anyone left?" Kallon's hard voice cut through the dizziness of her thoughts.

She wrapped her arms around herself to stop the trembling.

Willing bravery, she locked eyes with Kallon, feeding off the strength she saw there. She hoped he was as capable as he seemed, with his confident bearing and the determined set of his broad shoulders. She thought of those left in the town. She could think of a handful. Good swordsman all, these men kept their heads down and followed the rules for the sake of their wives and children. They hated every minute of it, though. They refused to be totally conquered.

"A dozen, maybe more," she said, biting her lip. "But, like I said, the mind power—"

"We will handle that," Kallon said in a harsh tone. "There are only a few Inkna, and they are weak. It is why we chose this town." He glanced toward the back of the barn. "Give her something to wear. We have no time to waste."

A horse stomped as solid shapes emerged from the shadows. Men and women, all wearing the same style of clothing, walked out of the black like spirits. Hard lines on their faces from stress and fatigue didn't mask the gleam in their eyes, or the smirks on some of their faces. If Jezzia didn't know better, she'd say they were excited.

"Quick kills and we move on," Kallon said as he drew a knife for each hand. "Close quarters. Aim only for those most skilled. Let the townspeople have their revenge on the others."

"And the officer?" the curvy woman asked, holding a dagger at the ready.

"Quick kill, like the rest. *Chulan* said to make haste. This is a distraction from our true purpose."

"A nice distraction, though. Killing Graygual is a wonderful hobby." A man who had come out of the shadows gave a throaty laugh. He nodded at Jezzia before tossing her a well-worn shirt.

"Who are you?" Jezzia asked as she pulled the garment over her head gratefully. It smelled clean, regardless of its appearance.

"To you?" Kallon glanced at her before turning away. "We are vengeance incarnate."

They moved out of the barn in a strange synchronicity, Jezzia steered by a middle-aged man with streaks of gray at his temples. Twelve in all, with at least another two left behind, the group stayed in a tight cluster, keeping her at the middle.

"You'll lead the way to this master," the curvy woman said as they moved along the outside of the barn wall, staying mostly to the shadows where they could. "We'll cut off his head for you. After that, you'll need to organize everyone. Sound the alarm."

"What alarm?" Jezzia asked, almost jogging to keep pace.

"The alarm that brings your friends out of their stupor," the aging man said. He was more severe than the others. As moonlight sprinkled down on them, she saw sorrow etched in every line of his face, a haunted look in his eyes. Jezzia wondered what he wanted more—to deliver death, or be taken by it.

"What has happened to you?" Jezzia whispered.

"The same thing that happened to you. My revenge will take longer, though. But I will have it, just as you will. We are kindred, you and I. Only in death will we be free from the pain."

"Tulous is an uplifting sort of fellow." The man who had laughed in the barn drifted to her side. "Not a great joke teller, though. Don't bother asking."

As they reached the edge of the square, their progress slowed. Two shapes lay near the middle, men lying on their faces. Silence descended around them.

"Who…?" Jezzia vaguely waved a finger at the bodies. "And…the men playing cards. Usually they stay up until all hours…"

The man next to her touched his temple. "I'm a crack shot with the ol' thinker, don't you worry. I'm no *Chulan*, but I'm no slouch, either."

"Sayas." Kallon's voice cracked like a whip.

The man next to Jezzia closed his mouth and winked at her.

"Split up." Kallon glanced to his right. At his nod, four people took off on silent feet, moving like wisps of smoke. Three more loped away left. Kallon's gaze landed on her. "Lead the way."

"But where are they going?" Jezzia whispered.

"They will take out the best of the guards. The ones keeping watch on your supplies. There are only a couple. We saw them coming in," Sayas explained.

Jezzia's eyes locked on the dead bodies in the middle of the square. When death had last graced the packed dirt, it had been her father and mother, holding her little brother as they had all tried to escape. She'd been ripped from their arms moments before the Graygual ran swords through them.

No one had tried to escape after that. They hadn't dared. Until tonight.

Agony welled up. Instead of turning to sorrow, as was usual, though, it flash-boiled into rage, matching the passion of those around her. She turned on Sayas, her mind fueled with fire. "If you saw them when you came in, why not kill them then? You obviously know what their kind do, so why wait until you're confronted with guilt before helping?"

"Ohhh." A smirk dusted Sayas' face. His eyes flashed. "She's got some fight in her. No wonder they want her. She'd produce great fighters."

"And if we were staying longer, I'd teach her how to use a knife so she could cut out your tongue for that comment," the curvy woman said in a dry tone.

"Forgive me." Sayas gave Jezzia a slight bow before nudging her toward the empty space of the square. Kallon had already started moving. "That was a horrible thing to say."

"We don't want to leave a trail for Xandre to follow." Kallon glanced back at her. "If we help everyone we pass, we will only save a few before the Graygual descend in large numbers. If we wait and reach our destination alive, we can hopefully save the whole of the land before the Elders call us home."

"So why now?" Jezzia's gaze constantly darted to the shadows. On a normal night, someone might be waiting in those shadows, watching. The watchers knew who moved around, and when. If anything looked suspicious, the Graygual would pay a visit. Soon after, the screaming would begin.

"You were right. Guilt." Kallon led the way to a small gap between two buildings. They huddled into the shadows. The vast, empty square pushed against their backs, reminding them that they were still largely in the open.

"Just over there is an alley," Jezzia said with an earnest voice. She stepped in that direction, but Sayas pulled her back. His smile was gone. He shook his head, keeping his eyes on Kallon.

A man, tall and broad, faced the wide-open square. The curvy woman looked away to the right. Kallon's head was tilted, his eyes on the woman, as if listening.

"Beyond the edge of the next building is the main road." Jezzia pointed in the direction the woman was facing. She glanced across the square to where the road went by the stables. "But you probably knew that. It'll have the most Graygual, though."

"Too many," the curvy woman said in a tight voice. "Too many for haste, and a waste mentally."

"Agreed." Kallon's gaze hit Jezzia again. "We'll take the alley."

Kallon jogged ahead, stopping at the corner and looking around. The tall, broad man crossed and waited at the other corner. Sayas remained by Jezzia's side as they hurried into the alley. The others poured in behind, quickly catching them up and overtaking, keeping Jezzia in the middle. Black pooled along the ground, only a filtered light from the moon dusting the walls.

"Mela."

At Kallon's voice, the curvy woman jogged out in front of the others, reaching the end of the alley first.

"Wait! There are usually—"

Jezzia broke off as Mela's sword flashed, drawn from its sheath. She turned the corner of the alley, lost from sight. A single cry of pain sounded a moment later, followed by a second.

"Which way?" Kallon asked, urgency in his voice.

"Left. We go left," Jezzia answered, out of breath.

Mela rejoined them as they reached the end of the alley. Behind her, filling a smaller lane, lay two Graygual. Blood pooled around their bodies. One's face held shock, the other, pain.

"A woman against two Graygual." Jezzia's voice was wispy. Sayas helped guide her. "A *woman.* Women fighting alongside men. I saw the weapons but I thought that was a rumor..."

"Which way?" Kallon said.

Jezzia led the way as her mind buzzed. Rumors and myths floated through her memory. Hushed stories of heroism and whispered words of hope rose to the surface. An end to all of this horror had been promised.

One name tumbled out of her mouth. "The Wanderer."

"Who is this Wanderer we keep hearing about?" Sayas asked as Jezzia doggedly came to a stop in the shadowed space across from Master's back door. The house used to belong to Sheridan, the town's most prosperous merchant. He was killed when he refused to let the Graygual through.

"There are three men in there," Kallon said, his head tilted to the side again. "And three women. Are all of those women…?"

Jezzia shivered, drawing in on herself.

Kallon nodded as if she had voiced her answer. He stood straight and still, staring at the house. As if on cue, the groups he'd sent earlier drifted back in from the sides, silent, but somehow communicating. It was like a practiced dance, each party having rehearsed the steps a million times, and now putting on a choreographed show.

"These Graygual are fat and complacent," one of the returning men said. "Easily taken down. Even the one with three stripes. They've seen no opposition in a while. They aren't expecting any resistance."

"It fits with what we've seen so far," Kallon said. "Townspeople?"

"We didn't make any sound. They are hiding in their homes, hoping no one comes knocking on their door. Like all the towns we've passed. Like our own town."

"Our town was lying in wait, not hiding."

"In these times, hopefully that is the same thing. We will see soon."

Kallon gritted his teeth. "Yes. Go back out. Kill every Graygual you see. Rouse the town. Mela, Sayas, and I will take these."

"All three of you?"

Kallon glanced back at Jezzia. "There are three captives. We bring the fourth. I want them safe."

"The Graygual are cowards," Sayas said quietly to Jezzia. "They'll kill all their captives if they think it will help them get out alive. Or if they are certain, they die. They will kill their captives at the first sign of trouble."

Jezzia gulped, fear bubbling up for her friends, one of which had moved into the town with the Graygual under golden lock and key. To the onlooker, they were pampered and treated well, given everything a rich wife might want. And if it were their choice, it would be a wonderful life, indeed.

If it were their choice.

Unspeakable rage welled up in Jezzia again. "Can I have a sword?" she asked.

"I don't think that's a good idea…" Sayas answered as the groups moved off as silently as they'd come.

"Why?" Jezzia faced him. "Because I'm a woman? *Your* women fight. *They* all carry swords. Why can't I?"

"They know how to use them. You might stab yourself."

"Here." Kallon handed her a knife, point down. Those hard eyes pinned her to the spot. As she took it, his other hand came up, fast as lightning, and covered hers. Seriousness bled through his gaze. "Killing will not make the pain go away. It will not cure your suffering, or heal your wounds. Recovering your freedom is the way forward. Peace and tranquility is what you seek. That is what your heart desires. I see it in your eyes. I read it in your bearing. I do not advise using this knife. Not if you don't have to, and with us here, you won't."

"Then why are you giving it to me?"

"Because we won't always be here. And because I can't tell you how to grant your own salvation. Only you can do that."

Tears welled up unexpectedly. When he let go, she brought the knife closer. "I understand."

He watched her for one more heartbeat before turning back to the house. Sayas stayed beside her, Mela next to Kallon.

They waited in silence. Just waited, and watched.

A hawk screeched in the distance. Someone shrieked in the house. Jezzia squeezed the handle of her blade.

A hoarse scream tore through the night from the distance. Flickering lights danced to life in a few windows. More screams and shouts.

Kallon and Mela started forward, as if one of them had said "go!"

"You stay behind me at all times," Sayas told Jezzia as she stepped forward after them. "You stay safe above all else. If the worst happens, run. Got it?"

"No. This is my fight, too."

"This will be your deathbed unless you listen to me."

Kallon and Mela scaled the steps gracefully, like dancers. Jezzia trudged after them, anxiety and adrenaline making her hands shake and her teeth chatter. She hadn't felt the cold like this for some time.

They burst through the door and hustled through the kitchen, pausing when showered with the illumination of a roomful of candles. Three girls jumped up from the couch, wide-eyed and terrified. Master burst out of his chamber, pulling on his shirt. The two other Graygual were each at a window at the front, no doubt alerted by the disturbance.

"Remember us, you sludge?" Sayas said in a voice out of a nightmare. He tossed a knife up in the air, caught it by the blade, and threw. The blade blossomed in the neck of one of the Graygual at the window. The man garbled out a scream, clutching his throat as blood welled up between his fingers.

Mela danced forward, lithe and agile, dagger in her hand. The other Graygual turned from the window, a sword coming up. His knees bent, ready for her. She stopped her advance just out of his reach, waiting as patiently as if he was pouring tea.

"I thought we had killed all of your kind," Master growled, holding up his sword.

Kallon stared at him through smoldering, hate-filled eyes. "That was the plan. Do up your laces. I'd hate for you to die thinking you could've bested me if only you had tied your boots."

Sayas chuckled as the other Graygual struck at Mela. She turned a fraction, the movement small, but his sword sliced through the air beside her, the blade so close it rustled the fabric of her top. She stabbed, the action as beautiful as it was lethal. Her dagger sliced his sword arm, making him grunt. His sword clattered to the ground, his hand going lifeless.

"Dismal. Very out of practice, ay?" Mela stepped forward and stabbed again. He tried to move as she had done, but his movements were jarring and clumsy. He couldn't get out of the way in time.

Her blade pierced his side. He grunted again, and staggered. His body fell against the wall. Blood stained the floor in bright red splashes.

The movement of Master drew Jezzia's gaze. She cried out as his sword struck. Kallon batted the blade to the side lazily. Master was ready again, lunging almost immediately. Kallon batted that one away, too, stepping back. Master stepped forward, striking. They had reached the mouth of the hallway, Master chasing the other man across the floor.

"Help him!" Jezzia cried, her knuckles white where they gripped the hilt of her knife. She stepped forward, trying to aid him, but Sayas grabbed her. "Let me go—he needs help! Master is an excellent swordsman."

"Kallon, we don't have time for this," Mela said.

Kallon showed his teeth to the Graygual in a silent growl. "Our duty is keeping you from the slow death you deserve." He stepped forward and to the side, his movements suddenly so fast they were nearly lost to the eye. His blade flicked and moved, like a living thing, slashing fabric and skin alike.

Master grunted, swinging his own blade, backing them away. His face went pale. Shock leaked into his eyes. Then fear. He lunged, wildly.

Kallon flicked the blade away, then stabbed. The sharp point parted soft flesh. Master's steel skittered across the floor.

"He may be an officer, but he did not deserve five stripes on his tunic," Kallon said in disgust. He wiped his blade on a heavy drape as Master kneeled, clutching his entrails. He struggled with a dying breath. Jezzia watched every last rise and fall of his chest. So did the other girls, unwilling to look away despite the carnage.

"That means the Inkna wanted this town. There's

no *Gift* here to stop them. They brought in the Graygual to maintain order. What were they after, I wonder?" Mela's light gaze passed over the mute and dazed girls huddled together on the couch before settling on Jezzia.

"Gems," Jezzia answered, shaking. "They aren't good for anything but decoration, so we didn't get much for them. They are worth a lot to the Graygual. More than anything else we trade. Until the Inkna showed up, anyway. They offered us more than we thought they were worth. We thought we were doing really well. At first. Then the Graygual showed up. They weren't interested in trading."

Jezzia's grip tightened on the knife. She'd probably never release it again. In a rush she asked, "Can you teach me to use a sword? In case they come back..."

A shadow crossed Mela's face. Her gaze turned apologetic. "We cannot stay."

Jezzia's chest tightened, fear and hopelessness warring. "But the Wanderer! You're sent to herald her coming. Aren't you? She's supposed to end all this. If you leave they'll just come back! Stay. Please, stay."

"Do you mean the Chosen?" Kallon asked, his brow crinkled.

Jezzia shook her head in frustration, and her gaze met those stormy gray eyes. Imploring.

The front door burst open. A blonde woman walked in with a confident stride. She took Kallon's focus. "It's time to go. The townspeople are finding their courage. Finally."

"They weren't raised to expect they'd lose all they held dear," Kallon said disapprovingly. "We cannot expect them to bounce back as quickly as we did."

"Is that what we've done? Bounced back?"

Kallon ignored Jezzia as the woman's gaze scanned the room, lingering on the women cowering on the couch. Her face softened. She glanced at Kallon once more and gave a slight nod before heading back out.

Kallon stepped closer to Jezzia. She couldn't help the tears streaming down her face; she was terrified of what would happen if they left.

In a soft voice that contradicted his hard eyes, he said, "You will need to keep to yourselves for now. If you let others know you have regained control, the Graygual will just send in more. You must maintain the illusion of being conquered if you want to keep your freedom. Watch for the tide to change. The Chosen has been named. We must join her before the Graygual discover our trail. One day we will return, and we will bring the Graygual's death with us. You must stay strong until that time. Organize these people. Lead this town. Wait for our return."

Jezzia felt something shift at that expectant gaze. His words tickled a place deep within her, unlocking a strength she didn't realize she possessed. Courage welled up, bleeding through her.

He was giving her a duty.

She squeezed the hilt of her knife, thinking of who in the town could train her to use it. "I will stand ready for when the time comes. I won't let you down."

This man was heralding change. Somehow he was connected to the Wanderer, she could *feel* it. War was coming.

CHAPTER 2

"WHAT ARE WE doing?"

"We're waiting."

"We're not supposed to wait. We're supposed to find S'am." Marc's voice was hollow. He sounded as nervous as Leilius felt.

"I know. Shut up. I'm thinking." Leilius rubbed his temples. He hated these exercises. If he couldn't sneak up on S'am by himself, there was no way he could lead a bunch of big-footed nitwits to do it. She expected far too much from him.

"We don't have all day for you to try and rub two thoughts together," Rachie blurted.

"Would you *shut up*? She might be in earshot." Leilius dropped his hands and glanced at the felled tree to the right. It lay in a broken mess, rotting into the green grasses, shimmering with wetness. To the left of the path grew a white flowered plant, shaded by the large trees that surrounded it.

"Okay." Leilius took a deep breath and tried to block out the eyes staring impatiently at him. "This is the beginning of the non-*Gift* area. Her mind power won't work in this area of the trials… I mean, what used to be the trials. S'am is waiting somewhere in there. I think—"

"This place creeps me out," Gracas interrupted, rubbing his upper arms as if he was cold. "It's got a weird vibe to it."

"Can you imagine going through here by yourself?" Rachie asked, looking through the trees with wide eyes. "That would suck."

"Why are you leading again?" Ruisa asked from the rear of the loosely clustered group.

Leilius swatted at a fly. "Because I'm the only one who has worked with S'am on spying, that's why! She seems to think I can help you guys get better at sneaking."

"Fat chance," Marc muttered. "Leading this group is like herding cats."

Leilius pinched the bridge of his nose and willed patience. He had no idea how S'am trained this bunch of ninnies. They couldn't follow even the simplest of directions.

Of course, they were always attentive and respectful when S'am worked with them. They had to be—she'd kick them in the head if they weren't.

Wondering if he could get away with the same thing, Leilius glanced back. His gaze skimmed each of them before stopping on Xavier's huge shoulders that topped his sizable frame. He thought back to the battle with the Graygual only two months before, remembering how quickly the large kid had moved. How effective he was with his sword. He'd plowed through men with twice his experience and come out the victor.

Leilius turned back slowly. Best not to stir the pot. Leilius would just get his ass kicked.

"So here's the plan," he said in a hush. Time to quit stalling. "We spread out. Stay off the trail. Stick to the trees and try to work within the leaves, but don't shake any branches or anything."

"Walk in the leaves, but don't shake any…" Rachie spat, something he did when he was irritated during training. "That doesn't make any sense."

"Just…try to keep under cover, but don't disturb your surroundings, you know? Quiet movement." Leilius' voice had risen an octave, something *he* did when he was irritated.

"We've stalked game; we know what we're doing." Xavier motioned them forward. "Let's go."

Leilius shook his head, but he stepped forward anyway. This wasn't going to go well. "Just watch what I do."

Everyone moved slowly off the path and into the area where mental powers were supposed to go dead. Leilius didn't know anything about that. The lush green landscape of the Shadow Lands seemed consistent across the whole of the island, wet and alive. He'd heard the Captain and S'am talk about huge fluctuations in their powers in certain areas, and he'd paid attention, but he couldn't feel any difference from one place to the other.

The guys and the sole girl spread out slowly like a fan, ducking under reaching branches but still shaking every small piece of flora they walked past. Gracas went so far as to set a whole branch quivering.

"Stop. Stop!" Leilius said, pausing in a leafy hollow.

Xavier stopped, shifting to look in Leilius' direction. A twig cracked under his weight, making the large guy wince. More pops sounded off to the left where Rachie and Gracas were, and a rustle gave Ruisa away. The only person who was as silent as Leilius was Marc. Something Leilius pointed out.

"I'm the worst with a weapon," Marc explained with darting eyes. "I'd be the first one to die if I got caught. Or, in this case, the first to get punched. The need to survive has taught me how to blend in. I just wished that worked with S'am…"

"Well how the hell are we supposed to walk through the damn leaves without making them jump around like dancing frogs?" Rachie snapped.

"Just…" Leilius sighed. "Watch me."

"I *did* watch you. You walk like a girl!" Rachie said.

"I'll kick your teeth in like a girl, how would that be?" Ruisa barked.

Leilius took a deep breath and held up his hands, trying to calm everyone down. His flaring nostrils probably gave away his irritation, but he had to try. "We're all jumpy. I know that. We'll be leaving the protection of the island soon and going back to the danger of the mainland. That's a scary thing. I get it. We might—"

Rachie's fist came out of nowhere. It was nothing more than a skin-colored blur.

A moment later, Leilius groaned as he picked his head up off the ground and wiped at the mud stuck to his cheek. He shook his head to clear it, his vision a little blurry.

"You've gotten much quicker," Leilius said, wheezing. Apparently, Xavier wasn't the only one to watch out for. S'am's lessons had really started to pay off.

"Don't talk to us like we're scared," Rachie growled, emulating Sanders. "I'm not scared."

"I'm scared," Marc said.

"Can we get on with this before S'am shows up?" Gracas looked around the trees with wide, expectant eyes.

Picking himself up slowly, Leilius chose a different technique. "Just...watch me."

Well, it was the same technique while hoping for

different results.

They started out again, everyone allowing him to go first. They moved slowly, rustling, cracks, and pops sounding off every so often. If this was enemy territory, they'd be caught by anyone half decent. But just like they had with weapons and fighting, they'd all get better.

Hopefully.

After about ten minutes of walking, the trees started to compress around them. The light, once filtered and soft, was now strangled, barely making it past the foliage. Above, a bird gave one shrill cry before the beat of wings announced its hasty exit.

Leilius held up a hand. The others paused behind him.

Silence reigned.

The murkiness sifted between the trees. Chilled air gently coated his skin, stagnant.

Eyes drifting closed, Leilius tried to *feel* like S'am had taught him. He concentrated on every sound, picking up the heavy panting behind him. Marc. To the side he could hear a scratchy slide, leaves against someone's jacket. Other than that, nothing.

S'am would've come this way, scaring away most of the birds. If she'd kept going, many would've come back to settle, fleeing for a second time as Leilius and his herd tramped through. But only one had taken flight. It either hadn't left when S'am had come through, or had been brave enough to return.

S'am could stay so still and quiet, animal life filled in her surroundings. But it took time.

She was in the area.

A thrill shot through Leilius. If she was in the area, she knew he was, too. If the Honor Guard took too long to find her, she'd sneak out and scare the crap out of them before waging battle.

Shit. They didn't have much time.

Trying to calm down, ignoring his thumping heart, he focused on that special survival sense, as S'am had called it. He tried to feel for a presence hiding within the trees. Waiting. Watching. Ready to attack.

A bead of sweat dribbled down Leilius' cheek.

The heavy panting behind him became more intense.

Unable to help himself, he glanced back.

Marc stood rigid, pale and shaking. He was looking off to the right with unfocused eyes. Xavier, only three paces away from Marc, on bent knees, his practice sword in his hand, stared off in the same direction. He noticed Leilius looking before minutely flicking his head in the direction of his focus.

Xavier couldn't be quiet, but it seemed he could do that survival-feeling thing.

Leilius turned his head slowly, moving no other part

of his body. He scanned the wall of green, looking for S'am's shiny black jacket or her light hair. Marc's huffing was the only sound. Time was fleeting.

He should move. She knew they were in the area. She had to.

I hate this part.

One foot in front of the other, Leilius slowly made his way, eyes constantly moving. He checked pockets of shadow large enough for a person to crouch. His gaze skimmed bushes and peered into caverns created by branches. He couldn't see her!

"*Pssst!*"

Leilius froze. He closed his eyes in disbelief.

If S'am hadn't known they'd been sneaking closer before, she *certainly* did now.

He glanced back at Rachie with wide eyes. No one else had moved since he started his advance in S'am's direction. They wanted him to get beaten up first, it seemed.

Rachie jerked his head to the left.

Confused, Leilius followed the prompting with his eyes.

Dense brush covered the ground. Weeds grew in thick patches, knee high, leaning against the trunks of trees. It could mask someone lying down, probably, but unless that person planned a rolling attack, it wasn't great for an ambush.

Leilius crinkled his brow and shook his head, trying to convey his irritation, anger, and thoughts on that hiding place all at the same time. Rachie's expression closed down before he looked back at that brush. He edged back slowly.

Leilius rolled his eyes. He looked again at that wall of green. She could be *anywhere* in there. Ready to spring.

This was a bad idea.

Leilius picked up a foot, but before he could put it down, a shape dropped out of the sky.

"Look—shit!" Marc screamed.

Leilius flinched and brought up his sword as S'am dropped right in front of him. He hadn't thought to look up!

He had his foot still in the air, not knowing if he should charge or run, and a blur with blond hair was upon him. His sword was wrenched out of his hand, batted away. The air gushed from his lungs as pain welled up from his stomach, S'am's kick landing hard and fast. He bent over and punched feebly, only to get his wrist grabbed and pulled. He threw himself onto her fist, doing the work for her as he fell.

Knuckles hit his cheekbone before he crumpled to the ground. "I give up!"

With weeds almost obscuring his vision as he played dead, he saw S'am descend on Xavier with her near legendary fighting grace. She feinted left, drawing his sword strike. He realized it was a ploy halfway through, making him jerk his hand back. Too late. S'am brought the flat side of her sword blade across, smacking him in the head.

"Ouch!" Xavier staggered, his sword still raised, ready to try again, but S'am had already moved on.

"Team up, team up!" Gracas yelled, waving Rachie toward him. "We can take her together."

"There's something—oh holy hell! Run! Everybody run!" Leilius heard heavy footfalls as Rachie followed his own advice.

Marc started screaming like a little girl.

"How do you fight a wild animal?" Ruisa yelled in desperation. Rachie sprinted by her, in a hurry to get away.

Leilius barely had time to get up to see what was going on as a cry like an enraged infant widened his eyes.

"Oh shit!" He hopped up, sword forgotten. Without thinking, only aware that Xavier was between him and the animal, and therefore would give him cover, he took off. S'am could punish him later for cowardice—that cat had sharp teeth.

SHANTI WATCHED WITH a quirked smile as the training

session unraveled around her. She could hear Rohnan laughing with big body chuckles from the branch above. Leaves drifted down around her.

"That's not fair, S'am!" Marc screeched as the big cat studied him.

Shanti's smile grew. "You should never run from a wild animal, Marc," Shanti instructed as Xavier bent his legs, his gaze fixed on the predatory, black animal.

"Too late!" Marc ducked behind a tree. Ruisa still stood with her hands out, eyes rounded, frozen in place. Everyone else had taken off.

"They can climb trees," Rohnan said. It took Shanti a moment to realize he was talking to Marc, who was trying to scrabble up the trunk of one.

She huffed as the cat stalked toward Xavier slowly, its light blue eyes sighting him as prey. Xavier's hand tightened on his wooden practice sword.

"I admire your courage, Xavier," Shanti said with a flick of her wrist. The cat halted its advance. "But what did you plan to do with a small piece of wood against a half-grown animal with teeth and claws?"

"I didn't get that far. I was too busy being scared."

"I'm amazed at your honesty. Usually you try to hide behind your bravado." Shanti walked behind the tree and grabbed Marc by the back of his shirt. She gave a tug. The doctor-in-training clung to the bark with his nails, ripping flakes off as he fell away. He landed in a sprawl in a prickly bush.

"Rohnan always gives me away." Xavier straightened up slowly, then started backing away from the animal. "We found you, though. If it hadn't been for this cat we would've had you."

"You did find me, yes." Shanti glanced at Ruisa, who was shaking out her limbs, eyes still on the cat. "Good work, Ruisa. That was the right way to ward off an animal like this. Usually, unless they are really hungry, they'll leave you be."

"And if they're really hungry?" the younger woman asked, still out of breath from her tightly contained panic of the moment before.

"Then you'd better hope you have more than a stick to save your life. Go find everyone else. Tell them we'll do night training. Maybe trying to do this without eyes will help your awareness."

Shanti barely heard Ruisa groan as she jogged away.

"Do I have to go tonight?" Marc asked, plucking a thorn from his arm with a grimace.

Rohnan jumped down from the tree, a grin still on his face from the pandemonium.

"Yes. Walk with me, Marc." Shanti started back toward the city. The panther she'd made an orphan followed her without prompting. As kicking a predator to scare him away would only result in a painful bite, she decided to just let the big cat do what he wanted.

"What did I do?" Marc asked in a whine. "You know I wouldn't run from an enemy, S'am. But you don't count. It's just stupid to stand around while you wind up to punch me in the face. What's the point in that?"

"Xavier, come with us," Shanti said as Rohnan fell in beside her.

Xavier's shoulders tensed up. His head drooped, before he jogged to catch up. He wouldn't voice it, but he had the same questions as Marc. Probably with a similar whine.

"I'm impressed with the way you identified me, Marc," Shanti started as they made their way through the thick, wet trees. "I've been trying to teach Leilius that. How did you do it?"

"Oh." The tension left Marc's body. "At first I just paid attention to Leilius. He's pretty good at picking up small cues. But then when he stopped and looked scared, I just…kinda…I don't know. Felt your presence somehow. Or maybe I was just scared."

"Fear, *Chulan,*" Rohnan said thoughtfully. "That is the ingredient. I told you."

"Yes, Rohnan, you know everything," Shanti said dryly. "Don't you have somewhere to be?" Shanti nudged Marc to the right so they could cut through the hole in the thorn fence.

"Yes, *Chulan,* by your side. As always."

Shanti took a deep breath as her *Gift* surged back into her. It spread out, tumbling across the ground. Her world opened up, producing a clearer picture as her extra sense filled in the gaps. She felt someone loitering in the trees away to the right, enjoying the solitude of quiet contemplation. A small animal skittered away to the left.

"I am happy to have been blessed with the *Gift*," Rohnan said with a sigh.

"And you, Xavier?" Shanti asked the large youth walking beside her. He seemed like he gained muscle by the day, already tall, but now filling out. He was as big as any Shadow fighter and he probably had another growth spurt ahead of him. Given his skill, and potential, Xavier would be great. If he lasted that long.

If any of them did.

Shanti wiped that thought away. It wasn't helpful.

"I saw one of your tracks, then I saw Marc tense up," Xavier explained, twirling a flower between his fingers. "Whenever Marc tenses up like that, you usually pop out a moment later. I just paid attention."

"Can you blame me?" Marc mumbled.

"Nope." Xavier bent to pick another wild flower as they turned onto the heavily trodden dirt path leading north. It was a different color to the one he'd already collected.

Shanti hid her disappointment in their answers.

"You guys head back, then. I'll see you at dusk."

"Good. I'm hungry." Xavier sped up.

"You're always hungry," Marc, lanky in comparison, said as he kept pace.

Shanti watched them for a moment as they ambled away, their minds blissfully focused on the moment. She envied them that trait—only noticing the here and now. They weren't troubled with the battles to come, the unrest in the land, or the fact that, even now, Xandre sat somewhere, going over that last battle. Documenting. Analyzing. Coming up with a strategy.

Shanti turned off the path, Rohnan at her side. She didn't have the luxury of only thinking about this moment. They would have to leave the seclusion of this island soon, and confront the misery and danger in the land. Shanti would, once again, have the lives of Cayan and his people weighing on her.

"It does you no good to plague your mind with what's to come, *Chulan,*" Rohnan said in a soft voice. "We are all on the journey. They are in no more danger now than if you had passed them by all those months ago. The unrest has swept across the land. There is no hiding from it."

"I know." Shanti looked back, noticing Xavier stopping to pick a third flower. She smiled. "I wonder which of the girls he'll give those to."

"He will give one to each of the three, I believe,"

Rohnan said, his gaze following hers. "I could feel the different emotion with each flower he picked. He, like his Captain, knows how to woo a woman."

Shanti gave Rohnan a sideways glance. "Cayan only brought me flowers to say he was sorry for…" Her brow furrowed. Why had he been sorry? She couldn't recall.

"Because he wasn't sorry. He was showing his feelings."

She rolled her eyes. "No. He was sorry for something, and wrongly figured I would melt like the women of his land."

"Instead you gave him a beautiful black eye."

"Exactly."

"And since you weren't planning to, I informed him that women fighters of our land usually use violence to show affection. Although, based on the bites on his torso, and the satisfied air about him, he probably knew that."

"Those bites were given in battle."

"Yes. A naked battle."

Shanti's lips thinned. "That's still a battle."

Rohnan laughed. "Just admit that you love him, *Chulan.* I do not understand the point in denying it."

"I don't have to remind you what happens to those I love, Rohnan. I'd rather keep things simple. You know that. *He* knows that. Why won't you all just shut up about it!"

Rohnan ran his fingers through her ponytail. "You're stubborn."

Shanti thought about the boys and Ruisa. In two months, her Honor Guard had come farther than any group of people she'd ever worked with, including her own. Something in that last battle had unlocked a hidden potential, now flowering out and growing like a weed. Every new thing she taught them they picked up lightning fast, using it as if they'd been born with the knowledge. They had held their own with the Shadow fighters, a feat the rest of Cayan's men were struggling with, and still they looked for more knowledge. More ways to improve.

"Cayan isn't sure what to do with the boys when we get back. They won't fit into the army mold," Shanti said. A woman walked along the path toward them. She gave a tiny bow to Shanti and a wink for Rohnan as she passed.

Shanti glanced sideways at Rohnan again. She raised an eyebrow.

The edges of Rohnan's lips quirked upward. "The Captain isn't the only one who knows how to woo a woman."

"Did you use flowers?"

"Of course not. I am not that predictable."

Shanti laughed despite her mood. "Anyway, the boys will be out of place."

"They'll stay with you. Fate has brought them to you. They have a purpose, and that purpose will be with you somehow."

"Fate. I bloody hate Fate. He's such a nosey bastard."

They emerged from the tree line and into a small practice field. Much like Shanti's people, the Shadow trained mainly in the trees all over the island. For groups training together, often on sword work or with horses, they used this clearing, made bigger by felling trees.

Two men fought with practice swords in the center. One, with a thinner frame, had bright red hair pulled into a knot at the top of his head. The other, tall and robust, with thick cords of muscle running the length of his body, had raven-black hair tied at the nape of his neck.

"Sonson just will not let it lie," Shanti said in exasperation as the red-haired man thrust forward. Cayan blocked with a rough, brutal defense before stepping forward quickly to counterattack.

"The Captain is using a style like Sanders." Rohnan's voice competed with the clatter of the wooden swords. "He is offsetting the graceful style of the Shadow people."

"For now. He'll—" Shanti stopped as Cayan's style morphed into a smooth strike, catching Sonson off guard with the quick change. The tip of the wooden sword grazed Sonson's side. "There. See? He's realized Sonson is slow to change his defensive strategies. Sonson is capable of it, as he's dealt with so many different swordsman over the years, but he hasn't had experience of combating three different styles all in the same man."

"Not many are. Cayan is rare."

Shanti couldn't help a surge of pride in the observation. In the last two months, Cayan had received a great many challenges in all forms, and he had never lost. Some battles had been close, especially with her and Sonson, but he remained the one true victor, a record not even Sonson held on this island. It had surprised a great many. If anyone had any doubts about the new Chosen's fighting prowess, those doubts were soon put to rest.

"Pride in a simple bedmate, *Chulan*? That seems abnormal." Rohnan clasped his hands behind his back as they stopped to watch the swordplay. "Or are you nearly ready to admit to love after all?"

"You could give Fate a lesson on being a nosey bastard."

Cayan jabbed forward, drawing the counterattack. He bashed the sword strike aside, having anticipated it, and struck with strength and speed. His sword drove home, hitting Sonson's stomach and bending him over.

"I yield!" Sonson yelled, groaning as he went to one knee. "Yield. That was a kill strike."

Cayan straightened up. He wiped the sweat from his brow with his forearm before his gaze swept the area. It landed on Shanti. The spicy hum deep within her lit on fire, bubbling up through her body and making her chest tight. A smile curled her lips as she recognized the fire dancing in his eyes and felt the answering heat course through his body, through their *Joining*.

Cayan handed off his practice sword and walked toward her with balanced, agile steps. When he reached her, his eyes found her lips, but thankfully he kept his distance. He wouldn't show affection on the battlefield, thank the Elders. It was just everywhere else he pestered her.

"*Mesasha.*" Cayan's deep voice sent tingles racing up her spine. "How did the training go?"

"About as expected. I'll try darkness and fear tonight. Maybe that'll help them develop their extra sense to detect presences. I can't think what else to do."

Cayan wiped off his face with a cloth, leaving his glistening chest to air-dry. Shanti ripped her eyes away from the defined muscles and tried to ignore her throbbing core. His presence was starting to get distracting.

Rohnan's smirk was irritating.

"Well. I need to chat with the Shadow Lord." Shanti

turned, only pausing when she noticed Sonson straightening up, his smile aimed at her.

"When does she think to send the first wave to the mainland?" Cayan asked, the twinkle in his eyes dimming.

"Still a month. She can't cut down the time. You've heard from Lucius?"

"Yes." Cayan turned so his body was facing a stiffly approaching Sonson. "All is well. The Duke's men are fitting in fine and the supplies are steady. They've seen no Graygual."

Shanti's brow furrowed, unease niggling at her. "I suspect Xandre will be mulling over his loss. He will analyze it before he acts again. I had anticipated a smooth crossing to the mainland. But where did the Hunter go? He doesn't seem like the type to hide."

"He does seem like the kind to wait, though," Cayan said.

"The Hunter." Sonson swung his arms to loosen them up. "That was the Superior Officer on your heels on your journey here?"

"Yes." Shanti pulled up her hood to shield from the moisture sifting down on top of them. The sky was spitting, threatening them with the rain to come. "He failed in the task Xandre assigned him, which was guarding Burson. Burson was a prize. Xandre's underlings have been tortured for far less. The Hunter's fate won't be pretty."

"And why wouldn't he hide?" Sonson asked.

"Why don't I?" Shanti squinted into the distance, thinking. "There is nowhere to go that Xandre wouldn't eventually uncover."

"The Hunter is not one to hide," Rohnan echoed with a soft voice. "No one with his training and prestige will give in to failure. They are not bred for it. Their training forbids it. He is out there somewhere. Waiting."

"Is Burson in jeopardy?" Sonson asked.

Shanti shrugged, exhaling her frustration with the unknown. Burson had left soon after she and Cayan had jointly gained the title of Chosen, saying he had to spread the word. He'd landed safely in Clintos, as he'd said he would. After that, there had been periodic updates, informing them of the smoldering unrest in the land. Word of both the Wanderer and Chosen had spread like wildfire. Uprisings had appeared, but been quelled just as quickly. The land was holding its breath.

They were waiting for her and Cayan, it seemed.

Xandre wouldn't wait forever.

None of that helped with the whereabouts of the Hunter, though. His battle was targeted. At her. She had every belief he'd pick up Burson if it was convenient, but the Hunter wanted to capture his prey: the elusive violet-eyed girl.

So where was he?

"Chosen. Sonson." A man ran up to them with harried movements. "Portolmous needs you. He says it's urgent. He's received a message..."

A sense of foreboding filled Shanti. It was as if the Elders had heard her question, and were now sending an answer.

CHAPTER 3

Lucius' face struck the wall. The guard held him there with a palm to the center of his back while he opened the door. He grabbed Lucius roughly by the shirt and yanked him off the side of the house before tossing him through the doorway. Lucius' feet dragged against the floor. He stumbled and fell. With his hands tied behind his back, his face smacked against a hard surface for the second time.

"Tallos, that is no way to treat our captive."

Lucius gritted his teeth at that calm, cultivated voice. He rolled to the side so he could look up at the speaker. Sharp, defined cheekbones, thin lips, and a straight, pointed nose that ended in a slight hook, giving him a predatory quality, accentuated by those horrible, dead eyes. Lucius hated looking directly at him. Hated the cold calculation in those soulless eyes. It wasn't natural.

"Sorry, sir." Tallos grabbed Lucius by the back of the shirt again, hoisting him up. Using less force than he had on the walk there, Tallos guided him to a leather couch and dropped him down.

"There. That's better." Staring at Lucius from the Captain's living room chair, the man adjusted his crisp black uniform. Eight red slashes adorned his chest like blood. Taunting Lucius. Silently threatening him.

"Would you like some tea?" the man offered in a genteel sort of way.

"No, thank you." Lucius jerked his head, trying to get the hair out of his eyes.

"Yes. You are in a state, aren't you." The Graygual officer, called the Hunter by his men when they couldn't be overheard, glanced at Tallos. "See to it that he is cleaned up. I do not like to speak to filth."

"Of course, sir." Tallos didn't bother looking in Lucius' direction. And he wouldn't bother to tell the barber to take it easy, either. If Lucius' throat wasn't cut as he was being shaved, it would be a miracle.

"Now." The Hunter held up a piece of paper. "I've taken the liberty of crafting a letter for you. As before, you will look over it, point out anything that doesn't fit your phrasing, we'll fix it, and you'll sign the bottom. And as before, if you do not do as expected, I will kill one of your women. Understood?"

Lucius ground his teeth.

The Hunter's bleak eyes studied him for a moment before he glanced up at Tallos again. "Bring her."

"No!" Lucius yanked at his hands. The tight rope

rubbed against his sore wrists. "No. I'll do it. You don't need to bring her."

The Hunter's flat stare didn't waver. "On the contrary. A slight hesitation means the desire for disobedience. It is a power struggle. You forget that you have none. To prove this I must, once again, punish you."

A door opened somewhere in the back of the house, emitting a woman's whimpers. Bare feet slapped against the hardwood floor in sporadic patters. As they grew nearer, the sobs became more evident.

Lucius yanked at the rope again as Alena was forced into the center of the room. A beautiful woman with large, brown eyes looked at him from under her tear-soaked lashes. A large bruise covered her right shoulder and yellowing skin colored her jaw, half hidden behind lank brown hair.

The Hunter waved one finger.

"No!" Lucius yelled.

A house guard stepped up and slapped Alena across the face with the back of his hand. The force sent her reeling. She fell onto the brickwork at the side of the fireplace, sliding down to the floor. Before she could get up, the guard was yanking her up by her hair and pushing her back toward the middle of the room.

"Please," Alena begged, falling onto her hands and knees.

Without passion, the guard pulled back his foot.

"No!" Lucius yelled again, struggling to his feet. "I said I'd do it! *I said I'd do it!*"

The Hunter's finger waved for the second time. The guard put his foot down and stood impassively over the sobbing woman.

"What kind of animal are you?" Lucius spat at the Hunter.

Something akin to humor sparkled in the man's gaze. "I want a small task completed that is easily within your power. If you do this task, you would save her the pain and embarrassment of violence. Yet you still try to defy me. One might say *you* are the animal, not I."

"Show me the letter." Lucius watched the woman on the floor with a pain in his heart. He couldn't bear to see her hurt. To see any of the women hurt. Fighting Shanti had been one thing. He could easily block out her femininity with her masculine fighting ability. Landing a punch or kick had been a small victory, short-lived. But the women of this land were soft. They weren't used to fighting or defending themselves.

He bowed in defeat as Tallos took the letter from the Hunter and approached. He read it quickly, not really needing to. It said what it always did: the city was fine, trade was undisturbed, and there was still no sign of the Graygual. It had few embellishments but left nothing out. The Hunter had intercepted a couple of letters before he stormed in a month ago and had learned Lucius' style well. Almost frighteningly so. He bet the Hunter could've signed it as well without alerting the Captain.

"It's fine," Lucius said softly.

"Good. Now you may sign it and be on your way."

Tallos stepped behind Lucius and undid the rope. He then delivered a writing board so Lucius could carry out the Hunter's instruction.

A thousand thoughts flooded Lucius' mind as he finished signing his name and approached the Hunter with the letter. His hands were loose and body primed, the desire to cave in the officer's head so fierce it made his limbs shake. Adrenaline spiked as his heart pounded.

Just him and the Hunter.

He could be at the Hunter's throat before Tallos could intervene.

The paper quivered in the air as Lucius handed it over. His fingers tingled as the Hunter reached up for the document. The Hunter's expression remained impassive.

Lucius stared into those cold, dead eyes for one full heartbeat, daring himself to attack. Willing himself to rid this city of the ruthless officer.

The breath gushed out of his lungs. He stepped back. Then dropped his hands.

There was a reason the Hunter didn't immediately have Lucius tied up again, or guarded tightly as he delivered the letter—his fighting prowess was unrivaled. Lucius had tried when he was in this situation the first time. Sterling had too, but to no avail. The Captain might've had a chance—maybe even Sanders—but no one else. The Hunter was on a level of his own. As long as he ruled this city, there was nothing Lucius could do to get them out of it.

That didn't stop him constantly thinking of possibilities, but it prevented him from needlessly attacking someone that would permanently injure him if he tried. Being a cripple wouldn't help his city.

That argument only mildly soothed the sting of cowardice.

ALENA FLINCHED AS the guard grabbed her upper arm. She remained slightly limp, allowing him to pull her to her feet. Her face pounded from the slap, and her arm stung from scraping against the brickwork, but other than that, she was fine. She should be able to complete her mission.

She gave Lucius a watery smile, wishing she could tell him to stop spending so much time dwelling on what was wrong with the city, and start focusing on what was right. Like that the Graygual thought the women were just as weak and useless as Lucius and the army men did. Or that the Hunter didn't have a taste for the women of this city, or maybe for women in general, and wouldn't let his guards partake either, unless it was consensual. That was a huge stroke of luck. Those two factors gave the women just enough wiggle room to be able to help.

Hopefully. Otherwise, it might be just enough wiggle room to get them all killed. In a few days, when the Women's Circle's first steps to rid the city of these captors took effect, they'd know for sure.

Her mind went to the tiny vial hidden in her bosom. Apprehension zinged up her spine.

Alena filled her lungs with air and held on to the importance of her courage with two fists. It all began with her. Right here.

The guard jerked her arm, the cue to get going. She swayed, taking two extra steps and forcing the guard to jerk her again, into the right path. After that he let her go, pushing her to get her to hurry up. She dragged one of her feet and let the force of the shove take her to the ground. Whimpering, she straightened slowly, playing up the wounded dove routine.

She walked through the arch and into the Captain's large dining room. Two Graygual, each with three slashes on their breast, leaned over their plates. Neither looked up as she passed.

She tried to keep her body from going rigid as she entered the kitchen where Ragna stood at the large pot over the fire. Steam curled around her face, enhancing the rosiness of her cheeks and fluttering her gray hair. She looked up when Alena came through.

"Oh my poor dear!" Ragna rushed over, grabbing Alena by the shoulders.

Alena ignored the dull pain in her shoulder as she fell toward the woman. She let her head fall to Ragna's thick shoulder while turning slightly, angling her chest away from the eyes of the guard. Quick as a striking snake, she snatched the small vial out of the pocket sewed into her dress.

"C'mon!" the guard grabbed Alena's hair and tugged her back.

"Ah!" Alena reached back with her free hand and ran it along Ragna's arm down to her palm. Ragna's fingers closed over the vial.

"Okay!" Alena said breathlessly, turning and stepping toward the guard. She let out another whimper as he yanked her head.

"Stupid woman. *Go!*" The guard shoved her toward the door.

It took everything she had not to glance back to make sure Ragna had safely tucked the vial out of sight. Instead, she scampered out of the kitchen, catching the door with her injured shoulder on the way outside. Off balance, she spiraled into the dirt. A rock jabbed her knee, sending shooting pain down her leg.

She rolled onto her butt, flinching as she then had to pull the jagged stone out of the cut.

"Go!" From the doorway, the guard made a shooing gesture with his hand, his expression impatient.

A flash of anger filled her before she could quickly stash it away. Hopefully the emotion hadn't touched her features.

Not waiting for the kick that would soon follow the guard's command, Alena got up and limped down the street. The sun sprinkled down, warming her just enough to excuse the chill of the air. Graygual littered the streets, their gazes hard but expressions impassive. Always impassive. It was like they were in a trance, watching with no real feeling. It wasn't human.

Alena noticed Molly ambling down the other side of the street carrying a basket of laundry. The woman glanced at Alena, her brow slightly raised. Alena gave one nod, conveying that the handoff had been made and the job was done to satisfaction.

Molly looked straight ahead again.

Molly's guard, a graying man with a surly disposition, prodded Molly in the back. "Don't dally."

"Can't I notice my friend?" she asked with spice. "You'd think we were as unfriendly as you lot. I'm a friendly sort of person. I need someone to talk to once in a while, I do. I can't just stay silent. It's not natural!"

"Shut up!" the guard badgered, pushing her again.

"Oh yes, big man, pushing a helpless woman. Big man indeed." Molly huffed as she continued along.

Alena couldn't help a small smile and a surge of pride. Molly had been their guiding light since the first sign of attack. The men had rushed to the city's defense, but it was evident almost immediately that the city would be taken. No one could withstand the mental assault. It scrubbed at a person's mind and chased away all coherent thought. Alena had been terrified, not only of the pain, but of what would come. The city had been attacked before, but the Captain had always been there to rally the defenses. With him in charge, everything seemed to work out.

This time, though, everyone had withered at their posts. They couldn't even raise their weapons. The Graygual had dropped over the walls like sludge, disarming or killing as they went. The gates had been opened and Alena's worst fear had come to pass. They were captives.

She shivered, just thinking about it. She remembered wondering if the soldiers would knock down the doors and take the women or kill the children. All manner of horrible things had panicked her to the point of suffocation. Those first few days had been lost in a fog of fear. She barely remembered them.

Finally, on the fourth day, Molly had walked through the door with a stubborn expression and determined set to her shoulders. She'd given Alena a big, tight hug, then slapped her across the face.

"Shanti always slapped people across the face," Molly had said with an insistent gaze. "She stared down the Captain, she fought off the Mugdock, and she changed people's way of thinking. It started with a slap in the face. So you shake off this fear, Alena. You shake it off. There's work to be done. We need to protect this city like our mothers taught us. The men are no good to us. This is a woman's job. Get yourself cleaned up and get to the Circle meeting tonight without getting caught. We need to take charge."

Alena ducked her head and wiped the smile off her face as she passed another hard-eyed Graygual soldier. Molly had caused enough havoc to get her own guard. But now that plans were set in motion, the essential thing was to keep their heads down and draw the least amount of notice possible.

Crying a lot also helped. The Graygual thought crying was a sign of weakness. It never hurt to let them continue thinking incorrectly.

After a miserable walk across the city with an aching shoulder, throbbing face, and pounding knee, she stumbled into Junice's house and found her way to the kitchen. As expected, Junice sat at the kitchen table, working at needlepoint with a worry knot in her brow. At Alena's entrance, she dropped her chore and bounced up.

"Did you do it?" Junice tsked at Alena's cheek. "That looks like it hurts."

"It does hurt." Alena allowed herself to be directed to a chair at the table in the modest kitchen.

"You'll live." Junice wet a cloth and put it to Alena's face gently.

"No sympathy from you, huh?" Alena grimaced as Junice dabbed. She must've gotten a cut—the treatment stung. "And yes, I passed it off. Now it's in Ragna's hands."

Junice exhaled noisily. "Well, we're in it now. There's no backing out."

"Unless she doesn't use it."

"She will. When the time is right, she'll do what needs to be done." Junice looked at Alena's shoulder, and then her knee. "You'll need some salve. It'll help."

"Dipping into Sanders' stash?"

"Of course. He came home with more scrapes and cuts…" Junice chuckled, but sadness and worry colored her tone.

"He's okay," Alena said softly. "Wherever he is, he's okay."

"Of course he is. That man is too stubborn to die, that much I know. I just wonder if I'll be okay. What we're doing...it's dangerous..."

"Why do you think we have such a great army, Junice? The Duke's men couldn't keep up with our guys. And do you know why?"

Junice paused in her doctoring. "Because we breed strong men," Junice recited.

"Exactly. *We* breed strong men. We give birth to them, we mold them, we shape them, and then we hand the Captain a warrior half formed. We do all the hard work; all he has to do is put a sword in their hand and show them how to use it."

Junice laughed. "You're starting to sound like Molly."

"A lot of us are. If there is one thing the women of this city know, it's quiet strength. Someone has to keep those bullheaded men in line!"

"Yes. I know something about bullheaded men."

"Ow!" Alena sucked a breath through her teeth as Junice dabbed her face. "That salve stings."

"Speaking of quiet strength—you could use a heavy dose of both..."

"I still don't know why the Women's Circle gave me this job," Alena complained. "I think they must hate me."

"Lucius is still trying to hold strong, huh?"

"Obviously. I don't think they'd bother bringing me in if he wasn't. The Hunter is calculating that way. It seems like he's only nice, or only mean, to manipulate.

His smiles aren't genuine, and he never shows anger. It's..."

"Terrifying."

Alena grimaced. "Unpredictable."

"Exactly. Which is terrifying." Junice put a bandage over the cut on Alena's knee. "As to why you, you're the toughest of Lucius' ex-loves. He knows you well. It hurts him more when you're in pain."

"He dumped me, actually. Or don't you remember when I lost it and destroyed his house?"

Junice smirked. "That was years ago."

"I don't know why we don't just tell him to do as he's told. If he knew what we were plotting, he'd go along with it."

"And if he just went along with it, the Hunter would wonder why. No, this is the best way."

"Just my luck." Alena sagged against the table.

"My only fear is that the Captain falls into the Hunter's trap before we've done our part. The Hunter is supposed to always be one step ahead of his enemies."

Alena reached over and covered Junice's hand with her own. "The Hunter will *think* he's one step ahead, but what he'll really be is distracted. We'll be the snake in the grass. We just have to stay the course."

"I hope you're right." Junice picked up her needlepoint, her brow knotted in worry again.

"I am." Alena sincerely wished she felt as confident as she sounded.

CHAPTER 4

"How do you know?" Shanti sat beside a rigid and silent Cayan, facing Portolmous as he sat behind his desk. Sonson's brother and the second in command after the Shadow Lord, his face was grim. He'd just told them that the Graygual had moved into Cayan's city and taken everyone hostage.

"Burson put it in his weekly report." Portolmous handed the folded letter across the desk. Cayan reached for it slowly—his hands were steady, but his eyes were on fire.

"And how does he know?" Sonson asked, standing by the window with a solemn expression.

"One of the men in his Wanderer network traded with Westwood Lands a couple weeks ago. He was trading water treatment agents. Apparently, there is a bad stomach flu going around the Captain's city. Two things stood out, of course. The first was that it's unlikely that a people wouldn't suddenly have an issue with their water. But someone foreign to that area might. The second was that this person moved and had all the mannerisms of a Graygual officer. They don't move and act like a normal trader would."

"So Burson isn't certain, he's speculating," Shanti clarified.

"Yes." Portolmous clasped his hands on the desk. "But that, combined with sightings of a large host of Graygual headed in the general direction of the city, would indicate that he is right."

"Yes, it would," Shanti mumbled, her mind whirling.

Cayan gave voice to her thoughts. "It seems the Hunter isn't in hiding, he's laying in wait."

She turned to look at him slowly, trying not to feel the guilt eating away her insides. It was hard, though. She'd told him his city would be safe. That the Hunter would follow her. And he had. He'd done what Shanti had expected…until she'd stopped expecting anything at all. She hadn't thought far enough ahead. She was still thinking like she was the only one on this journey, making her focus singular and shortsighted.

She dropped her shaking head.

"There are other matters to discuss," Portolmous said in a tight voice.

Shanti looked up in confusion, seeing that his hard stare was aimed at her.

"We have reports," Portolmous started. "Not all the Wanderer's heralds are in Burson's network. Of the pockets of people rising up against the Graygual, the most effective advocates are light of feature and far from home. They've said they are looking to join the Chosen. Always the Chosen, they say. Not the Wanderer. With each town they help, or each time they dodge the Graygual, they plant themselves more firmly into legend. They are bolstering Burson's network like no one else…except you."

Shanti met his stare with her own, not sure why this should anger him. He'd known Shanti wanted a bird sent. Originally the Shadow Lord was going to take care of this, but after Shanti had talked it over with Cayan, new plans were formed. None of this was a secret.

Portolmous' jaw tightened. "The Graygual have been mostly complacent about these small uprisings. Our thought was that they expected it with the news of the Chosen. But now…this has created a different atmosphere."

"Have they been sighted?" Shanti asked in an even voice, the desire to see her people so strong it dripped through her stomach like acid.

"A handful of times. They make good time. Amazing time, given the distance from your home land to their most recent sighting…"

Shanti shook her head in irritation. "I explained this to the Shadow Lord. A select group of my people hid during the last battle. We knew Xandre's armies would be too much, so I chose the best and brightest to hide themselves away until they were needed. Just as I had to flee capture, they had to escape from death. After everything settled, they snuck out in order to station themselves in remote locations, waiting for the call to arms. At least…that was the plan. Until this news, I didn't know if they had made it."

"And you have directed them to the Captain's lands."

"Well, I couldn't very well invite them here. There was no guarantee that we would be here when they turned up," Shanti said with a flash of anger. "What are you getting at, Portolmous?"

"The Graygual have taken an interest in these so-called heralds. They want this band found and killed. They're also taking more interest in the other bands of rebels cropping up all over. In short, the Graygual are starting to react on a larger scale."

"We knew that would happen eventually," Shanti countered.

"Not so soon, though. It's shortening our time to get organized."

"Wars aren't planned with a timetable," Cayan said, standing. "They are a game of cause and effect. Is that everything you have? I need to talk to my men."

Portolmous stood as well, staring at Cayan with intelligent green eyes. "Wars aren't planned with timetables, no, but when someone such as Burson gives them to you, it's best to listen. He said you should wait—not to act right away. He said that would greatly improve the chances of success."

"Noted. Now, excuse me." Cayan glanced at Shanti before striding from the room.

She looked at Portolmous. "Can you be ready any sooner?"

Pity entered Portolmous' eyes. "No. I'm getting our people ready as fast as I can, but you are talking about massive relocation. It takes more than a few months."

"We'll have some people at your disposal." Sonson dropped his hand to the hilt of his sword. He gave his brother a look of warning. Portolmous' mouth snapped shut. "Planning is great, but sometimes action is better."

Sonson looked back at Shanti. "Whoever we can spare, we will. Just let me know what you plan."

Shanti gave him a nod of gratitude before she walked from the room. She crossed the city quickly, using her *Gift* to track Cayan to Sanders' quarters. A few of Cayan's men were already there looking up at their leader with the same fire in their eyes.

"When do we leave?" Tobias asked, his furry brow raised in expectation.

"Now, obviously. Tonight." Sanders paced at the back of the room. "They'd better have a ship available."

"Burson said in his letter that we'd benefit from

waiting a month," Cayan said carefully. "He says it will be a trifecta. Our chances will be better."

"A trifecta, sir?" Tobias squinted in confusion.

"I take that to mean that he expects three groups of people converging together—or near enough."

"I don't give two shits about a trifecta." Sanders stopped pacing and stared at Cayan. "Burson is a few bricks short of a house if he thinks I'm going to sit around here, playing at swords, when my wife is in danger. No way, sir. It's time to go."

Cayan nodded and glanced at Daniels. The older man, sitting regally in the back of the room, sat forward. His gaze was contemplative. "As devil's advocate, Burson has always been right. Always. His methods are strange, of course, being from his...gifts—"

"Cut to the chase, man," Sanders barked, temper making his face red.

Daniels' expression hardened. "It might be a better outcome, like he said, if we waited."

"It would be a better outcome for whom?" Sanders shot back. "The war, or my wife? Because why are we fighting the Graygual if not to protect our loved ones? No. I'm sorry, sir, but no dice. I will leave this army right now if it means sitting around here for the next month, with our thumbs in our assess, while our family and friends are subjected to the treatment of the Graygual. No fucking way, sir, pardon my language."

"Why is the Hunter keeping the situation a secret, I wonder?" Marc said from a chair in the corner. When eyes turned his way, he hunched and looked at his hands, scrubbing at his nail.

"He isn't very well going to alert Shanti that he's holed up in the city, now is he?" Sanders said, pacing again. "She'd turn up with Shadow and mind power and all sorts of ideas on how to kill them all and get my wife out of this. At least, she'd better." Sanders shot Shanti a *look*.

"But—" Marc's face retracted into his collar like a turtle as Sanders' gaze swung at him.

"But what, cadet?" Sanders prodded.

"He wants her. And probably the Captain. And I'm sure he must know—oooh." Marc scrubbed harder at his nail.

Sanders stopped walking and stared at Marc with wide eyes. His face was a dangerous shade of red now. Shanti stepped in. "Say what you have to say, Marc, before Sanders brains you."

"Oh." Marc cleared his throat, not looking up. "He probably assumes that if he asked you to trade yourself for our city, you'd want to do it, but all of us would stop you. Right? Because that would save our people for now, but without you and the Captain, we'd all die eventually. We're a marked city. So trapping you and taking you is probably the safer approach for him."

"There's no point in going if we don't have mental workers," Cayan said in a low voice. Shanti could feel the pain in him, and also the anger and desperation to get moving. He wanted to leave every bit as badly as Sanders. As she did. But he didn't get where he was by being hasty.

"There's you and her," Tobias said. "You guys rocked the Graygual at the last battle. This wouldn't be a big deal for you, would it?"

"Everything depends on what he's got behind those walls," Shanti said in contemplation as the rest of the Honor Guard came running in, out of breath and wide-eyed. Without a word, they went into the back corner with Marc, clearly knowing they'd be told to leave if they interrupted. Shanti continued, "Using the mind is just like the sword. You're an excellent fighter, Sanders, and can take five men on alone if they are decent. You can take two if they're good. One if they are topnotch. Just you against twenty, though…"

"What level of mental assault will the Hunter have gathered, do you think?" Cayan asked.

Shanti braced her hands on her hips. "It's hard to say. So far, he's had some of the best. I've had a hard time combating them, especially since he knows to keep them in pairs or in groups. But he's an outcast now. I have no idea what he may still have at his disposal."

Cayan shook his head and looked out of the window. "We can't just sit here. *I* can't just sit here. Not when my people are in danger. We need to get closer and assess."

Shanti felt a knot in the pit of her stomach. The Hunter was cunning and ruthless. There was no telling what he would do to Cayan's people to get what he wanted. She only hoped they weren't already too late.

CHAPTER 5

KALLON CROUCHED IN the tall grasses with his sword at the ready and his fighting brothers and sisters all connected with a mind link. The horses they'd either stolen or been given were all tied in a cluster of trees just over the hill. In front of him, sitting around a fire with cups in their hands and self-assurance in their bearing, sat a host of Graygual and Inkna.

"We are outnumbered," Mela said softly, crouched beside him holding two throwing knives. Night had fallen, making everywhere beyond the firelight a hiding spot.

"In number only. Those Inkna are weak, and I doubt the Graygual can match our swords." Kallon glanced to his right and met eyes with Sayas. His sub-leader's team was in position. Kallon looked left, finding Tulous. He was ready, too. Expectation buzzed through their merged *Gifts*.

"Okay, let's get ready." Kallon nodded to the others, increasing the buzz of expectation within their merge. He felt a pulse of eagerness. *Ready!*

He moved out in slow, deliberate steps. Everyone else stepped out at the same time. The half-circle of fighters closed in around those in the firelight, completely unaware. Kallon started to pick up speed, increasing the buzz in their minds. Their *Gifts* coiled, ready to lash out. He was jogging now, his footfalls slightly louder, but still lost to the unobservant.

A horse, tethered outside the camp, neighed. A few more started giving sounds of unease, stamping hooves and shifting stances.

At last, one of the Graygual glanced up. Kallon couldn't see his eyes in the low light, but the plane of the Graygual's face pointed at the horses for a long moment. Kallon could almost see his thought process cranking to life with rusty spokes. The Graygual glanced around.

Kallon started running. The rest followed, shifting to form more of a circle before closing in, suffocating the enemy in perfect synchronization. They surrounded the Graygual before the enemy even knew what was coming.

"Look out!" one yelled, jumping up and ripping out his sword.

Too late. Tanna, excellent with knives and close combat, descended on him. She batted away his weapon with her sword and stuck him through the gut.

A blast of mental pain stabbed at Kallon, then swept

around his group. Tulous took point, *thrusting* a single point of pain at the mind, fracturing it. Sayas *frayed* the other two Inkna, deadening their thoughts.

Kallon rushed at two Graygual who were standing, their swords not finding their hands nearly fast enough. Kallon pulled out a knife as he struck with his sword, piercing the chest of one. He stabbed the other through the lower neck. Both men buckled to their knees with screams of pain.

Stepping over someone Mela had taken down, Kallon lunged at another, slashing with his knife to clear the man out of his path. He skirted the fire, as he entered their midst, a lethal phantom.

A sword strike came at him. He dodged to the side and then struck. His blade sliced flesh. He was already moving on.

Dannon, the largest and strongest of their people, grabbed a Graygual throat with his bare hand. He clamped down and tore, ripping flesh. The enemy scream ended in no more than a gurgle.

Kallon dodged Mela, who was making short work of a grungy Graygual, and found their officer. He was hanging back, watching the melee with a cunning stare. Even as Kallon advanced, the officer inched back toward the horses. It was clear leaving was on his mind.

"You've forgotten your training," Kallon said as he advanced.

"It *is* true. You live."

"Yes. Were you there? Did you cut my people down?"

Fear worked into the man's gaze. "I was told to. Those were the orders!"

White-hot rage stole Kallon's breath for one moment. He felt its mirror race around the merge. Cooling himself, he advanced on this disgusting creature with a sure step. "As I said, you've forgotten your training."

A small crease wormed between the man's brows. He licked his lips, showing his nervousness. "I haven't forgotten anything."

Kallon lunged. His sword tip cut through the air toward the man's side. The defensive block came too late, and the answering strike was slow and clumsy. In confusion, Kallon stepped back, still in his ready stance. "You weren't trained as an officer..." He eyed the four stripes on the man's breast.

The man licked his lips again. He didn't offer an explanation.

Kallon struck, slicing the Graygual's other side. "Why do you hold this position?"

A mad gleam lit up the man's eyes. "Because I took it, that's why! We were offered women and rewards. I had mine already picked out. They said I could have my pick!" He rushed Kallon, his sword work all over the place.

Ringing steel echoed through the camp, Kallon not doing more than blocking. Panting, the man fell to his knees, floundering.

"How did you kill an officer?" Kallon asked.

The man climbed to his feet painfully. He spat. "We were all promised rewards. They weren't delivering. So we took what was ours, including this uniform. He wasn't so good with a blade in his sleep. People do what you say when you wear this uniform. They go along quietly. And when they don't, you're free to force them. I can take the rewards due to me now. It's within my power."

A crawling sensation filled Kallon's stomach. His hand tightened on his sword. "I could make you suffer. I could exact justice for the things you've done." Kallon wiped and then sheathed his blade. The man staggered, clutching his sides. "But I could never torture you the same way your brethren will."

Kallon turned and walked toward the horses. "Swap out our rides for any that are better, and send the rest of the horses on their way. Leave his food."

"Wait…what are you doing?" the man begged. He staggered toward Kallon.

"I'm leaving you to the Graygual." Kallon threw a bag of food to the ground.

"No! Please." The man stumbled, falling to his hands and knees. "No. Let me go."

"Not so sure of yourself now, are you?" Mela asked with a disgusted expression.

"You must've known this would happen." Sayas put his hands on his hips, surveying the man. "Obviously you were going to get caught eventually. Any fool would have known that."

"The army is stretched too thinly." The man reached out imploringly for Sayas. "The officers are in short supply. Please, I can show you the way. After I killed the officer, I've been avoiding the Graygual for months."

Kallon jingled a satchel of gold and silver, then put it into his pocket. "It looks like your luck has run out."

A shock of pain ripped through Kallon's mind. The Inkna on their trail were in range.

He threw up his shields and felt everyone else do the same. "Grab the horses. Go! We're out of time."

"They're gaining on us, Kallon," Mela said, slapping the butt of a shaggy mount. She grabbed the reins of another. "We have to move faster."

Kallon hesitated for a moment. He felt the Chosen's call. He felt the need to go to her with a strength he hadn't experienced before. Something in him said she was in grave danger, and the disorganization this Graygual deserter spoke of was due to Xandre focusing his mind elsewhere. There was only one person who would distract Xandre.

On the other hand, if he ran now, he'd continue to be chased. He would lead the Graygual to the Chosen's doorstep. If she wasn't prepared for it, or had her own battles to fight, Kallon could single-handedly end this land's hope.

His gaze hit Mela. He was not able to decide if he should go or stay. A flat look of resignation gazed back.

She'd had the same thoughts, and her choice was clear. They had to protect the Chosen with their lives if need be.

They would have to stay and fight.

Kallon looked around, analyzing their location. They were cutting across the land on a northern angle, aiming for the more densely wooded areas clustered at the base of the small Westwood mountain range. Currently their surroundings were mostly flat and open, great for a battle between large armies facing off, but horrible if their force was outnumbered. If they fought here, they'd be slaughtered.

"We'll go until we find a place we can defend," Kallon said, action again. "We need to be smart about this. Let's get moving. We haven't much time."

CHAPTER 6

"OH MY GOD, I've never wanted to see dry land so much in my life!" Rachie staggered off the dock and fell to his knees in the mud.

"What about the first crossing?" Shanti asked, shouldering her pack as she stepped off behind him.

"Too far back to remember."

She scanned the banks and the roads off to either side. There was not one Graygual uniform, as they'd seen from the approach. Unless their intentions were shielded from her *Gift*, as Burson's might be, no one paid them any special attention, or seemed to be watching for them. They could've been any strangers landing on the banks.

A sense of foreboding filled her as she walked toward the street leading up to the city.

Rohnan fell in beside her. "How long will we stay here?"

Shanti started toward the road leading to the heart of the town. "Just tonight. Cayan and the guys are eager to get home."

"I don't blame them, and in their place, I would want to do the same thing, but I'm not sure it is the right plan."

"It's not. It can't be. Cayan and I can't beat whatever the Hunter has prepared, and Sonson is a week behind us, at best. We're probably walking into captivity."

"And yet you are still willing."

"I walked away once already, Rohnan. I walked away from our people being slaughtered. I will not do it again. Cayan and his people have given me life, they have sent men with me to gain the title of Chosen, and they trusted me when I said their people would be safe if I left. I was wrong. And now I will try to make that right. I will gladly trade places with his people if that is the only option."

Rohnan nodded once. He didn't comment.

"You don't have to come," Shanti said quietly.

"You have to go for the Captain. I have to go for you. Sanders was right. If we aren't fighting for family, what are we fighting for? Besides, you'll need someone to rescue you. It's my turn."

"You'll probably have to fight Sanders for that job." Shanti felt a surge of spiciness licking up her core, something she usually felt in the more intimate moments with Cayan. She turned back as she crested the hill, spotting him immediately as he stood at the end of the dock. His men were unloading the ship, walking past him to lay their needed travel equipment and supplies together on the ground.

He didn't move; he didn't need to. She could feel his warning fizzing up her spine before it turned into a spike of fear. Finally, the complex feelings carrying a clear directive softened into overall warmth, infusing her body and tingling out through her limbs. He was telling her to stay out of trouble, but if she landed in it, to inform him with a shock of fear. The last was his mental version of calling her *mesasha.*

She blew out a breath. They were almost better at speaking without words. They'd been practicing without meaning to, communicating with their *Joining* while in training, or from across the Shadow Lands. Or when entwined in each other's bodies. It almost felt better to feel the meanings than hear the words.

"I've really stuck my foot in it," she mumbled, calling up the weighty feeling he would know as disgruntled acknowledgement.

Shanti glanced around them, looking for anything suspicious. Her mind spread out, feeling for the same thing. The lateness of the afternoon meant many of the patrons had gone home, and now the traders' stalls were being taken down and put away. A few people ambled along the path around them, one drunk and staggering. Nothing seemed out of the ordinary. It was almost…normal.

She mentioned the latter.

"It *is* normal, *Chulan*. These people are living their life. They won't understand the danger of the Graygual until it is upon them. Until then, they'll carry on, looking after their families."

"The Graygual were here. It should've been upon them…"

"When Xandre came through, he didn't want his presence known. You were his goal, not this town." Rohnan's eyes were scanning faces. "I wonder about the way back, however. Why not capture the town then? Where are the Graygual now?"

A spark of unease emerged in Shanti. Her mind raced, running through implications. "He's clearing the path for me. He must be. He's allowing me safe passage back." She shook her head, the unease turning into a fire of doubt. Cayan's response welled up, half supportive to calm her down, and half anxious, wondering what the problem was. "He is allowing me to get settled again. He must've made obvious deductions about my ties to Cayan."

"I'm not sure I follow."

Shanti stopped in the middle of the lane, thinking. She'd spent her life learning about Xandre's habits. She'd studied his battle awareness, his tactics, his movements. She was sure of his need to always acquire intelligence before carrying out his plans. She'd shaped him that way. In turn, he was studying her.

She wandered off to the side of the street and leaned against the wall, contemplating. Looking for deductions Xandre might've come to. And then she knew. As plain as day, she knew. She wasn't a wanderer—Burson had gotten that wrong. She *needed* to be a wanderer.

"What have I always done, Rohnan?" Shanti said as a sick feeling turned her stomach.

"I can't… I'm not following your emotion, *Chulan*."

She gave him a direct stare. "Our people knew Xandre would come for us. We *knew* it. And what did we do?"

Rohnan's brow furrowed. "Prepared…"

"No. We waited. We dug in our heels, stayed right where we were, and we were annihilated. *Then* I left. And what did I do?"

"You found a new place to call home." Rohnan's voice turned grave. "And now you are returning to it."

"Exactly." Shanti rubbed her temples. "He *is* waving me through. Our people are not wanderers. We make a home, and we defend our home regardless of the odds. Despite my knowing I'll never have one, I want a family. I want to live in peace with my mate. If I could choose, I'd choose Cayan and his city for that."

"You did choose…"

Shanti hung her head. "And Xandre knows it."

"Do you think the Hunter is acting on Xandre's orders?"

"I doubt it. The Hunter's failure should be shoved in everyone's faces as a warning. But if Burson has figured out where he is, Xandre would've. He's the bait to lure Cayan home, and me with him. *Flak.*"

A passing woman jumped and clutched at her child, throwing Shanti a startled expression.

Shanti pushed off from the wall, anger burning through her. "He is trying to strip from me everything I love, Rohnan. One at a time, he has peeled away the things that made me smile, leaving only death and decay. He is fighting only one war. I saw to that when I bested him the first time. His war is against me."

"You are fighting only one war, *Chulan.* Always were. Against him."

Shanti felt the weight of her sword heating her back. "Yes. Exactly. I've been blind. We don't need armies, Rohnan. We don't need to consolidate forces. We need stealth and the cover of darkness. We need Burson and our people, not a city and its resources." She blew out a breath and thought about punching something. Rohnan took a step back. "I can't leave Cayan, though. He is the other half of my power. Together we are a force. I was right about that."

She clenched her fists and eyed the wall.

"I do not recommend punching a hard surface, *Chulan.* Surely you've learned that lesson by now."

Shanti flexed, trying to work out the frustration. "I need to speak to Burson. I don't know what to do."

"Will you send Cayan on alone?"

Shanti flexed again. She shook her hands and swung her arms, trying to work out the aggression. "No. How could I? Xandre's got me by the lady-balls."

"He moves slowly. You move quickly. His strengths are in planning, yours are in action. We need to play to your strengths to keep him from using his."

Shanti rolled her head, loosening up her neck. Rohnan was right. She needed to take action. But one thing at a time. "This is turning into a bad day."

"You started it."

"A bar fight might be in my future."

"Let's find a place to stay, and then we'll find a *different* place to start a fight."

It was sound logic.

They walked down the wide lane until they came to an inn with a chipped sign and paint peeling off the front. "They'll let us in, I bet."

"They'd admit a flea-ridden dog." Rohnan plucked at her shirt. "Let's go somewhere that doesn't make us scratch for the rest of the journey."

She glanced down at her clothes. They were the Shadow stylings, but with holes, some stains, and the general smell of sweat and filth from being at sea for nearly a week without a bath.

"I've been refused lodgings when I've looked this travel-stained before, Rohnan."

Rohnan pulled her toward a glistening sign featuring a plow with a backdrop of stars. "Your journey must've been awful, *Chulan*. You have my sympathy. But then, if you were in any way personable, things probably would've been different."

He walked into the inn like he was nobility. His white-blond head, messed and a little greasy though it was, was held high. His shoulders were straight, even with the rumpled and stained coat he wore. His eyes glittered with self-importance and his face was pointed at the world regardless of the smudge of dirt on his cheek. It was as if he wasn't aware of what he looked like.

"*Hello*," he said in the trader's dialect, his lips quirked in an almost-smile.

The man behind the counter looked up from his book and surveyed Rohnan. His brow creased in distaste. At Rohnan's continued gaze, his expression bent toward confused. "*Yeah?*"

"*Yes.*" Rohnan gave him a slight bow. "*I will be needing several rooms, baths, and meals for the night.*" Rohnan's hand dropped, grazing the slight bulge in his pocket. Gold?

Did Cayan give Rohnan gold? Or did he steal it...

The man's gaze turned shrewd. "*I've got five rooms.*"

The man leaned his hammy arms against the counter. "*Three gold pieces each.*"

"*Oh my no, that is outrageous.*" Rohnan smiled and took another step toward the door.

Shanti rolled her eyes as she felt Cayan drawing closer to the inn. In their shared language, she said, "I'll get the horses. I don't have the patience for your style of bartering."

"That is why you're used to sleeping in bushes."

As Shanti left the inn, she muttered to herself, "You never get used to sleeping in bushes."

She saw Cayan walking up the lane. It was hard not to. His shoulders were wide enough to knock down buildings with each swing. The things should've had a warning attached.

"What's the problem?" Cayan asked as he drew near. A woman across the lane with her eyes glued on Cayan stumbled on a rock and swerved into the wall.

Served her right for gawking, Shanti thought.

"Nothing," Shanti said, trying to calm her turbulent emotions from her conversation with Rohnan. To Cayan's quirked eyebrow—lying was no longer an option with him—she followed with, "I'll talk to you about it later. Rohnan is inside getting us rooms, so I figured we could—"

"There isn't anything nicer?" Cayan looked at the inn front with distaste.

"Would you rather a castle? Elders have mercy!" Shanti started off toward the outskirts where Sea Farer, the ship's captain, had said the main stables were located. "Let's get some horses instead of standing around nickpicking."

"*Nit*picking," Cayan said as he fell in beside her.

They caught Sanders coming up the path, a few of the Honor Guard walking doggedly behind him. "I caught these idiots pooling money to go to the whore-house." Sanders threw a thumb behind him at the three boys with red faces. "A bunch of nitwits, the lot of them."

"Rohnan is getting rooms at the inn." Cayan pointed back the way they'd come. "Rachie and Gracas, you go up and meet him. Leilius, head back to the docks and get more gold. I have a feeling I didn't bring enough up. Have Xavier carry it. You lads will have less problems that way."

"I could do with a problem or two." Sanders punched his palm. Just like Shanti, aggression rolled off him. He was spoiling for a fight.

Shanti would invite him to her party later. That flea-bitten inn would probably be great sport.

"Yes, sir," Rachie said as he and Gracas walked on, their faces still bright red and pointed at the ground.

Leilius turned around and started jogging, not daring to look Shanti or the Captain in the eye.

Sanders cracked his neck before glancing off at the boys hurrying away. "I was curious at that age, too. Didn't think they'd want that question answered with a ruddy-faced working woman, though."

"They'll thank you for it when they get older," Cayan said as Shanti led the way to the horses, not at all surprised when Sanders fell in with him. He knew horses better than anyone else in their group.

"Are we sure we want to waste time staying in this town?" Sanders asked as they approached the stables. A row of stalls spread out in front of them, horses neighing and pawing at the ground. A loud thump sounded toward the end. Then another. It sounded like a horse was kicking its stall in a temper.

"Everyone is tired. A bath, a hot meal, and a good bed is needed," Shanti said as they stopped in front of a mangy brown animal lethargically chomping oats.

"These are pitiful." Sanders put his hands on his hips and spat. He meandered down the row of stalls, checking out the offerings.

"Hello, hello!" A short, balding man walked up with a calculating eye and a relaxed demeanor.

"Is this the best you have to offer?" Sanders asked.

"Now, sir, these horses are some of the finest you've seen. Come from all over the land, they do. Fine horse stock here, yes sir. Mighty fine."

"Are you blind as well as a bad liar?" Sanders demanded. He gestured at the stall next to them. "That mare is hoping for a ride to the afterlife."

"Please, sir." The man turned to Cayan, his cunning gaze starting to fray. "Tell me what you're looking for and I will find it for you. Does the missus need…" The man looked at Shanti. He squinted a little. "A plow horse, maybe…"

"Do I have shit on my face or something?" Shanti asked in exasperation. "It's not like I'm wearing rags."

"Usually respectable women don't look like the underside of a shoe," Sanders said as he passed by, walking toward the other end of the line. "What do you have on the other side?"

"Oh." The man looked at Sanders with a grave expression. "They are *very* pricey on the other side. But we have some fine ones over here. See?" The man hastened to an older animal that looked more like a mule than a horse.

"Show us the other side," Cayan said in a loud, commanding voice.

"Don't like it when people think you're poor, huh?" Shanti smirked at him.

The man hesitated, something in Cayan's voice drying up his protests. His shrewd gaze slid over Cayan's frame, tall and broad, with a fighter's grace. Calloused hands drew his eyes next, then the hilt of his sword. Finally he nodded. "Follow me."

"Are they made of gold or something?" Sanders growled as they followed the man to a second row of stables.

As they got within sight of the horses, Sanders let out a low whistle. Compared to the first set of horses, these might as well have been made of gold. Large, shiny steeds neighed or bobbed their heads. Fierce-eyed and well groomed, they stood within their stalls expectantly. Or at least that was the way it seemed. Shanti didn't need to know horses to recognize the breeding in these. She'd seen it up close.

"Graygual stock," Sanders said under his breath as he passed in front of Shanti and Cayan, his scowl ever-present. "Hiding the good stuff, huh…?"

"Gustov, sir. The name's Gustov. And no, sir. No, no. These are expensive animals, though. Too much for the common man."

A loud thump sounded at the end of the row, followed by a whinny.

"Good thing we aren't the common man," Sanders said as he slowed his walk to a sort of stroll, his scowl still firmly in place. He eyed each horse in turn, completely ignoring the sales tactics of the stable man. When he approached the end, he stopped with a jerk and stared. His head turned slowly until he was looking at Shanti.

"What?" she asked.

"You won't believe it."

Brow screwed up in confusion, Shanti stalked to the end, Cayan in tow. As they drew near, Shanti sucked in a breath.

There, in the very last stall, was her bloody bastard of a horse. Shining like a star, sleek and obviously of excellent breeding even compared to the others, he huffed and neighed, shaking his head with all the ire and temper he was known for.

"That one—bad attitude, that one. He's a horse for breeding." Gustov shook his head.

"He'd bite the mare." Sanders spat before pointing at the black stallion Cayan was standing near. "That one's ready to bite, too. I'll bet half these horses won't take a rider."

As if on cue, the black stallion stepped closer to the gate. He pawed the ground. His nose went forward, but he didn't bite. He nudged his previous owner.

Cayan had found his horse, and Shanti bet he didn't plan to pay more than stable fees to get it back.

She smirked before noticing Rohnan's horse was here, too, standing placidly as it watched what was going on. Someone had rounded them up after the battle, along with any other horse they could capture, and locked them up.

"I wonder what happened to Burson's," she said quietly.

The Bloody Bastard kicked the wall in a fit of temper. He blew out breath and stomped the ground.

"My, my." Shanti stepped up to the fence. "They let you get away with this temper, huh?"

"I don't advise that, lady. That horse is wild!" The stable master reached out to pull her back.

The horse kicked, thrashing the wall, adding a hoof imprint to the plethora of others. It shook its head, scaring the man enough that he jogged backward again.

"How'd you even get him in there?" Sanders asked, eyeing the animal.

"We captured the others first, and then—" Gustov cut off when he realized what he'd said.

Sanders' eyes sparkled. Graygual didn't subscribe to the rule of "finders-keepers," and everyone who dealt with them knew it. Poor Gustov had just handed Sanders a giant bartering chip.

"Can you still back that one down, *mesasha*?" Cayan jerked his head at her horse. "He'd be great to have, but there's no point if he'll be too wild. This is about haste…"

"Open the cell," Shanti instructed.

"It's a *stall,*" Sanders said with an eye roll.

"They're prisoners. Cell fits. Open it."

Sanders looked at the stable master and shrugged. "It's her funeral."

"No, no. I don't—"

"You can close me in," Shanti said. "C'mon. Let's get this done. I'm stinky and I want a bath."

Gustov undid the latch slowly. As Shanti stepped up, he swung the door open and reached out to push her in. Before his hand could make contact, Cayan reacted, hard and fast. He snatched Gustov's hand out of the air and leaned forward, dominating the stable master with his size. "You don't touch her."

Gustov's eyes rounded. Horse forgotten, he nodded adamantly. "S-sorry, sir. I didn't mean—"

"Who's wilder, the horse or the man?" Shanti laughed.

"This poor bugger is going to pay *us* to take these animals after we're through here." Sanders stepped closer to the stall.

Without wasting any time, Shanti sauntered into the small area, thoroughly aware that this horse was twice her size, much stronger, and had more hard surfaces with which to hurt her. She didn't care. This bastard would not get one over on her. She'd already put up with too much crap where it was concerned. There was no way she was going to let it off easy by spending its life knocking up mares. If she couldn't hang around and have sex all day, neither could it. Fair was fair.

"*You're coming with me, you bloody bastard!*" Shanti said in her native tongue, ready for action.

It neighed at her, shaking its head.

"*Now. Are you going to play nice?*" She reached out to pet its neck.

It neighed again, and this time, it threw out a hoof. She jumped out of the way just in time.

"Oh!" Gustov yelled. "Watch out!"

"*You get one more chance to be nice, and then—*" She narrowly dodged another hoof. The horse kicked behind, banging against the stall.

"*Enough is enough!*" Shanti punched. Her fist connected with its cheek. "*Knock it off or I'll buy you just to make a stew out of you!*"

The horse gave its weird equine growl, a sound unlike any other horse she'd ever heard. It stomped.

She lifted her eyebrow, and then reached out again.

Another stomp.

"Careful…" Gustov cautioned.

Shanti's palm touched the horse's dirty neck. Then, slowly, remembering when this horse had let her hug its neck for comfort, she lightly placed her palm on its nose. The horse bobbed its head and blew out a breath, but he stilled. Shanti touched his nose again. After a moment, she rubbed.

He remembered her.

In a soft voice, she said, "*I need an animal I trust on the journey ahead of me. Will you be that animal?*"

"What is that tongue she speaks?" Gustov drew out

his words suspiciously.

"Never you mind about that," Sanders said, losing interest in Shanti and walking down the line. "What other stock have you got?"

Gustov stared at Shanti for a moment longer. When she glanced at him, she saw a flicker of realization. His eyes widened, but he didn't say a word. Instead, he hurried after Sanders.

In confusion, she watched him go.

Shanti took her hand away from the horse and stepped back. When the horse took a step, she backed out of the stall and closed the lower half of the door. The Bastard put his head over the barrier, allowing her to pet its nose one last time. If she let him, he'd probably follow her back to the inn. If he were human, he'd probably grumble the whole way.

"He'll be fine," Shanti said to Cayan.

"Good. Sanders?" Cayan waited for Sanders to glance up from the other end of the stables. "Take care of this."

"Yes, sir."

"I'll send Tobias and the boys over to help move the animals."

"Yes, sir." Sanders turned back to the horse. "Now this one is seriously lacking. I hope you don't want much for it—"

Shanti felt Cayan's warm hand on her back. "Let's

get back."

"I thought you were worried about having enough gold?" Shanti asked in a low voice, hoping Rohnan had finished getting them rooms.

"Sanders seemed confident. He'll make it work." They walked in silence for a moment before Cayan said, "That stable master had a strange reaction to your eyes."

"You noticed. He must've heard about me, but he didn't say anything. That hasn't happened before." The uncertainty started to niggle Shanti again. "And if he knew I was Chosen, he would've known you are, too. Yet he never gave you a second glance."

"I don't like this, *mesasha.* There was a large battle in this town only a few months ago. There was a huge battle in the Shadow Lands shortly after. Things are changing, but that isn't reflected in this town. Why?"

Shanti should've told Cayan about what she suspected, but even if she did, it wouldn't account for these people's lack of interest in her and Cayan. It was as if everyone was purposely putting on blinders, trying to forget all the strife around them and focusing on their daily life.

Maybe they were. Maybe, as a people, they were shocked into not noticing the change coming. She wouldn't blame them.

"First things first—we need to free your city," Shanti said as they saw Rohnan standing with Ruisa outside the inn. "One step at a time."

A FEW HOURS later, after they had all taken a bath and eaten dinner, Shanti sat quietly at a table with her fingers curled around a pint of ale. Cayan sat beside her with Sanders and Tobias opposite them. All were quiet, but unease and anxiety poured out of them and coated Shanti's mind.

"I almost wish there had been Graygual here," Sanders growled before taking a big swig of his drink. "I could've used the outlet."

"I'd planned to visit that rough inn down the lane," Shanti said, looking out over the strangely placid bar. A man at the far table glanced up, catching her eye. His gaze lingered for a moment, before he looked away. A moment later his lips moved, bending the head of the woman next to him. Shanti could read expectation emanating from both of them, but for what, she couldn't say. They showed no sign of aggression and they weren't preparing for a battle—what were they waiting for?

Shanti felt the minds of the other patrons. "The people in this inn are guarded." Another pair of eyes met hers, a woman's this time. She sat with two men; both of them were keeping their eyes firmly on their mugs. "When have you ever known an inn not to have a card game going? Or dice?"

"Never, and it's a damn shame." Sanders glowered. "I still say we should've gone to that rough place down the lane like Shanti suggested. Maybe someone would've tried to rob us on the way there. Or back."

"I could use a skirmish," Tobias said before he took a sip.

"I don't like the feel of this town." Cayan's gaze swept over the room. "At first I thought no one knew us, but now I think something else is happening. It's like we're being shielded."

Sanders' head snapped up. A fierce light glimmered in his eyes. "From who?"

Cayan shook his head, looking at Shanti. "I don't know. I can't feel any threat."

"Your mind power can't feel anything?" Tobias asked.

Cayan's expression was troubled. "No. All seems quiet. So why is this town on edge?"

"They're not on edge, they are expectant." Shanti pushed her mug away. "But we can't deal with that now." She stood, waiting for Cayan to do the same. "We need to free your city. That has to be our first priority. We'll leave at first light."

"I agree," Sanders said, his eyes scanning the room. "But I'd just as soon bash a head or two before I go."

Shanti smirked as she led the way. More than one pair of eyes glanced up at her leaving, but none lingered.

Tingles worked up her spine as she mounted the stairs to her room. Something big was happening, she could feel it. The press of expectation was begging her to notice something below the surface, ever-present but hidden from view. It was like a secret was being whispered around her, but she just couldn't hear the words.

She let her *Gift* comb the room before opening the door to emptiness. Cayan closed the door behind him. She felt the buttons on her tunic being undone. Her body warmed from the inside as her clothes slid to the ground.

"I can feel your reservations about moving on," Cayan said. His lips skimmed her bare shoulder. "Is it because you know I will want you to live with me?"

More tingles. She really should've mentioned her earlier realization before he got his hopes up. This future he was planning would never come to pass. Not with her. She had a different fate than the one he was hoping for.

She should've, but as he laid her on the bed and climbed between her thighs, she didn't. It would only kill the mood, and she needed to think of something other than what lay directly ahead of them. So she clutched on tightly as his body entered hers, filling her in a way that blanked out her surroundings and soaked into her thoughts. As he moved, wrapped in her limbs, she longed for a time when they could do this without the ever-present danger hanging around them. She wanted to stop taking the herbs that kept her childless and see if their like-*Gifts* might grant them new life. She wanted any fate but the one she had been given.

The climax came almost out of the blue, stealing her breath away. In the aftermath, as she lay with him quietly, the road ahead encroached on the moment. "Ruisa is positive the women of your city will fend for themselves."

"She's young and idealistic. It's one thing to have the knowledge to defend yourself, but another to stand up to tyranny."

"She thinks they'll just poison everyone and be done with it."

Shanti barely heard Cayan's sigh, but through their *Joining,* she could feel the crushing anxiety he somehow kept hidden from the world. "Again, she's young. It's a large city with probably a fair number of Graygual. They wouldn't be able to get everyone at the same time. If even one *hint* of doubt strikes the Hunter, I imagine he'll react hard and brutally to quell the uprising. I would, and I have morals. Surely the Women's Circle will see that. They are all smart women. They pay attention. They'll know the danger they're in."

"So you don't think they'll act at all, huh?"

"Hard to say. But if I had to guess, no, probably not.

They've always had the army to fight while they hid. They might handle an abusive husband, but that's because if things got out of hand, the law would step in. Now, there is no law. They're completely on their own, and I don't know who would have the courage to stand against it, much less organize a defense. I try to remain optimistic, but..."

"Hopefully they can hold on, then. We can be there in a week. Then we'll figure out how to get them free. How to get them safe. They just have to hang on."

CHAPTER 7

ALENA FROZE IN the darkness. She clutched her hands to her chest and pushed her back against the wall of the stone prison. A bead of sweat trickled down her back despite the chill.

The deep voice of a Graygual sounded around the corner. Another answered.

She glanced around her location, looking for a place to hide. The dull moonlight didn't completely illuminate her, but with no trees or cover, she looked like a lumpy wart on the side of the wall. She'd be found for sure.

A grunt and another rattling of foreign words had her heart beating wildly. He was getting closer.

She glanced at the corner, knowing that the two guards and the prison entrance lay just on the other side. Her gaze landed on the nearest tree, and then she bent to the packed dirt below her feet. If she started running, they'd hear her. Even if she moved slowly, like she had been, she might still be found.

What do I do?

Trying to calm her body so her noisy breathing didn't give her away, she eyed the way she'd come. She wanted to go home. She wasn't cut out for this. Every moment she broke the rules acted like an anvil on her chest, crushing her with fear. But the Women's Circle needed her. They had faith in her.

Her grip on the package tightened. She licked her lips. Should she stay or go? Hide, maybe, until the coast was clear?

As she was about to back away, the Graygual voice sounded again before heavy footsteps pounded the ground. She sucked in a breath, ready to run…but no one came around that corner. He was going in the opposite direction.

"You there! What you looking for?" the guard shouted. It sounded like he was going back into the prison.

As if to prove it, a clink of metal slowly repeated until it turned into a regular rhythm. A tin cup against the bars, probably. The midnight guard liked to bully the prisoners.

Steadying her breath, Alena moved closer to the corner. Once there, she inched her face along, trying to show as little of herself as possible in case anyone was looking.

An open doorway flickering with soft light greeted her before the groan of a wooden chair from within the prison. Shadows draped across the building.

Alena checked her timepiece. It was more than an hour since Gretchen, one of the cooks, had slipped a sleeping draught into the guard's food. He should be getting drowsy by now.

Another deep breath and Alena was around the corner, inching toward the door. She gripped her hands tighter to try and still the tremors. Her legs quivered, begging her to run away from danger and head straight home. Hiding in her house wouldn't be safe, though. Nowhere in this city was safe, not while it was occupied.

At the door, Alena froze one more time, making sure all was quiet. Usually after midnight no one moved around the city. The citizens were supposed to be in their houses, and the army men were all locked up either in this prison with the officers, or in the park with the enlisted men. The guards, complacent with the long, slow hours of the night, often dozed or stood at their posts with vacant stares. *Usually* they stayed put—she had no idea what the second guard had wanted with the first. She only hoped he didn't plan to return.

Aside from a few shuffles, some heavy breathing, and the occasional cough, silence reigned.

With her heart in her throat, Alena inched her head around the doorframe to peer inside. A candle flickered somewhere off to the left, sprinkling the bars and softly illuminating a mess of bodies sprawled out on the floor.

She could barely make out chests rising and falling, her army's men sleeping. Two ankles, one on top of the other, stuck out from the wall. The guard was definitely sitting, and appeared to be relaxing. This was good news.

She inched her head in a little further, glancing around to look down the other side of the row of cells. Moonlight from a few high windows barely lighted the ground where another mess of bodies lay. Since the city didn't see many captives, the prisons were small and cells few. The Graygual had stuffed as many of the officers in as they could.

She clutched her precious cargo tighter to her chest. Her stomach constricted with fear. She stepped in.

The guard was sitting with his head drooped to the side. His meaty arms were crossed over his chest. She couldn't see his eyes, but with his head like that, he had to be asleep.

Breath shallow, she inched forward, tingles of fear making her joints tight and jerky. Unwashed bodies assaulted her senses. More than one man lay in an awkward position, pressed up against the bars or other men, limbs jumbled together. The fact that they could sleep like that was testament to the extent of their overall suffering. They were so tired they could sleep anywhere, in any position. They'd grown used to the horrible conditions because they had to. It was that or die.

Alena's heart ached. Three already had.

No time to think about that now.

She scanned the cell in front of the guard where there was the most light. Gretchen had said Lucius and Sterling were both in that cell, carefully watched. They were the highest-ranked officers in the city.

Dark heads danced in the flickering orange light. Dull blue uniforms, coated with dirt and grime, became a sea. Boots of all sizes stuck out of odd locations within the bodies.

Squinting and shaking her head, she stepped a little closer, her senses on high alert. She caught sight of a head with short hair. Looking closer, she could just make out the strong jaw, perhaps a small cleft in his chin? He seemed handsome enough, but she could barely see him. It could be her mind playing tricks on her.

He had short hair, though. It *had* to be Lucius. The Hunter kept him relatively well groomed.

He lay near the back, tangled up like everyone else. Tiptoeing, careful not to shuffle, Alena edged toward the cell. She had to get this done.

She bent to the nearest shoulder and touched it gently, belatedly realizing it was a childhood friend—Barus. His eyes snapped open, sighting her immediately. A faint line came into his brow in confusion, but he didn't move.

Alena put a finger to her mouth. She pointed to the bundle clutched to her chest, and then pointed to the back of the cell. She mouthed, "Lucius."

Barus' gaze flicked toward the guard, then back up at her. He shook his head. "Go."

Oh good, he was going to try and tell her what to do from inside a jail cell. Very helpful.

She shook her head and whispered, "Get Lucius!"

Barus' eyes flicked to the guard again. The furrow in his brow deepened, but not out of confusion this time. He was disapproving.

The sands were pouring through the hourglass as she stood there, dickering around with the fool. He'd get her caught while trying to make sure she was safe.

She touched the body next to him. The man moved, waking up slower than Barus had. When his head turned, she saw it was Timken, an older army man who refused to retire. He was probably kicking himself for that decision now.

Confusion stole his expression as his gaze fell on Alena. Just like Barus, his eyes then flicked to the guard.

"Lucius." Alena added a point to her whisper.

Unlike Barus, Timken took note of what she held. His doubt cleared instantly. He gave a curt nod before shifting in order to get his right arm, previously pressed against the bars, into the air. With a wheeze of effort, he gave the man next to him a hard poke.

The wake-up period and following confusion ate more time. Alena could feel the sting of anticipation. She glanced at the guard behind her, only a little comforted by the steady rising and falling of his chest. Someone could come through the door at any minute, though. She needed to speed this up and get out of there.

She made circles in the air with her hand, hoping that they would get the message. *Let's go!*

The next man woke up, then the next, each a little quicker now that more of them were awake. Barus shifted position. A button scraped against a bar. Everyone froze.

Alena did the motion again. *Hurry up!*

Finally someone jabbed Lucius. His eyes snapped open. His head came up, and he scanned the men on the ground before his gaze settled on her. Confusion and fear stole his expression, the fear a remnant from when they had punished her for his stubbornness.

Alena looked down at her bundle, and then motioned him forward.

A chorus of breath being released blew through the cell as a message was passed along.

"Pass it through," Timken said quietly.

"I can't. I have to explain the plan to him directly."

"Whose plan?"

Was now really the time to be nosey? "*Just pass the message on!*"

When the message reached Lucius, the real issue came into effect. For him to get up and get to the bars, they all had to move. Fabric rustled. Bodies scraped against the stone floor. Someone grunted as another let out a muffled "Ow!"

Alena started bouncing in place, that open door pressing at her back. She glanced at the guard, then at that airy void through the door. More grunts and shifting. A groan of pain.

This is a very bad idea.

The guard snorted.

Alena spun, fear crawling through her. Her stomach rolled as his head came up and a grimace took over his face. Eyes still closed, his head bobbed.

Gretchen hadn't made the sleeping draught strong enough!

Holding her breath, Alena glanced down at her package. Then at the men in the cell, all frozen, staring at her or the guard with wide eyes. Then at Lucius, agony in his gaze. She knew he would rather die than for her to be captured by the guards and put to death. The men of this city hated women being in harm's way, and the Hunter had made the punishment clear for those defying his rule. She should run!

Without warning, Shanti's face flashed into Alena's

mind. She didn't know the foreign woman personally, but she envied her freedom of will, her fearlessness and brash attitude. Shanti had never been afraid of anything. She'd always gotten the job done.

Then Alena thought of Molly slapping her across the face. If she ran now, she would leave a hole in their planning. And with just one hole, the whole thing would unravel.

The Women's Circle was counting on her. She could not fail.

A new wave of courage washed through her. Hardening her resolve, she continued to wait for Lucius. The guard shifted, moaning once more, before settling back with his chin on his chest. He shifted again, uncomfortable. He'd wake up again soon. Alena didn't have long.

She turned back to the cell and motioned Lucius forward. "Hurry!" she mouthed.

"Go!" he mouthed back, flinging his hand toward the door.

Timken pushed someone out of the way, the rustling of fabric blaring through the silence like a hammer on an anvil. He grabbed Lucius by the shirt and jerked, making him step forward.

Lucius stepped on someone's leg. Then an arm. Grunts sounded like popping corn. The guard moaned behind her.

C'mon. *C'mon!*

"You shouldn't be here!" Lucius' words were barely more than a rustling of wind.

"Take this." Alena passed through the bundled collection of vials. "There are two potions in there. One is a fast-working poison. All you have to do is introduce it into the enemy's body any way that you can. Mouth, eyes, a cut..."

Lucius nodded with the info, taking the package through the bars.

"The other is a deep sleep draught. It'll make you appear dead. *You,* Lucius. Sterling, too. There are three draughts in all, so you can choose one other. Those vials have a red lid. It'll work within a few hours, and then your heart rate will slow to the point that it is undetectable. You'll go cold to the touch, you'll go still—you will look dead. That will last for about a day, maybe less. Do you understand?"

He frowned. That was a no.

"When the Captain comes, and things start to get hairy," she explained quickly, "swallow the contents of the red vial. Appear dead and they'll put you in the morgue where there are no locks. You can help from the inside of the city while the Captain is on the outside. Do you *see*?"

"What about the poison?"

Boots scraped against stone. The guard moaned. Alena's heart started to thump wildly. She pushed the bundle against his chest, hearing the guard moving again. He was fighting the sleeping draught now.

"That's for everyone else. Spread it out. We are trying to get a little to everyone. When the Captain starts the attack, and things are getting more chaotic, you can use this to cut people down. We'll try to get you knives, but those are harder to hide from the guards. This'll work if you don't have anything else. Just a tiny bit will do the job—it's very potent. Splash it in their face to get it into their mouth or something. It's all we could think of to give you guys something to use."

"Have you had word of the Captain?" Lucius asked, his voice dripping with hope.

"No, but he will come. That's what the Hunter is banking on. And when he does, he'll bring the foreign women. Molly is positive that together they will cause havoc."

Lucius nodded slowly. "Wise. And yes, they will." He reached through the bar and took her hand. The warmth seeped into her, vibrating through her in a long-forgotten way. "Thank you. For your bravery."

She felt the rush of pride. It was short-lived.

The chair behind her creaked. Alena jumped and spun. The guard's head lolled before bobbing up. He blinked, dazed, before rubbing at his eyes.

"Get out of here!" Lucius said in a fierce whisper.

The guard rolled his neck and then shoulders,

straightening up. Alena didn't waste any more time. She hiked up her skirt and ran. The soles of her shoes slid as she took the corner too fast. She crashed into the doorframe.

"What—?" The chair creaked again, the guard getting to his feet.

"Move!" she heard Lucius urge. As she swung around the corner, she caught sight of Lucius pushing someone. She could just make out Barus barreling into someone else, drawing the guard's attention, before she was gone.

She had to tell the Women's Circle she'd succeeded in her task. There was only one more plan to put into effect, before they were ready for the Captain and the bloodshed to follow.

That was when the real danger began.

CHAPTER 8

SANDERS REFUSED TO feel the ache in his legs and back from their constant riding. The horse under him, as well bred and sturdy as it was, panted from fatigue. But the end was in sight. Already the land was changing, morphing from an acquaintance into an old friend, reminding him of childhood hunts and excursions. They were almost home.

A shock of fear punched him.

Junice.

He gritted his teeth and looked out to the side, clamping down on the stream of worst-case scenarios that rolled through his mind. Junice would be okay. She was a fighter. She had never let Sanders get his way, much less order her around, so there was no way she'd let some stinky Graygual push her around.

"The Hunter will be civil to his captives unless his demands aren't met," Rohnan said in his stupid singsong, caressing voice. It had a calming effect.

Being too calm could get a man killed.

"Stop reading my mind, gorgeous," Sanders said

sarcastically. He looked back to the front. He didn't need anyone seeing how anxious he was. He needed to be the strong focal point of this outfit, backing up the Captain and keeping everyone else confident. That damn twin of Shanti's was just confusing matters.

Sanders blew out a breath, feeling both relief and fear as they crossed the first landmark identifying the border of their land. His horse's head started to droop, and his wasn't the only one. These horses were near the brink. They'd ridden hard over the last week, and if they didn't give these animals a break, they'd be walking the rest of the way.

Another landmark came and went as they moved deeper into the lush trees. The first sentry post loomed on the right. Sanders could tell it was empty. That was normal. Sanders hadn't stationed people in that crow's nest for years. It was too far out for the present time of peace with the surrounding lands.

After this, though, it might be time to stick a Shadow person with mind power up there. Peacetime was over.

In a hundred yards or so, the next sentry post came up. Also empty. After this, they should be manned, assuming the Hunter hadn't killed everyone.

"Let's halt," Shanti said in a faraway voice. Her horse pranced sideways instead of stopping. That horse didn't like to stand still when it sensed a battle coming.

"Bloody horse," Shanti muttered before sliding to the ground.

She glanced back at Sanders before walking to the Captain's horse, away from the rest of the men.

"She wants you with them," Rohnan said as he swung his leg over his mount.

"You don't have to be a mind reader to catch the obvious," Sanders said, jumping down.

Daniels joined them, too. The Captain hadn't gotten down from his horse, though. He looked out toward the distant city with unfocused eyes.

"The sentries aren't yours," Shanti said to the Captain. "I don't know how good their range is. I don't want to risk moving any closer yet."

"How many can you sense?" Daniels asked.

"Two. The first two, and just barely." Shanti matched the Captain's distant look. "I'm at the very edge of our range, and there is no one in the land who can match us. But those two are strong, and if they have more and they are all merged, they could come close to being able to reach us. Very close."

"We're a long way out," Sanders said, eyeing the men. They all sat rigid in their saddles with clenched jaws and severe expressions. It was all coming to a head. "We can't do much from here."

"We need a plan," Shanti said.

"The Hunter probably expects us to have an army of

Shadow at our back." The Captain sat straight and tall, steady as a rock. His eyes were vicious. "It would make sense for him to put his best men up front."

Sanders ground his teeth again. Instead of the army of Shadow, they had a team. That team was still a week behind them, at least. If the Graygual took an interest in them, though, they might never get there at all.

The Captain's knuckles went white on his reins. "The wise thing to do would be to wait."

"The *wise* thing to do would be to get an idea of what we're up against." Shanti fingered the knives on the holster around her upper thigh. "My problem is, I don't know how to do that. There's no sneaking in when someone with the *Gift* is watching for me. As soon as I'm in their range, they'll have me."

"They'll have you in more ways than one," the Captain said, his voice getting harder. "They'll vastly overpower you with the *Gift*. You might as well just offer yourself to them. It's you the Hunter wants."

"And you, now." Sanders braced his hand on the hilt of his sword. "He must know it was the two of you that made the wave of mind-death. He'll want you both."

"Sir…" Daniels' expression was one of contemplation. "The Hunter has no idea you know what's going on. He will be expecting you to come home, and then find these foreign Inkna in our sentries' positions. I think he'll make allowances for your reaction, don't you?"

The Captain and Shanti both looked at Daniels. Neither said anything, probably thinking that through.

"He doesn't know Shanti is here," Daniels continued. "He knows less than you, actually. Creating a diversion with a large release of power, and a few deaths if we can manage it, may open the way for Shanti to sneak in. And maybe one or two others. The question will be, can she get into the city? And if so, can she hide once she does?"

"That raises a lot more questions," Sanders said, hating the situation they'd been forced into. "If she gets in, how does she communicate with us? She'd be right under the Hunter's nose. All he'd have to do is scoop her up."

SHANTI FELT A whirl of nervousness as what Sanders had said sank in. But underneath that there was nothing but fire and determination. Aside from Xandre and his guards, the Hunter thought he was on top of the food chain. He thought his plan to come here and hold Cayan's people hostage would grant him an easy capture.

Shanti wanted to see the look on his face when she proved him wrong.

"I can communicate with Cayan, after a fashion," she said, glancing up to meet those burning blue eyes. "I'll get inside, I'll figure out what's going on, and then I'll find a way to relay news. We're connected. You'll feel me the whole time."

"If you can actually get in," Sanders said. "If they catch a whiff of you, the jig is up."

Cayan shook his head in small jerks, his jaw clenching. He didn't like this—she could feel the uncertainty and possessiveness raging through him—but there was no other choice. He couldn't go—he'd be spotted immediately—and no one else, not even Rohnan, could sneak in the way she could. She was the person for this job.

"Daniels is right," she pushed. "The Hunter is blind right now. And he knows we work well when surprised. He'll expect our hard reaction, but then he'll expect to capture us. He'll also expect us to stick together."

"Not to piss on the parade, but what about the Inkna in the city?" Sanders asked.

"He'll have the strongest out here," Cayan said, staring off into the distance. "He needs a strong first line of defense to keep us out. Within the city, he probably only needs to maintain order. We didn't leave anyone with the *Gift* behind. Keeping order in a city of non-*Gifted* won't take much."

"And by now, I'm sure everyone is laying low."

Daniels rubbed the growth on his chin. "They'll be complacent. Troublemakers would've been subdued or killed by now…"

"Do you dig up graves with that dispassion, too, Daniels?" Sanders growled. "That is your city you're talking about."

Cayan swung a foot over his mount and gracefully jumped to the ground. He came around the horse with burning eyes directed at Shanti. "I don't like this."

"This is the only way, Cayan," she said. "You must see that."

"I do. Doesn't mean I like it." His big hand gripped her upper arm. He pulled her to the other side of his horse, mostly out of view of everyone else. Once there, his gaze roamed her face before settling on her eyes. "This is the *only* way, *mesasha,*" he said quietly. "But you *will* come back to me, do you hear me? You will not go in there and give yourself to the Hunter to protect my people. That is not the best way. Sacrificing yourself will just mean *all* of our deaths in the long run."

"I know, Cayan," she whispered, falling into that blue oasis. "That is the last resort."

His jaw clenched. He shook her a little. Pain bled through his gaze. "No. You get eyes in there, and you come back. I will accept no other plan." He shook her harder, his emotion threatening to break free. "I will not lose you, Shanti, do you understand me?"

As he stared down at her, Shanti felt his fire and rage and war. Muscles flexed down his body, raw strength tempered with a terrible grace. His *Gift* swirled around them, crouched and ready, currently emulating a *Warring Gift* ready to unleash destructive force with only one result. Death.

The Hunter had no idea of what he'd called up by taking Cayan's city. Maybe none of them did.

"I love you, *mesasha.* And I will marry you. This is the city where we will join our peoples and raise our children. So you *will* come back to me safe, and we *will* destroy the Hunter while keeping our home intact. Together."

Yet another terrible time to tell him the truth about her duty. He wasn't making honesty easy.

"Okay," she said. Then, feeling like that was maybe an anticlimax when on the precipice of perhaps saying goodbye forever, she threw it all on the table. "I love you. Don't make me regret it."

A ghost of a smile brushed his lips as his thumb ran over her chin. "I told you I'd get my way in the end."

"You are ruining this moment."

His lips quirked, threatening to unleash his dimples. He gave her a hard, bruising kiss. A kiss of war, and triumph. A kiss of returning.

She really hoped the kiss wasn't out of place.

AS THE LIGHT retreated from the ground, allowing darkness to consume the day, Shanti waited in the shelter of a cluster of trees. Leilius, Ruisa, and Gracas squatted just behind her. Leilius was as still as death, waiting. Ruisa was fidgeting madly as worry poured from her. Gracas had a crooked grin. They'd all be going behind enemy lines to see what could be done from inside the city.

The trees rustled. Rohnan crawled through. His hair had been pulled back and dirt smeared on his head and face.

"You look terrible," Shanti said, turning back to the silent night.

"I wanted to look more your level." Rohnan stopped just beside her, peering out through the branches as she was. "Are we bird watching?"

Shanti rolled her eyes and sat back on her haunches. "Just because we can't see anything at present, doesn't mean there is nothing to see."

"Whatever eases your mind." Rohnan sat back, too. "The Captain is almost ready."

Shanti looked at the others. Only Gracas was excited, but that was because he was too young and full of energy to realize he should be scared. "My asking you to go is just that, *asking*. If you don't think you are ready for this, you should stay behind. You'll be safer left here."

"And ridiculed? No way!" Gracas said in exuberance.

"I chose to go on this journey with you because I wanted to defend my home," Ruisa said in a somber tone. "And now my home is under attack. So I will defend it."

Gracas' face screwed up. "That makes no sense. Do you want to stay or go?"

"Stay, idiot." Ruisa elbowed him. Gracas' mouth snapped shut. He rubbed the offending spot.

"Leilius?" Shanti asked, ignoring the other two.

His eyes darted to her. "I'm terrified, S'am. But I'm the best trained for this. You know, besides you and Romon."

"Romon?" Rohnan asked in confusion.

"You can tell how wound up he is by how badly he chews up titles and names." Shanti put her hand on Leilius' shoulder, hating to put him in this position.

"I don't need that slip-up to tell," Rohnan said softly, his eyes on the younger man. "But he looks calm and sure. You found a great thing in him that is now starting to bud."

"I'm sitting right here, you know." Leilius frowned, his eyes darting away.

"I can give you three the gift of courage," Shanti said, sensing Cayan's readiness. It was about time. "But this is not a battle, and if you have no fear, you might do something stupid. Something stupid might not just get you killed, it might get all of us found out, and your whole city killed. So I leave the choice up to you."

"The gift of courage?" Ruisa asked, her hands shaking as she fidgeted.

"Give it to her," Rohnan said, gesturing at Ruisa. "She's not like the boys. Fear will make her hesitate."

"I don't need it, S'am," Gracas' said, his eyes widening for no reason Shanti could fathom. "I know what I'm up against. I can do it."

"I'm okay. Fear is good sometimes." Leilius slowly wiped a bug off his face. Rohnan was right—if Shanti couldn't read his extreme apprehension, she'd think Leilius had done this a million times.

Focusing on Ruisa, Shanti envisioned stripping her of all her fear, then she injected a shot of courage into the girl. Almost immediately, Ruisa's body straightened up and the lines of worry were erased from her face.

She looked down at her steady hands with wide eyes. "Wow."

"It's cool, huh?" Gracas grinned again. "You can run right at ten guys with swords when you feel like that."

"Hopefully not." Shanti turned back, looking out at nothing. She could feel Cayan gearing up for something, readying his men. He didn't need the *Gift* to inspire courage, he just needed a few moments of speech.

"Ready?" Shanti asked.

Horses sounded away to the left, hooves beating the ground as they charged. A roll of thunder rumbled along the ground, Cayan unleashing his substantial *Gift*. Screams filled the air a moment later.

"Let's go!" Shanti took off at a jog. She led the others around the perimeter of the closest Inkna's range, waiting for the signal from Cayan. In another dozen footsteps, a blast of urgency pushed through her head. *Here we go.*

She turned toward the city, speeding up. They wouldn't have long. As soon as the Inkna had any relief from Cayan's barrage, they'd scan the sides. Shanti had to be through their net and to the city by then.

"Hurry," she urged, putting on a burst of speed. The others kept up easily, younger and harder to tire. Thank the Elders for giving her young people to train.

They passed within sight of one of the Inkna's perches. The man was leaning over his wooden bird's nest, looking away from them. No doubt trying to catch a glimpse of Cayan.

She shut down her shields, just in case, and ran as quietly as she was able. They cut through some branches, using the trees as cover, passing another perch. Then another. Rumbles of *Gift* still blanketed the area. Based on the rigidity of the Inkna she passed, they were working together to fight it. Cayan wouldn't have long.

He was mighty, but he was up against too many who were pretty damn good.

"Almost there," she said, panting, her words lost to the sound of their breathing and footsteps. The city's side gates loomed ahead of them. Closed, as expected. There was a lone guard at the top, facing toward Cayan's assault. It was a Graygual, thank the Elders.

Pain from Cayan trickled down her sternum. The Inkna were getting through his defenses.

"Cut it off, Cayan!" she mumbled, passing the gate behind thick growth. She stopped at a stretch of forbidding stone wall, taller than two men standing one on top of each other. Focusing on feeling relieved so Cayan would know she had made it, she pushed the others into cover.

"How are we supposed to get over that?" Gracas said, his head tilted up to see the top of the wall.

"Walk right through." Leilius rolled his eyes. He panted for a moment to catch his breath before saying, "In all seriousness, though, S'tam. S'am, I mean. I'm not very good at climbing these walls. I mean, I've done it a few times because you made me, and then a few times to practice when you were gone, but I skidded down the other side really often. It hurt. I sprained my ankle once."

"There are compost piles on the other side," Ruisa whispered, looking at the wall. "It'll be a soft landing.

Mostly."

"How do you know?" Gracas demanded.

"I've snuck out a time or two."

"Quiet now," Shanti said, inching her *Gift* over the wall. If she met an Inkna, all this would be for nothing.

She felt a female mind, determined, scurrying past, but nothing else. Pushing a little further, slowly, she felt nothing but emptiness, just as she expected. "Okay, into enemy territory we go."

CHAPTER 9

QADIR SAT BESIDE the open window in the comfortably furnished and spacious room. A chill breeze blew in, smelling of greenery and nature. He hadn't spent much time in this part of the world, being too northern and warm for his taste, but he could see its benefits.

"Sir. They've been pushed back."

His second in command stood with a straight back and blank expression. His eyes were tight; little lines gave away his inner turmoil. Something had not gone as planned.

"Are they stationary?" Qadir asked.

"Yes. They wait just outside of our reach."

"Have you sent someone to engage?"

"Not yet, sir. They took out three of our Inkna."

Numbers flitted through Qadir's head. Plans shifted. A kernel of frustration lodged, already chafing. He didn't have an endless supply of resources anymore. When he'd lost the old man, he'd lost the Being Supreme's favor. What he had under him now were the remnants of his command before the hiccup. If he kept losing these high-powered Inkna, the violet-eyed girl and this Captain these people loved so much would easily shove him aside. He needed to be more careful.

"Send someone out. Deliver the terms."

"Yes, sir."

Qadir took a deep breath of the fresh-smelling air. So cleansing.

One thing he knew about these people—they hated to see innocent people killed. Especially their own.

CHAPTER 10

SONSON FELT THE urgency as the ship was being unloaded. The black cats raced by him and up the bank, excited to stretch their legs and play. After them lumbered thc larger beasts, having already traveled further than anyone in their party. Townspeople and traders alike eyed the animals nervously before skittering away, clearing the area with grunts and wide eyes. They gave Sonson and his people fleeting glances before doing double takes and stuttering in their steps.

The warriors of the Shadow people were coming to the mainland. They weren't trading, or buying supplies—they were going to war. Change had come, and fear would spread out before them and through the land, heralding the myth born into blood.

When people realized that the Shadow didn't cook people in giant pots and then eat them with their fingers, or plague the night with death and destruction, the anxiety would dissipate. For the innocent, anyway. The Graygual would see the nightmare come to life.

"Should I get us rooms?" Punston asked as he

stopped beside Sonson at the end of the dock.

"No. We need to keep moving. We'll go into town for supplies, but then we'll get going. We have half a day of light left, plus a strong moon for tonight. We can make good ground."

Punston sighed softly. It was no secret that he liked to visit a certain woman that lived in the area.

Sonson glanced behind him, seeing packs for the horses being unloaded. It had been a calm voyage, as far as the seas were concerned, but they'd had a large amount of livestock. The trip had been draining.

"Do we need any supplies?" Sonson asked, feeling for the man.

"No, we've…" Punston hesitated for a moment. "There are a few bits we could pick up while the rest is being unloaded. And it's always good to get the news from the town…"

Sonson nodded once. "Get Salange and Denessa. We can make a quick trip."

A few moments later they were walking up the hill to the bustling port town. Sonson had been in and out of this place his whole life. Most of the Shadow had. But the change this time was obvious.

"What do you feel, Salange?" Sonson couldn't help his voice dropping.

Townspeople looked their way with tight eyes and wary glances. Traders in their stalls had rigid backs and most of their wares still out for sale. They'd had a slow day. That suggested fewer travelers.

"Unease," Salange said in a hush as they walked past the merchants. "Some are afraid."

"Of us?" Sonson asked.

"No. *For* us, I think."

They continued onto the main thoroughfare through the town, the strip where most of the inns stood. Denessa stiffened before loosening again, her hand drifting down to her sword hilt.

Graygual loitered in front of shops and outside the drinking houses, watching people pass with hard eyes. Many had three and four stripes. One had five.

"Duck into this inn," Sonson said, veering slightly to his right.

Three Graygual spotted them. Their bodies snapped erect. Their balance shifted into a ready stance. They were preparing to fight.

"We should go back," Punston said as Salange opened the inn door. "We need to stick together."

"Salange?" Sonson said in a hush.

"I can't feel them from here, but those passing are gearing up. Tension is starting to boil. The Graygual are not loved in this town."

"Are they anywhere?" Sonson went inside and sought out the innkeeper immediately. He was at his desk, looking over a ledger.

"Boris." Sonson leaned against the wall as his eyes traveled the main room beyond. Mostly bare; the few patrons he could see sat quietly over their pint or food. Barely a whisper drifted out through the door. "What's happening in this town?"

Boris glanced up and then eyed the door. "The Graygual are moving in in numbers."

"I didn't see any sign of a scuffle at the docks. Did you witness the Chosen making it through?"

Boris licked his lips. "Without a problem. It's been the damndest thing to watch. After the battle, the Graygual came back here in droves. They made a right mess of things, trying to take control, telling us how to run businesses—but they didn't hassle any folks. There was no death, no fighting…we counted ourselves lucky. Then most of them left. Evaporated. It was a strange hollowness, I'll tell you. Relieving, but strange after all the pandemonium. We didn't know what to think."

"How long before the Chosen?"

Boris raised his eyes to the ceiling, thinking. "The city was completely empty of Graygual…probably a month before. Three weeks. Not a single one was here."

"And now? Why are they back?"

Boris' stare held a warning. "They were never really gone. A host stayed behind the others. They left the city, but they didn't leave the area. They stayed deep in the trees. Out of sight. Oh, one or more would come in dressed as common folk for supplies or whatnot, but out they went again. You can tell one of their officers by the way they carry themselves. It was them, all right."

Salange shifted, her expression troubled. "They could easily have waited at the docks and taken the Chosen's party when they were disembarking. Hiding doesn't make sense."

"They moved back in the day the Chosen left. That very day." Boris licked his lips again. Nervous.

"They are trying to cut us off from this land." Sonson felt the urgency returning. "We need to get going before they organize. They'll try to block us from the Chosen. Sorry, Punston. You'll have to see her another time."

"One thing, sir." Boris reached out to Sonson. His expression was grave. "I didn't get to see the violet-eyed girl, but I have a message." He lowered his voice and leaned in. "The Wanderer's network is ready. We're set up and waiting. All we need is a sign."

Sonson stood in confusion for a moment. "What sign?"

Boris straightened back up. "That's for her to decide. But we're ready. We're watching. We just need the sign. We will know it when we see it."

"Time to go," Denessa said, drawing her sword.

"Are there Inkna?" Sonson asked Boris in a hasty release of breath.

"Yes, but not many. You'll have no problem there. For now. You'd best get more Shadow in this city, though. Someone will be claiming it—it had best be you."

The door to the inn burst open. In poured three Graygual, all armed. Salange melted to the outsides of the group, knife in hand. She wasn't the best fighter but she'd run cleanup if she had to.

"Get a message to Portolmous!" Sonson yelled to Boris. "He's run out of time."

The first Graygual advanced without regard to the interior of the inn. He kicked a plant at Denessa before he swung his sword. She blocked and *struck,* her mental power slashing through his mind. He gritted his teeth and wobbled, but his sword came up again, fighting through the mental pain. Those behind him pushed closer, throwing the first Graygual's body toward Denessa. Her sword found purchase in his gut.

The other two continued to shove until their dying man had knocked Denessa out of the way. One Graygual advanced on Sonson, lunging. Sonson battered the sword away and *raked* his mental power across both Graygual as the other charged at Punston. They stumbled, grunting as Sonson *stabbed* mentally. He followed with a physical thrust of his sword, piercing the Graygual through the heart. Punston swung his knife down at the hunching Graygual, stabbing him high in his back.

"Sorry about the blood, Boris," Salange said as she yanked the first Graygual off Denessa by the hair.

"I'm sorry, too," Denessa said, looking down at herself covered in crimson.

Sonson was the first out of the inn, looking around with his *Therma* for the other Graygual he knew where there. Sure enough, five formed a semicircle, allowing them no easy escape. Except…they didn't have any Inkna with them. This was no contest.

Sonson joined power with the others, feeling it bolster and pound, before each unleashed a *kill strike.* Their mind *slashed* into the Graygual, finding no resistance. Screams pierced the afternoon as each of them lost the strength in their legs. Sonson was moving a moment later, sword flashing in the sun. He cleaved into a Graygual neck, almost severing the head to quicken the man's death. Salange was beside him, stabbing her knife repeatedly into a Graygual chest and stomach.

When Sonson turned to the others, all he found were impatient Shadow standing over a pile of bodies.

"Let's go." Sonson started a jog through the town. He made it halfway to the traders' stalls before a blearing heat seared his brain. He slammed up his shields as his head swung to the side, seeing the Inkna hiding between two buildings a moment after he felt their presence.

"I'll take him," Denessa said, putting on a burst a speed toward the vastly outnumbered Inkna. She reached him with a bundle of aggression before thrusting. Her sword stabbed through his chest.

"There are more up ahead," Punston called.

Graygual fanned out at the mouth of the street leading down to the docks. They were preventing escape. Still without any Inkna.

"For officers, they aren't very bright." Before Sonson could attack mentally, arrows flew from overhead. They landed in soft bodies, the fletchings quivering as they stuck.

Surprised shrieks and grunts accompanied the Graygual clutching at the wood sticking from their midsection. Another three arrows found their mark then Denessa was upon them, hacking and slashing to kill them faster.

"She needs to bed someone," Punston said, watching Denessa with a quirked grin. He didn't rush forward to help. "She has too much pent-up aggression."

Sonson could barely make out people disappearing from the nearby rooftops, slinking out of sight once the deed was done. "Let's go. We need to keep moving before they call in more."

They reached the docks to find more bodies strewn about. Most had marks of claws and teeth, with shredded necks and torsos. The animals stood over them, blood splashed across their faces and trailing from their feet.

"The Graygual are trying to keep us from moving on," Boas called as he tied a pack to a horse.

"The animals came in handy." Punston gave one longing look back toward the city before he jogged to his mount. "How close are we to leaving?"

"Just about ready." Boas glanced at the other horses and riders. "Will we alter our path?"

Sonson shook his head as he found his own horse ready and waiting for him. "No need. Staying off the main travel routes is still the best option."

As they got underway, Sonson's mind drifted back to what Boris had said. And then to the archers helping from the rooftops. The people would take back their homes.

The question remained, would the Chosen know how to call them into action?

CHAPTER 11

"INCOMING, SIR!"

Cayan finished off the last of the mud-like draught Marc had made and passed the cup back. The youth had found a concoction that would rejuvenate the *Gift* in record time. It was made of plants from the Shadow Lands, and since those plants didn't grow around here, would soon be in short supply. Thank God for it, though, because Cayan had drastically overdone it against that band of Inkna. He'd held out as long as possible, but there were too many of them. If his men hadn't shot the first few Inkna out of the trees, he wouldn't have lasted a quarter as long.

"Who've we got?" Cayan asked, wiping his hands and tossing the cloth at Xavier. He met Sanders on the city side of their hastily erected camp. Three men on horseback came their way, all Graygual.

"They don't mean to fight, that's obvious," Sanders growled, his hand resting on the hilt of his blade. "How's your head?"

"It'll do for non-Inkna."

Sanders grunted in response.

All officers—two Graygual had three stripes, and one had four. They stopped a few paces away, sitting straight in their saddle. With a city full of Graygual, they had the upper hand here, and they knew it.

One of the Graygual, a smug-looking man with thin lips, spoke. "I wish to speak to the Captain."

"That is me." Cayan stepped closer.

"We are here to deliver the Hunter's terms." The man with the four stripes waited a moment before he spoke again. "He wishes for Shanti of the Shumas and Cayan, the Captain of these lands, to present themselves to him. He will then escort you to the Being Supreme without pain or hardship. In return, he will quit these lands and leave your people as they are, completely unharmed. If you fail to abide by these terms, he will kill the majority of your people. You have a few beauties in this land. They will be distributed as entertainment."

A flash of rage boiled deep in Cayan's blood. He stared up at the dead man sitting on his horse. "And how do we know he'll keep his word?"

"As evidenced by his upkeep of your city so far. He has not harmed anyone who followed the rules. He has no interest in these people. His interest is in you and the violet-eyed girl."

"You say he has kept my city intact, and yet he won't let me near it. How can I be sure?"

The officer hesitated. "We can bring out one of your people to declare the state of the city."

"The Hunter must think he is dealing with an imbecile." Cayan paused a moment, wondering if the Graygual would comment. When nothing came, he said, "As I'm sure he knows, I need to view the city myself. As I'm sure he also knows, walking inside those walls would be putting myself in a situation where I'll be caged in. Shanti isn't here. She is traveling with the Shadow who were delayed. So you can't have us both at present, and Xandre doesn't want just me. He needs her. So really, you're wasting my time."

The Graygual's hand flexed and then formed a fist again. It was the only movement revealing his irritation. "You have very few men out here to back up these words. I wonder, what makes you so cocky?"

"I just took out three high-powered Inkna. And look at me. I'm ready to take out three more. I retreated to give you a chance to play nice. I don't want my people harmed. I also won't sit here for long, *allowing* you to reside in my city. The sands are running through the hourglass. I'll give you until Shanti gets here, and then I will walk in and set matters to rights."

The Graygual smirked. "You blow a lot of wind. But as you say, we need the girl." The officer sat, looking down from his horse. Analyzing.

Cayan let the extreme, burning hatred show in his

expression. He let his desire to skin these men alive bleed through his gaze. And he stayed perfectly balanced, as though holding a sword and ready to swing it, to foreshadow what would come in the end. The Hunter may have the upper hand *at present,* yes. But as soon as Shanti took the lay of the land, they'd even the odds. He and she were a remarkable team, and his men were some of the best. They just needed time to prove it.

"Very well," the Graygual finally said. "I'll take your message to the Superior Officer. Expect an answer you will not like."

As the men walked their horses away, just as slowly as they came, Cayan barely prevented himself from exhaling in fatigue.

"I have a bad feeling about this," Sanders said.

"I do, too. If we see them approach again, keep the men back." Cayan's gut twisted. "I don't want them seeing what the Graygual will probably bring. I don't want that on their conscience."

A thundercloud crossed Sanders' expression. "You know that Shanti won't let them kill someone. Rather than worry about the Graygual response, we need to figure out what to do when she turns that whole place upside down."

"And then what to do when she trades herself for everyone else's life," Xavier said in a hollow tone. He waited by the tents with a solemn expression. "I don't think we have a week, sir. We might not even have a few days."

SHANTI FELT A rise of fear and then angry determination from Cayan, distant though he was, as she and the others crouched behind a house in the shadows. She pushed his emotions to the side. She'd need to block him out in order to keep her focus. She couldn't afford the distraction.

Two Graygual stood down the lane, silent and watching. Their minds were dull and movements slow. Normal men would be sleeping on their feet. These men were either trained very well, or terrified of failing at their duty. Probably both.

Shanti *searched* the familiar landscape of the city, delicately spreading her *Gift.* Most of the Inkna were spread around the wall, no doubt watching for Cayan. Her light mental touch, only lingering for a moment before retreating, had gone unnoticed by all but two of the strongest. As soon as she backed off, she was forgotten.

The Inkna in this town were complacent. At least for now.

"The males seem to be under more scrutiny," Shanti said quietly, checking out the pockets of mental minds. "I recognize a few, like Lucius and Sterling. They are in the prison."

"That makes sense," Ruisa whispered. "The higher officers are the most dangerous, right?"

Shanti gauged the emotions of the men. They were restless, uncomfortable, and their hope was starting to dwindle. The confinement, or something else, was breaking them down.

A broken man was an easy man to control.

"When I was in the Graygual camp," Rohnan said, "my guards had a key to my chains when I needed to be moved, but otherwise the key was kept elsewhere. They thought, correctly, that I could find a way to take the key if left in my vicinity. When the keys were absent, I was poked and prodded at all hours. I rarely slept for long periods of time. Sleep deprivation and humiliation muddled my mind. I can only guess that the practices are similar here."

Rachie moved a little closer. His smile hadn't returned since he had slid down the wall on his face. "Not many army men could fit in the prison, though."

"No. There are many more within the park. Graygual surround them, helped by a few Inkna." Shanti couldn't help a scowl. "There are so many Inkna in this city. The Hunter is prepared."

"And our force is small."

"Very small. Thank the Elders that Cayan has excellent intuition with the *Gift*. But he's still largely inexperienced." Shanti mapped out the land as well as she could, constantly worried about finding an Inkna that might be paying attention. She learned quickly that areas with a greater male population also had more guards. Those with more females were controlled by a smaller enemy presence. It seemed that the Graygual segregated parts of the city, probably putting the more dangerous of citizens in one location. The Hunter was well equipped for taking over hostile territory.

Shanti's mind stumbled over a cluster of active women. She felt their minds spark and burst with various emotions, as though in lively debate. Given how late it was, that was more than strange. One mind within that group she recognized immediately. "Molly."

Ruisa perked up. "Is she with anyone else?"

"Yes." Shanti told Ruisa what she could feel with her *Gift*.

"We need to get over there!" Rohnan slapped a hand over Ruisa's mouth to stop her words. She peeled Rohnan's fingers away and continued in a lower tone. "That's the Women's Circle. We need to meet with them."

"I agree," Shanti said, mapping out the quietest route. "We'll see how much they know about what's going on."

"They'll know a lot." Ruisa nodded adamantly. "They'll be right in the heart of it, I bet."

Gracas rolled his eyes.

"What about the orphans?" Ruisa asked.

"What about the orphans?" Shanti repeated. "The Hunter wouldn't kill children unless he needed to control an uprising."

"Are they together?" Ruisa's eyes were intent.

Frowning in confusion, Shanti checked that area of the city. As expected, a horde of kids were gathered together, a mess of energy regardless of the late hour. "They're fine, as far as I can tell."

"We should check in with them. Even stay in the orphan house tonight if we can. They can help."

"She's cracked," Gracas whispered to Leilius.

"They know the ins and outs of this city better than anyone," Ruisa fired back. "Whatever holes lie in the Women's Circle's knowledge, the orphans will be able to fill. It's always been that way. Trust me."

Shanti didn't want to waste the time arguing. Nor did she discount the sentiment. Instead, she stood, waiting for the others to stand with her. "First we'll visit the women and see what they can tell us. Ruisa, Leilius, which one of you knows this city best?"

Ruisa said, "Me." At the same time as Gracas and Leilius both said, "Her."

"Okay." Shanti pulled the girl to her. After telling her where the Graygual were stationed between their current location and the women, she said, "We need to get there without getting seen."

"Easy." Ruisa turned and scurried back toward the wall.

"The orphans are like rats after dark," Leilius said as he followed behind Shanti. "They're the ones you should've trained to spy, S'am. I've been in trouble loads of times for sneaking out, but the orphans hardly ever get caught."

"*Shh!*" Ruisa ducked into a shadow between two houses. She peered around the corner.

"There's no one there," Shanti helped.

Ruisa stepped out and hurried to the next sheltered area, peering around the corner. After a few more times of Shanti telling her they were clear, Ruisa finally learned just to keep going until Shanti had her slow or stop.

Halfway through the city, having used narrow alleys and small paths Shanti hadn't known existed, the first cluster of Graygual stood in their way. Ruisa looked at Shanti from beside a pungent garbage bin. She shook her head a fraction.

Shanti *searched,* trying to remember if there was a way through the holes of Graygual from her limited experience of the city. She didn't know of one. Peering through a bush to the shadowed street lit by a few oil lamps, she saw the Graygual, standing idly. Two chatted with each other, their minds troubled.

"Let's wait until one or more moves on," Rohnan said, looking away, watching their backs.

Shanti squinted up at the sliver of moon, and then back at the street in front of them. "If we wait, we'll probably miss the Women's Circle."

"*If we go, these kids are sure to get caught,*" Rohnan said in the Shumas language.

"Go...kids...caught..." Gracas put his hand on his hip. "We aren't as good as you, but we aren't hopeless, either. I can stay quiet."

Shanti and Rohnan stared at Gracas for a moment. Shanti had no idea he was learning their language. She had no doubt that Marc must have had a hand in that.

"He's right, though," Shanti said, biting her lip in indecision. "They aren't great, but they are passable. These Graygual don't even suspect anyone in the city. They worry, but there is no urgency in it. I'd bet their concern is with the outside threat, or from the Hunter."

"This is a big risk," Rohnan warned.

"The risk is where to stash the body," Shanti replied.

"I can think of three places," Ruisa said.

Shanti blinked, shocked mute for the second time. Regaining herself, she said, "Then the risk is being able to hide the Graygual absence. Regardless, we are wasting time." Shanti gave Rohnan a level stare. "Do you have a better idea?"

"Ideas are your territory. I am but the voice of reason."

Gracas huffed. Shanti had to agree with the sentiment.

"Okay." She looked at Gracas, then at Ruisa. Finally at Leilius. "Follow us, but you don't have to be our shadows. We are a team, but we are not glued together. If we need to split up, try to stay close, stay quiet, and stay hidden. If you get separated and in trouble, hide. I'll come back for you eventually."

The three nodded, their brows bent in concentration and determination.

Shanti set out at a fast but light walk, her back bent, sticking to the shadows. The rest fanned out behind her, doing the same, but picking different crevices or shadowed areas in which to travel. Besides Rohnan, Leilius was by far the most accomplished at this, having had a lot more practice. The other two were doing well too, though. Without twigs and branches to constantly step around, or the concern of leaving tracks, they could concentrate all their effort on moving as quietly as they could. Shanti rarely heard a sound from any of them.

She approached the two chatting Graygual and slipped between a bush and the wall. Hunkering for a moment, she waited until the others stashed themselves out of the way. She threw a rock. It skittered down the lane.

The two Graygual didn't even glance in that direction. Their conversation was their sole focus. Good.

Beyond them, partially obstructed by the corner of a house, was a solitary Graygual, watchful but static.

Shanti hurried to the next shadow, watching the Graygual as she felt the others move behind her, inching closer. She ran to the next shadow, then waited. Twice more she did this, hating how tedious this was with a group that weren't very well synced. Finally, though, she was in earshot of the hushed words.

"I'll find out. I'd rather stay in here than have to confront that colossal," one of the Graygual said in their home language. "I hear he's a giant."

"All these men are giants. Even the shorter ones are stacked with muscle." The other Graygual looked out over the street. "The Captain is supposed to be unbeatable, though."

"Exactly. I'd rather guard the weaker ones. Do you think the Hunter is going to send out sacrifices?"

"I don't know. I hear there are not many of them out there. They're waiting for more."

"Then he'll probably send out the best." The man sucked his lip in thought.

Shanti felt Rohnan's impatience behind her, but she wanted to hear this out.

"The girl isn't with them, though," the first said, wiping something from the front of his uniform. "The Inkna didn't see her or feel her presence. She's with the

Shadow."

"Or else she hung back."

"What good would that have done? Nah, from what I've heard, she's always running around, killing people. If she wasn't in the battle, she's making her way to it. The Hunter agrees, so…"

"The Hunter should capture that Captain before the girl gets here," the first Graygual said with a knowing tone. "It'd be easy. This city is full of bleeding hearts. They'll roll over and play dead if a woman is smacked. I say that if the Hunter just starts killing people, that Captain will walk right in and give himself up. I guarantee it."

"He's going to. The Hunter, I mean. You know how he works, though."

The other man spat. "For a guy that has no problem torturing, he sure has a funny set of rules."

"That's just it. Rules." The man looked around and leaned closer to the other. He dropped his voice to a level that Shanti could barely hear. "If I'd known what I was getting into, I wouldn't have bothered to join up, know what I mean?"

"*Shhh!* You're going to get us killed." They started walking toward the middle of the street. Their hushed voices turned into nothing more than hissed whispers.

So Cayan had said she hadn't come with him. He didn't really have any other choice. The Hunter would be suspicious, though. Any foul play in the city, and he'd turn his Inkna inward, searching.

She took a deep breath. This was not a great situation.

Wasting no more time, she started moving again, increasing her pace. She could feel the women starting to relax, their focused determination drifting into overall angst. They had to be getting ready to sneak back to their homes.

Shanti turned the corner and ducked behind a hedge as the solitary Graygual standing near the far wall shifted his stance. His body swung in their direction, his gaze following a moment later. Rohnan dove behind a cropped bush, the thud thankfully going unnoticed. Gracas half ran to the side, ducking behind a wall just in time. Leilius had already hidden himself in shadow. Ruisa, though, was halfway across the street, aiming for a deep patch of black, when the Graygual lazily scanned in her direction.

Her shoe scuffed the street as she slipped into the nearest shaded area, nothing more than a crevice in the architecture of a house. The Graygual's body went rigid, his shoulders swinging around to match the direction his face was pointed. At Ruisa.

"Hey!" He pushed off the wall at a brisk walk, heading in her direction.

Ruisa, caught, jumped out of her hiding place and

tore off down the street. The Graygual ran after her, just as quick but with longer legs. Before she could turn the corner, he was on her, tackling her in someone's front yard.

"*Flak!*" Shanti emerged from her spot at a run, her knife in her hand and Rohnan at her back. She reached them as the Graygual was dragging Ruisa to her feet.

"I have grass stains now, because of you!" He grabbed her by the hair and pulled his other hand back, ready to slap her into submission.

Shanti slipped in behind him, silent as the grave. She stuck her blade into his back. She slapped a hand over his mouth to muffle the scream. Before she could slit his throat, Rohnan was there. With two quick hands, her brother grabbed the Graygual's head, a look of pure hatred on his face.

A loud crack announced the end of the scuffle.

"Slitting his throat would have meant a lot more blood, *Chulan*. You're getting sloppy." Rohnan wiped his palms on his pants, trying to catch his breath.

Shanti cleaned her blade on the man's uniform before looking around for a place to put the body out of sight. The women were starting to break up now. One had already left.

"Why didn't you just use your mind, S'am?" Leilius said as he jogged over, his eyes darting around the empty street.

"The Inkna would've felt the release of power it takes to kill." Shanti stared down at the body. "Damn. Well, let's hide him. We can come back for him later."

"Sorry, S'am. I—"

"Don't." Shanti held up her hand to stop the younger woman from explaining. "It happens. This is why we carry knives."

"Yes, S'am." Ruisa dropped her head.

"Gracas, help me lift him." Rohnan moved to the head of the fallen man. "And mind your clothes. We don't want to get to blood all over. It doesn't wash out."

"Hurry up, you guys. We have to go." Shanti traced the rest of the way with her *Gift*. "If we roof it, we can avoid any more Graygual."

"How are we going to get on the roofs?" Gracas grunted as he picked up the legs of the dead man. "This guy is heavy."

"Roof it. Like…go fast."

"Hoof it, you mean," Leilius said, eyes still darting.

"Oh. Ah, yes. Like a horse. That makes more sense." Shanti put her knife in the holster.

"Ready." Rohnan wiped off his hands again.

They took off at a jog, everyone but Rohnan staying distractingly close to her. Luckily, apart from a sprint that was needed to cross a street, the way was clear. They reached the house where all but two of the women were still present.

"They are going to be so happy to see you!" Ruisa gave three light knocks, then two, paused, and then five more.

"What would've happened if I didn't have that code?" Shanti asked, impatient to get inside and out of sight.

"They would've all hid before someone opened the door."

"She's just trying to show off." Gracas shook his head in disdain before looking out at the street.

The door opened a crack. Then swung open all the way. "Hurry!"

Ruisa slid through the doorway, followed by the two boys. When Shanti finally crossed the threshold, the first person she saw was Molly.

"Shanti!" Molly's hand came up, impossibly slow. Not knowing why it was happening, but wanting to fit with custom, as strange as it was, Shanti stood still. Molly slapped her across the face.

CHAPTER 12

SHANTI TILTED HER head as Rohnan came in with a confused frown. The door closed behind him.

"I…did something wrong?" Shanti asked.

With tears in her eyes, Molly barreled into her, wrapping her thin arms around Shanti's frame and squeezing. Sobs racked the woman's body.

"I don't know what's happening," Shanti confessed.

"You're here to save us!" Molly straightened up, looking Shanti in the face with a giant smile. "I knew you'd come. I said she'd come, didn't I, Eloise? I did. I said she'd march right in here and save the day!"

"Well…we snuck…"

Ten women gathered around them, some assessing, some smiling in delight, some wringing their hands.

Eloise, a stocky woman with a face like an angry bulldog, said, "Did the Captain come with you?"

"He's outside the gates. We haven't many with us. We need to feed them information." She left off the "somehow." It made her sound more confident.

Eloise nodded decisively, like she'd expected that

answer. "He knows when to send in a woman to get the job done. Our Captain is the best there is."

"Let's show them what we've got!" Molly, still tearful, ushered Shanti to the living room where empty teacups littered a low table.

"What about them?" one of the older women asked, pointing at the guys.

All the women slowed, then stopped, looking at the males in the group.

"What's the problem?" Shanti asked.

"We don't usually share our…art with men," one of the hand wringers said. Her hair looked like it was desperately trying to escape the bun it was confined in.

Shanti turned back, noticing that, for the first time, Gracas and Leilius both looked terrified.

"No." Molly fisted her hands and braced them on her hips, turning to the women. "Tabby, that is nonsense. Before Shanti came, the men didn't let women fight. We only practice our art because we weren't allowed to defend ourselves in other ways. But Shanti changed that, for better or worse. The Captain let Ruisa in, and I'll tell you something, I certainly wish I knew my way around a knife."

"Any good cook knows her way around a knife!" one of the woman said in a bold tone.

"But I doubt that cook knows where to stick one into an enemy," a mousy women in the back said quietly.

"It's no great mystery," the bold woman fired back. "It's a knife. Just put it in the body somewhere and you're in business."

"I've butchered a pig," someone else announced. "I know where the vital parts are. You just stick a knife in one of those."

"Well then, when we're overrun by pigs, we'll be sure to ask you!" another woman badgered.

"Ladies, ladies." Eloise put out her hands to stop the bickering. Her eyes were burning into Leilius and Gracas, in turn. "Molly's right. The Captain and Shanti, not to mention a gaggle of Graygual and Inkna, have brought change. There's no use trying to stick to the old ways, not now. We need to work together if we want to take our city back. These boys can help."

"I don't know the handsome one, but I know the boys. They are too dense to learn the complexities of mixing chemicals." Shanti couldn't see who uttered that, but she didn't bother to hold back her laughter.

"I could mix chemicals," Gracas muttered.

"Son, you'd melt your face off," Eloise said in utter seriousness.

Shanti laughed harder, joined by Rohnan.

"But that isn't to say you couldn't help us distribute this round of flu." Eloise gestured them over to the small table. A map of the city was spread out, small rocks dotting the landscape.

"The Graygual haven't caught on that you guys are causing the sickness?" Shanti asked, looking over the layout.

Eloise sat down with a weary sigh. She rubbed her knees. "Old bones." Glancing at Molly, she said, "Put on some more tea, dear."

Molly bustled off to the kitchen as Eloise explained, "We aren't really using a flu this time. It's a new creation. We're working on its potency, but I think we've got it. Tabby, do you want to explain?"

The woman with the hair struggling out of the bun stepped forward. "In the beginning, we created a sickness like we usually might. The Graygual thought it was the water. Since it only affected them, this made sense. When they started treating the water, though, we could only kill the ones that were the worst off."

"You've killed?" Rohnan asked, sitting on the couch opposite Eloise.

Tabby looked at the floor sheepishly, a shy smile playing with her lips. "Yes, of course," she said with a shaking voice. Nervousness and lust poured out of her.

Shanti hid a smile.

"The goal is to take back our city without alerting the Graygual to our tactics," Tabby continued, wringing her hands harder. "The trick is aiming for those not valued as highly. The Hunter doesn't seem to have friends. Or even people he likes. But he does value ability. So if someone who isn't a great fighter suffers, the Hunter doesn't seem to care. But if someone that he needs, or values, is in jeopardy, he looks into the problem. This is why he sent out for water treatment. We'd targeted the best and brightest at first. Unfortunately, that was a mistake."

"Nothing is a mistake until you get caught," Shanti said, looking at the map. "You learned some vital information."

The women nodded, muttering their agreement.

"Well. So…" Tabby glanced at Rohnan. He met her eyes patiently. She jerked her gaze to the ground, batting at the wisps of hair touching her face. "That was a stomach irritant. So while we tried to come up with something else, we hit the city with food sickness. Unfortunately, we had to include a few of our own or else it would be obvious."

"We didn't kill any of our own, though," Eloise said.

"No. None of our own, no." Tabby scratched her head. Her bun danced. "We targeted those who deserved it, anyway."

The women collectively nodded and muttered again. Leilius took a step away, his eyes darting to the door. Shanti could feel how uncomfortable he was.

"So we were able to kill off a few more that way," Tabby continued. "By the time that was cleared, we were ready to test this new formula. The first two batches didn't seem to work. Or not that we could tell, anyway. The third was too much. We partially paralyzed one of them. Thankfully he was whipped shortly after for touching Sabra inappropriately."

Shanti's throat squeezed. Not wanting to hear the answer, but needing to know all the same, she asked, "Have they put their hands on many…"

Eloise batted the air. "Oh no. We planted Sabra. She can seduce anyone, and then call up tears right after. It was a big problem when she was just growing into her body. She became curious, like we all do…" Eloise looked around the room with raised eyebrows. A few women smirked, some scowled, and a younger one bit her lip, looking anywhere but Eloise. "She didn't want to be given a label, though, or get in trouble, so she blamed it on the boys. Absolutely inappropriate."

"I bet you didn't poison her…" Gracas mumbled.

Eloise fixed him with a stare. "She was punished, I assure you."

Gracas withered from the scrutiny.

"Be that as it may," Eloise went on, "we had her get close, and then slip him the concoction. Then she cried and screamed. The girl can really put on a show. The man was visibly flagging when the Hunter had him tied to the whipping post. He died after only five lashes. The whipper thought he'd done it, as had the Hunter, so we got lucky."

"Yes," Tabby said. "So we remixed and tried again. We've got a winner now, I think. We've already seen the effects. We've increased the dose and are trying to get it into as many as possible."

"So it doesn't kill?" Rohnan asked.

Tabby went mute, her fingers turning white with how hard she was wringing them. She looked away from Rohnan in embarrassment.

"Oh for heaven's sakes," Eloise muttered. She answered Rohnan, "Yes, but it takes time. It's a slow-acting poison. I won't bore you with the details, but the body starts shutting down. First the signs are small. So small you have to look for them. Then the man is bled of energy. It's sapped from him and he has no idea how. He just feels very tired. On and on until he finally succumbs."

"We don't have that kind of time," Shanti said.

"It's already in the middle stages," Molly said as she delivered cups of tea. "Men are already feeling tired. Strained. They think it's stress, or just the climate. When you and the Captain take to them with your swords, they won't be nearly as able to defend themselves."

"Yet they will have no idea of their limited ability," Rohnan said, a smile budding. "That is cunning."

"Well." Eloise sipped her tea. "We couldn't just start

killing people. The Hunter is far more cunning than we are. He'd figure it out. Even now he is annoyed with some of those who are sleeping a little later and not jumping to his commands with the same enthusiasm."

"Did you give it to the Hunter?" Shanti shook her head at Molly, not wanting tea.

"Oh, go on," Molly pushed, letting the offered cup hover in front of her. "Have a cuppa tea. It'll make you feel better. Go *on*!"

Shanti took the cup as Rohnan quirked an eyebrow. "She'll just keep telling me to drink it," Shanti mumbled, taking a sip. "I lived with her for a time. I was waterlogged by the time I could leave."

"She has no sense of what's good for her," Molly said with a determined set to her jaw.

Shanti rolled her eyes as Rohnan smiled, his eyes twinkling. "I think I like these new friends," he said.

"We didn't give it to the Hunter, no. He is keeping this city reasonably safe for us," Eloise said. "He is insane, I think we can all agree on that, but he's as hard on his people as on ours if rules aren't followed."

"He'd know right off," a woman in the back said. "He'd sense something was off and worry at the problem until he solved it."

"You know him well," Shanti said as she tried to see the speaker. All she could tell was that it was a younger woman with brown hair.

"We've tried to keep track of guard positions and the times they change out," Eloise explained as she motioned at the map. "The problem is, they keep changing. They don't stay in the same place in the city, and they don't always change at regular times. It's all haphazard."

"That's the Hunter." Rohnan pushed forward to see the map. "I saw him change how the guards worked within his camp. He is excellent at strategy and diligent about defense. I often—"

The front door burst open. A terrified woman glanced around the room in panic. "Molly, your guard is coming!"

"Shit!" Molly threw an apologetic glance at Eloise, and ran for a basket of clothes by the door. "I'll run out now."

"It's too late!" The woman shut the door and pushed Molly away. "He's suspected these meet-ups, Molly. He means to catch us. *Why* didn't you just go home when you should've?"

"Do you all have guards?" Shanti asked, putting away her sword and touching her knives in preparation.

"Just me," Molly said, looking around the room frantically. Her eyes fell on the map. Panic shed from her in waves.

"Clear this away!" Eloise struggled to get up, gesturing at the map as well as the cups. "Clear everything away. Hide, everyone—"

The handle to the door wiggled. With the lock engaged, the door held. A fist pounded against the wood.

"Hide!" Eloise seethed, hobbling toward the lit candles. Her body was too old to sit for long and then move with any sort of grace.

Cups clinked as women grabbed them. One wobbled toward the edge of the table, then fell, shattering on the floor. Tabby froze, staring at the mess with wide eyes.

"Hurry!" Another woman grabbed the map, crinkling it. Rocks scattered across the floor.

The pounding sounded again, angry and insistent. "Open this door!" a man shouted.

"There's no time!" Eloise waved her arm, trying to scatter everyone with the movement.

All the women disappeared into the rooms, except for one. The younger woman who had had such great insight with the Hunter dashed toward the mess, sweeping the remnants of the mug under the couch with her foot. A smear of liquid glistened on the dull wood floor.

"Go!" Eloise walked toward the door, giving a last pause to look behind her as Shanti and Rohnan melted into the shadows within the room. The older woman flicked the lock and pulled the door open. A current of chilled air sliced through the room.

"Where are they?" the man berated.

"I don't know what you mean. Where are who? I was just up for a cup of tea. I can't sleep well these days. Old bones, you know."

"Get out of the way!"

Eloise's body jolted backward, and then fell, the woman sprawling on the ground with a grunt. Her head thunked off the floor, a sound like a bouncing melon. "There's no one here!"

A grizzled Graygual crossed Shanti's vision, striding into the house like he owned it. His gaze swept the area, pausing on the low table and immediately finding the fragments of the teacup. His eyes darted around the room. "The Hunter won't be happy knowing you filthy women are meeting in secret. He'll cut that right out. Toss one of you on the whipping post."

"I dropped that cup when you banged on the door." Eloise climbed painfully to her feet, wincing as she straightened up. A small trickle of blood dripped down her temple.

The Graygual noticed the rocks, and then walked toward the kitchen. "Where are they?"

"I don't—" Eloise cut off with the woman's shriek from the kitchen. Then another.

The Graygual walked into the living room again, his fingers curled around two fistfuls of hair. Tabby already had tears in her eyes, the other, a younger woman, had a crease between her brow, her large brown eyes sparkling with anger.

He flashed Eloise a malevolent grin, jerking his hands. Both women's faces screwed up in pain as their necks wrenched. "How many are you hiding?"

"I'm here." Molly walked out from the bedroom, her head high and her expression determined. Shanti could feel both her bravery and terror. "You came for me. I'm already watched by the Hunter for causing trouble. Take me. They were just trying to talk me into behaving."

The Graygual's grin turned sickly. He shook his right hand. The younger woman gritted her teeth, agony emanating from her. "The Hunter uses this one to keep that stubborn mule in line. What would he say if she is secretly plotting, I wonder? He'd be suspicious, methinks. And when that man is suspicious, people give answers, or they lose limbs…"

A shape rushed forward, swift and graceful. A loud crack sounded through the pregnant silence, followed by thuds as different points of the Graygual's body slapped the floor.

"He's really good at snapping necks," Gracas mumbled in awe.

"Disgusting, but useful." Leilius gulped and moved to the window. He'd always hated enacting violence. But then, so had Rohnan. In times of war, a person killed or was killed. There was very little middle ground.

The other women in the room stared down at the Graygual with wide eyes, their gazes stuck to the unnatural angle of his neck. Tabby retched.

Rohnan bent to check his handiwork. "Dead. We'll put him with the other."

Eloise shook herself, still braced against the wall. She recovered first. "That's going to be a problem."

Molly came out of it next, joining Leilius at the window and looking out. "No, it'll be fine. He wasn't well liked. I'll just tell the guard taking his place that this one took off a little early. He's done it before. It'll give us a day."

"Oh my God!" One of the women swooned from the doorway of the bedroom. She staggered into the wall.

The women who was a self-proclaimed expert at dicing pigs caught her, rolling her eyes. "He would've made sure the Hunter strung us up for this. That pretty man did the right thing."

"We killed another on the way here," Shanti said, standing in the middle of the room. "We need to make some decisions."

"Is there a way to get a note to the Captain?" Rohnan asked the women.

Eloise painfully lowered herself onto the couch. She put her ankle on the table. "There is a trading party that leaves in a few days." She leaned back and squeezed her eyes shut. "That's the soonest."

"A few days?" Shanti blew out her breath. That wasn't soon enough. "We need to figure out how to get the prisoners free."

"Without more people with the *Gift,* fighters will be useless." Rohnan straightened up. "Maybe we should sneak back out."

"And then what, Rohnan?" Shanti fisted her hands and released, then again, just to let out some pent-up frustration. "We can't pretend we never came. The Hunter knows Cayan is there, even if he doesn't think I am. He'll want Cayan and his men to hand themselves over. If they don't, the Hunter will force his hand."

"Force his hand... In what way?" the younger woman asked, standing behind the dead Graygual with an intent expression.

"The Hunter often slaps Alena around to get Lucius to cooperate," Molly explained.

Shanti looked at the attractive woman with a firm gaze. "You show great bravery to stand against the Hunter when you've seen his tactics."

The woman slumped just a little before straightening back up, her chin raised. She shrugged. Shanti could *feel* the strength in her character and her dogged determination. She was afraid—they were all afraid—but they were pushing through it.

"It's clear the women of this city are just as courageous as the men," Shanti said quietly. Her voice cut through the silence. "And that is saying something."

"Told you," Ruisa mumbled.

All the women in the room moved in some way, some straightening up, some shifting in embarrassment, and some puffing out their chests in pride. Courage bolstered. These women were fighters, and now they were being given their chance to prove it.

Rohnan smirked. "*Chulan* didn't think you had it in you."

"Have what? A solid backbone?" The woman who terrified pigs harrumphed. "I've given birth three times to giant babies. I can endure a whole lot more than those army men can, I'll tell you that!"

"Okay," Shanti said firmly. It was time to get to business. "Get that poison distributed as far and wide and as quickly as you can. Take only the smallest risks. *Do not* get caught." The women's expressions hardened. Most nodded, taking in that command. "Try to figure out how our guys are imprisoned, and how we can get them out. They'll help with the Graygual. Rohnan and I will need to figure out what to do about the Inkna."

"When we get close to making a move, we can slip a lot of people some harsh poison," the bold woman, Fabienne said. "That stuff is not pretty, but neither is snapping someone's neck. So there you go."

Tabby shivered. "True, I suppose."

"Great. Now—"

"What about him?" Eloise cut Shanti off, pointing to the dead man.

"*Chulan* and I will take him away and hide him, along with the other. We'll hope they go unnoticed for now, at least." Doubt radiated from Rohnan, but he did not let it show.

"We'll stay with the orphans tonight." Shanti glanced at Ruisa and received a nod. "Tomorrow, I'll want to roam the city as much as possible. So I'll need a disguise."

"A proper dress is all you need," the pig killer said.

"And some die for your hair. Blond will stick out, even with a hat." Molly's eyes twinkled.

Shanti sighed. "You will finally have your way, Molly. I will willingly dress like a frosted cake."

"I know just the dress, too. Lots of ruffles…"

"This situation just gets worse," Shanti mumbled, bending to the body.

Even with the dress, they'd set events in motion with those deaths. It was only a matter of time before the Hunter sprang the trap and locked her inside.

CHAPTER 13

KALLON STATIONED HIMSELF behind a jagged outcropping of rock, looking down on the winding trail. The Graygual would be climbing up at any moment, trying to follow the path made by Kallon and his people as doggedly as they had for the last couple weeks. This time, though, Kallon wouldn't run. He and his small band would stay and fight.

It felt good.

"It amazes me that they're still battering at our shields," Sayas said as he crouched near Kallon. "They are just draining themselves."

Kallon glanced behind him, making sure everyone was tucked away into their hiding places. He'd strategically placed them around the trail. As Graygual fought their way in, Kallon would spring the trap, crushing the weaker fighters to pulp. Graygual would then trip over one another, trying to find footing. That would make it easier to cut them down.

Kallon turned back, sword in hand, impatient to finally stand his ground and deliver the deathblow the

Graygual deserved. He felt the constant pokes to his shield, and ignored them. The Inkna were no match for the power Kallon had at his disposal, just as the Graygual were no match for the skill. Greater numbers didn't guarantee victory. Not when the defenders were Shumas.

"Your ego is too big," Mela said in a feminine hum, feeling his confidence. "When we see the Chosen, she'll work on beating it out of you."

"I have to make sure it is greater still, then, haven't I?" Kallon's grip tightened on his sword. "She is probably fat and lazy by now. I'll need to give her a large job so she can get back in shape."

"Fat and lazy." Sayas nodded. "That sounds like the Chosen I remember, yes. Fat, lazy, and full of sweetness. Fits her personality exactly."

"I wouldn't mind picking on Rohnan again," Tanna said with a smirk. "Goading him into fighting is one of my joys. Or was."

"Until he threw you flat on your back." Sayas laughed.

"That started a different pastime that was just as fun." Tanna's voice colored with humor. "He was always very obliging. I wonder what happened to him. I wonder if he ever found her. She didn't mention him in the letter…"

Kallon felt his heart squeeze a little. It wasn't the

time to think about who was lost.

The sound of a rock skittering over the sharp cliff to their right cut out the whispers. A moment later, heavy boots reverberated off the rock outcrop, announcing their enemy.

Kallon couldn't imagine being any louder. This was another example of the Graygual numbers growing too quickly for their resources. He bet this host was stuffed with poorly trained men from conquered lands, either trying to stay safe by joining the powerful, or looking for the riches the Graygual promised. Either way, he doubted an upper-level officer would travel with a group of misfits making as much noise as these were. The harsh punishments along the way would've knocked everyone in line, or it would've killed them.

Footsteps started to slow. Scuffs and scraps sounded just around the bend. The mental assault pulled back, not battering Kallon and his fighters as hard. The two forces were about to meet. The Graygual would be getting organized.

Kallon focused on his breath, maintaining calm. Keeping his heartbeat regular, feeling his fighting brothers and sisters around him. The bare dirt trail waited for travelers, idle and calm. All noise ground down to a halt. The only sound was the sorrowful whine of the wind through the trees higher on the hill.

Graygual, moving in single file, burst around the

bend, running with swords in their hands and grimaces on their faces. Kallon ripped off his *Gift's* shield, immediately feeling his fighting brothers and sisters mentally holding hands with him. Just as fast, the Inkna assault tore at his mind, trying to find purchase and rip his life from his body.

Kallon stepped around the rock as he felt Sayas take point with the *Gift,* creating a complex and potent counterattack. The Inkna wouldn't last long. He met the first Graygual with a sword strike, catching the enemy in the side. He stepped back, drawing the Graygual in while the men behind him ran on. Mela popped out next as Kallon blocked a strike and then lunged, piercing the Graygual in the chest.

Kallon stepped wider, allowing more Graygual to stream by, some with terror clearly painted on their faces. He hefted a knife, tossed it up, caught it by the blade, and threw. The weapon lodged between the shoulder blades of a Graygual. The man screamed and arched before sinking to the ground, trying to grab at the blade.

Kallon turned, confronted by two Graygual. He snatched out a knife and stuck one in the neck. He yanked and then turned, moving the body in front of him as the man screamed his death. The other Graygual stabbed, hitting his own man before reaching for the shoulder to drag him away from Kallon. Kallon used the momentum. He wrapped his fingers around the man's wrist and tugged, moving him off balance. He then whipped him around before pulling his blade free and giving it a new home in the chest of this other Graygual.

Before the body hit the ground, Kallon was away again, his sword finding purchase in a stomach.

A knife flew past his head, sinking into a shoulder of an oncoming Graygual. The man flagged before Kallon finished the job.

Another stepped up, a manic grin splashed across his dirty face. Kallon slashed him across the chest before kicking him, knocking him back into the man behind him. He threw another knife, sticking it in a chest as Mela danced forward to dispatch a deathly skinny man.

Another knife sprang out of a neck before blood gushed down the Graygual's front, and Sayas ran forward to get into the fray. The three of them stabbed and cut, slicing through the enemy as though they were toddlers and weaponless.

Their power surged. A killing strike for the remaining Inkna.

"They are going down too easily!" Mela shouted. "These men are not trained."

Kallon stuck his sword into a Graygual stomach before grabbing his shirt front and ripping to the side, clearing some room. He stabbed another, just as quickly. Just as easily. Mela was right. This wasn't an army, it was a badly trained militia.

"Let some through!" Tulous yelled. "You aren't the only one who wants to avenge our loss."

Kallon moved backward, seeing Mela and Sayas peel off to the side, following Kallon's lead. Graygual surged forward, stumbling and jerky. They jogged into the space, tripping over dead bodies and slipping on muddy ground, wet with blood.

As Tulous and the others moved forward to meet the enemy, Kallon took a moment to assess what they were dealing with.

Gaunt faces and sticklike arms badly waving swords caught his focus. Dirty and disheveled uniforms with only one or two slashes hung off malnourished bodies. Shifting eyes full of fear but driven by determination set off warning bells.

This wasn't the enemy. These men were trapped in a destiny they hadn't chosen.

"*Stop!*" Kallon yelled.

Already sensing their defeat, and clearly waiting for death, the Graygual probably figured they had nothing to lose. As the Shumas pulled away, following Kallon's lead and stopping the assault, the Graygual slowed. One by one, they stilled.

Kallon's mind whirled. Hardly knowing what he was doing, but somehow feeling the *rightness* of it, he lowered his sword. The Graygual man in front of him, bearing only a single slash, dirty and afraid, didn't move forward. He stared as terror polluted the air around him.

"*Who is your officer?*" Kallon asked in the Graygual language.

The man's brow furrowed. "*Officer...killed,*" the man answered in a bad accent. He glanced behind him.

"*The officer was killed a few days ago by an arrow,*" another man said as he stepped forward. His sword was held tightly in a quivering hand. "*We were cutting through a town. Chasing you. A little ways outside, we were ambushed by...townspeople, I think. They aimed for the officer and the other Graygual with at least three slashes on their breast. There were five in all. As soon as the officers were downed, the townspeople scattered. We...kept chasing you. That was our directive.*"

"What are you doing, Kallon?" Mela asked in the Shumas language.

"*Without an officer to keep you in line, why bother following the directive?*" Kallon asked, ignoring Mela. His gaze was rooted to the speaker. "*Why not return home?*"

The man looked at those around him. His mouth turned into a thin line.

Someone in the back staggered forward. Greasy black hair fell into his sunken eyes. "*They will kill our families. I know someone that deserted. When he re-*

turned home, his wife and children were hanging there for him. By their necks! His neighbors, too."

"*And your food? Do they not feed you in this army?*"

"*They've been taking the stores in the towns to feed the armies. There are many to feed. We were only called to fight recently.*"

Kallon raised his voice, trying to reach them all. "*We are not the enemy. We are not the ones starving you, or forcing you to fight. We are not the ones killing innocents. We are trying to stop all of that. The Chosen has come forward. We go to join her. Help us. Free yourselves.*"

"We don't have the resources for them to join us," Sayas warned.

"*What about our families?*" someone shouted. "*We'd just be trading one tyrant for another!*" someone else yelled.

"*Keep your tunics,*" Kallon said, his voice now booming. "*Pretend to stay enlisted. Check on your families. But when the time comes, remember who gave you a chance of freedom. And then look around you. Choose what to fight for. Don't let someone else make that choice for you.*"

"We're wasting time, Kallon," Tulous said.

Kallon turned to Tulous. "Can you put them to sleep without killing them?"

He frowned. "I've seen the Chosen do it, but…I'm

afraid I might kill them. I don't have her deft touch."

"I can't either," Sayas said. "I've tried before. I killed the man."

Kallon turned back to the unsure army one last time. "*We are leaving you here. Think on what I have said. If any of you follow us after this, we'll kill you. Your Inkna are dead. We don't need swords to take you down.*"

A few people's eyes widened. A few others looked behind them, probably wondering if the Inkna statement was true.

"*Are you really going to help the violet-eyed girl?*" someone asked.

Kallon turned to jog away as Mela said, "*She is the leader of our people. Together, we stand strong.*"

As Mela joined them, jogging away, Sayas said, "Poetic, Mela."

"I thought they needed a better end note than 'Don't come after us or we'll kill you.' It's all about presentation."

As Kallon and the others continued along the path, Sayas said, "That was genius, Kallon. There were a lot more of them than I'd thought. We would've taken wounds."

"I wasn't thinking about sparing us." Kallon reached his horse, tethered loosely on a dead limb. He climbed up and swung his leg over the saddle. As his horse picked its way carefully to the top and then over the winding path along the hillside, he said, "Those men weren't fighters. They weren't trained, and they didn't even know what cause they're fighting for. Showing them compassion might change the tide. When they see what their leaders are capable of, they'll think back and remember this."

"It might not help," Tulous said.

"We had to take the chance and hope the Chosen can eventually turn them to our cause." As Kallon led the way, urgency ate away at him again. The fate of the land lay at the Chosen's feet. He only hoped she could live long enough to fulfill her destiny. That any of them could.

CHAPTER 14

SHANTI BLINKED HER eyes open, then rubbed them, gritty from fatigue and begging her to go back to sleep. After squirreling those two Graygual bodies away last night, hiding them within a garbage bin where the eventual stink wouldn't be noticed, she'd stayed awake to get one last look at the city with her *Gift*. Graygual dotted the perimeter and within the park, where they must've felt they were needed the most, but within the city, the gaps between watchers was often large. They didn't view the women nor the older or workingmen as much of a threat.

Rolling her shoulders to try and work out some stiffness that had settled in her body, she started when she noticed the small face looking at her from the corner. Big, brown eyes with lush black lashes watched in silence. Barely blinking, the little thing didn't even move when she saw him. He just continued watching from where he sat, his arms hugging his knees to his chest.

He'd make an excellent spy.

"Don't your people have an issue with impoliteness and staring?" She pushed the hair from her face.

"Staring is caring." His voice was little more than a squeak.

She let a smile bud. "So they say. What do you want?"

His little shoulders jumped in a shrug. He didn't move any other part of his body.

She got off the bed and moved to sit beside him, taking in the room from his vantage point. Large windows let the soft morning sunlight in, sprawling across the ground and warming her disposition. Two beds occupied the room, one rumpled where she'd slept, and the other made where Rohnan had been.

"Is this your room?" she asked, hugging her knees to her chest like he'd done.

"Yes."

"And I took your bed, didn't I. I'm some jerk, I know."

His knees fell to the sides as he tucked in his ankles, relaxing enough to sit cross-legged. "It's okay. I get lonely in it, anyway, but Vale hates when I get in with him. So I got to sleep with Ruisa last night. She used to live here, too, but then she got to go with the Captain."

"Have you lived here long?" Shanti dropped her knees and crossed her ankles under her, mimicking him again.

"A year."

"What happened to your parents?"

He hunched a little. "I never knew my mom. My dad left. He didn't come back. Where are your parents?"

"My parents died when I was about your age. My grandfather took care of me until he died. So I'm an orphan. Like you."

He nodded with half his body, his chest rising and falling like his head. "Yeah. That's what Rohnan said. He said you're his sister because you were raised together. But if that's true, all the people in this house would be my brothers and sisters."

"And you wouldn't like that?"

He chewed his lip for a moment in thought. His legs flopped out before him, now straight. "I don't know. Saburo hits me all the time. And I get pushed around a lot. But I don't really have anyone else."

"I used to push Rohnan around a lot. He didn't have anyone else, either. Eventually we just started depending on each other."

He nodded with his body again, his legs spasming, making his heels thump on the floor. Shanti smiled with his energy.

"Well, I have to get up," she said in a put-upon tone. "They're going to try and dress me like a girl."

"Ruisa always hated when they tried to dress her like a girl. She likes wearing pants."

"I like wearing pants, too. That way, no one can see my knickers when I kick someone in the head."

The boy started laughing, hopping up when Shanti did. "I'm too small to kick someone in the head."

"Nah." Shanti pulled open the door, pleased when he followed behind. "You just need to learn the right way."

"But my foot can't reach."

"Then learn to jump." Shanti traveled through a corridor to the stairs. As she made her way down, she heard the boy's loud steps behind her. "What's your name?"

"Arsen."

"Hi, Arsen. I'm Shanti."

She rounded the corner, making her way to the large dining area. There, she found Rohnan in the middle of the kids, gesturing wildly. A peal of laughter greeted her.

"What'd I miss?" she asked, grabbing a bowl and slopping some porridge into it. "This stuff is the pits. Don't they feed you anything else in this place?"

Rohnan scowled at her. "As I told the *children* earlier, porridge is good for you. It gives you lots of energy and makes you grow up big and strong."

She sat down, looking at it dubiously. "It tastes like wood."

"You have only a few minutes, *Chulan,*" Rohnan

said, turning his focus back to the kids gathered around him.

Shanti grimaced as the gruel squished between her tongue and the roof of her mouth. A door opened and shut at the front of the house. Shanti choked down more of her breakfast as Molly bustled in with a harried expression.

"C'mon, dear, we have to get moving," Molly said to Shanti as she glanced over the children. "Good morning, everyone! Are you being welcoming to our guests?"

"Yes!" they chorused.

Rohnan rose as Molly shooed her into an airy room and made her stand next to a giant pile of bright yellow fabric.

"No way, Molly!" Shanti exclaimed. "The Graygual will have to shade their eyes when they see me."

"Well then, they won't recognize your face, will they?"

"No. I'll wear the blue one."

"That one is for Rohnan."

"What's this now?" Rohnan stepped out of the horde of children who had gathered in the arched entryway in observation. He wore a comical yet disbelieving smile on his face.

"You can't very well walk around wearing trousers!" Molly scoffed as she yanked down Shanti's pants. She turned to Rohnan with a warning in her eyes. "You have long hair and you're pretty enough to pass muster. So take those off or I'll take them off for you. C'mon. I have to hurry. My guard is waiting outside."

"What about the guard from last night?" Shanti asked, stepping out of her pants and putting on the unreasonably large undergarments. The white ruffled things were tight on her thighs and went down past her knees.

"I wasn't asked any questions about last night. Like I said, he'd done that before. But when he doesn't turn up for his post tonight…"

Shanti pulled off her shirt. Gasps filled the room.

"Shanti, for heaven's sake! There are *children* in here!" Molly ran at the kids, shooing them away.

"Why is everyone putting so much emphasis on the fact that there are children?" Shanti wrapped her binding around her breasts, needing to keep them in place in case she had to strip out of her dress later and fight.

"You seem to forget you are no longer a child. We are trying to remind you." Rohnan moved to the side of the room.

"You can't get naked in front of the boys." Molly huffed as she stepped in front of Shanti. She ignored Rohnan's "why?" as she tsked. Picking up the corset, she stepped up to Shanti with a scowl. "You have to wear this."

Shanti laughed. "We've had this fight, Molly. I will not wear that death trap."

"What is it?" Rohnan asked, stepping forward again, moving as far from the dress as possible.

"Shanti, now listen to me." Molly yanked at the binding, trying to rip it off her. "You need to look like—"

"How are we doing?" Valencia, the woman who had proclaimed herself an expert with a knife and a pig, bustled in with an expectant expression.

"Good, you're here." Molly pointed at Rohnan. "Get him going. And make sure those boys don't try to sneak in here. They're trying to get another look at Shanti."

"Your fear of the naked body is silly." Shanti swatted Molly's hands away. "That thing could be the difference between life and death, Molly. I cannot wear it."

Molly sighed as Valencia backed Rohnan into a corner. "I don't care how much you value your masculinity, young man. You will put on this dress, or I will *make* you put on this dress. Either way, you are leaving this house much prettier than you came in, if that were possible."

"I can move around this city without being seen. I do not need to wear that frightening thing to do it." Rohnan gently removed the woman's hands from his person.

"Then at least wear a girdle." Molly shook a band of

fabric at Shanti. It had strings hanging from it, promising an uncomfortable hug that bordered on painful.

"No. There is no need." Shanti slapped Molly's hands away again.

AN HOUR AND several arguments later, Shanti, wearing a horrible monstrosity that hugged her breasts and then exploded out into a sea of fabric to the floor, had her hair dyed black and styled. She was the only one, though. While having Rohnan disguised as a woman was a good idea, his shoulders were much too broad and muscular for him to pass as one. He'd have to stick to the sides and try to get around as best he could in broad daylight.

"I don't have a good feeling about any of this," Shanti said as she finally stepped outside. Molly had left after getting her dressed, not having an excuse to hang around any longer. At least none that her guard would buy.

"Neither do I, but we don't have any other options." Rohnan slipped in behind some shrubbery as the pretty young woman from the night before came walking toward them.

"Good, she's on time." Valencia pushed Shanti forward. "That's Alena. She'll be taking you around the prison. Okay, I have to run, girls. The kids make a horrible mess when someone isn't looking over their shoulders. And remember, keep a low profile."

Alena approached with an angry bruise across her cheek. She glanced at Rohnan in the bushes before focusing on Shanti. Her face turned a light crimson. She opened her mouth, probably to utter a greeting, but closed it again when Gracas stepped up.

"I'm ready, S'am." Two of the oldest orphans were with him.

"You know what to do?" Shanti asked Gracas.

"I got it, S'am. I can do it." He motioned the silent orphans forward. His body was much larger than theirs, stacked with muscle. He still had the youthful, floppy, and goofy way of moving, but he was a young man now, walking among boys. Hopefully the Graygual guarding the army in the park wouldn't notice his older age. She was counting on Gracas to get some information about how that system worked, and distribute more poison if at all possible.

Ruisa came out of the house next in a puffy pink dress. Orphans scurried behind her and then out to the sides. They each carried a purse filled with a potent version of the poison the women had devised. With their time running out, they needed to start affecting the Graygual now. Ruisa would distribute that poison to everyone she could, working it into food and water. The effects wouldn't be entirely noticeable for days, but the start of the damage would be quick—fatigue would set in only a few hours after ingesting the liquid.

Shanti had been dead set against involving the orphans. Children should be sheltered away from danger, not thrust into it. Unfortunately, they'd stolen some of the poison for themselves, and made it very clear they'd be helping Ruisa. She was one of them. And they all stuck together.

"Be careful," Shanti said as they left the house.

"I like using the orphans least of all," Rohnan said quietly.

Shanti sent a mental *kick* his way. That was supposed to be a secret.

Thankfully, Alena ignored it. "Shall we?"

Leilius slunk behind Shanti and joined Rohnan where he skulked behind the bushes.

"I know my way around the city," Shanti said before she started walking. "You don't need to put yourself in danger. I'm going to try not to engage, but…well, you just never know."

"From what they said, you only vaguely know your way around the city," Alena said, raising her chin. "I can help. I'm not afraid."

The woman shed fear like a dog shed fur in summer, revealing her lie. Shanti just nodded, and let her lead the way. She really hoped nothing went wrong.

CHAPTER 15

"SHHH. DO YOU hear that?" Sonson looked around with wide eyes.

Denessa paused, a cube of cheese on the end of her knife hovering near her mouth.

They sat deep in the trees, clustered around a small fire. They'd taken a northern route instead of veering south and using the Cross-Land Travelway, which ran along the plains. This way would take longer, but it kept them hidden and played to their strengths of fighting within the cover of woodland. The black of the night consumed anything outside the flickering glow of the flame.

A distant *snap* sounded, and then a rustle of plant life.

Sonson let his *Therma* travel out as far as it could, bolstered by the others. He could barely feel someone tickle his consciousness out in the night. He glanced to his side in time to see all three of the great cats melt into the blackness. On the other side, the three beasts raised their heads and looked out into the night, issuing a soft whine.

"They have no idea who they are dealing with," Boas said in delight. In the trials, he'd always been the lead in sneaking up on people during the still of the night. Only the Chosen had ever felt him coming. And only the Chosen could best him, Sonson included.

"They have no idea *what* they are dealing with," Denessa said with an evil grin as one of the animal keepers let Bonzi, the male beast, off his tether.

Sonson rose slowly and took out two knives. To the animal keeper, he said, "Those cats won't take a bite out of me, right? I'm a friend?"

The man hesitated. "If the Chosen were here, I'd say yes. They've been overly anxious since they were left behind, though. But…" He scratched his growing beard. "You should be okay."

Sonson gave Boas a commiserating stare. *Should* be okay?

"How many do you want to go?" Boas asked as he spread a little mud across his cheeks.

Sonson looked around at the eager Shadow, all hoping he'd point to them. These were the best, most versatile fighters they had. They loved their craft and wanted the chance to experience it beyond the confines of their island. Too bad Sonson didn't trust those animals, or he'd let them all go.

"Let's just see what we're up against." Sonson motioned for a few of them, including Denessa and Punston, to rise.

A small unit followed Boas' example, covering the paleness of their faces. If moonlight found its way through the thick canopy above, they didn't want it highlighting their presence.

One by one they drifted into the trees, stepping lightly, careful not to disturb plant life. Sonson felt the cool air coating his skin, and heard a small scrape of wood on jacket from somewhere to his right. This land was much drier than they were used to. It was harder to keep the noise muffled.

Sonson's awareness tingled as enemy minds sparked into his mental map up ahead. Another presence tugged at his awareness, and then made him jump as something ghosted by his leg. One of the cats, silent and deadly.

He worked around a large trunk and then paused, sensing movement in his direction. Dark shapes moved on the near-black background, hardly noticeable but for the sound. Footsteps crunched the ground. Leaves rustled.

Sonson felt Boas go tranquil, blending into the night to his left. Then Denessa did the same. They were getting ready to attack.

Sonson brought his knives up, nice and slow, bent his knees, and let his mind drift into the night. He felt his surroundings, his *Therma,* and his fellow warriors, as they synchronized their minds and prepared.

A low growl stopped all movement.

A creak of leather sounded.

The growl increased in pitch.

"*What's that?*"

The language was that of the Graygual.

"*I don't know,*" came the whispered response.

The growl grew more menacing. The beast was readying to charge.

"*Should we keep going?*"

Sonson could hear the uncertainty creep into the voice.

Boas launched himself forward. The wet slide of a knife was followed by a shriek of pain and surprise.

Sonson jogged in, grabbing the first shape and jabbing three times with his knife in different locations. His man jerked and screamed before he was falling to the ground. Sonson moved on as a black shape gave a feline cry before barreling to an enemy. Another cat joined the mix, taking down another man.

Wetness sprayed across Sonson's face as his hands clutched fabric. He yanked the man and brought his knife in, sticking him in the ribs. He aimed lower, hitting him rapidly twice more in the guts. The man slackened, his fight starting to die. Sonson brought his knife up and swept it across the jugular before tossing him aside and reaching for a man bringing up his sword.

"Mine!" Denessa's voice cut through a roar. She grabbed the black shape and went to work as the huge beast lumbered into the area.

"Give him room!" Tunston, the animal keeper, shouted.

The Shadow cleared out of the way, knowing that when the beast flew into a rage, it stopped noticing who was friend and who was foe.

The beast crashed through the trees, his growls and roars having the enemy pausing. It barreled into a stationary man, crushing him to the ground before going after another. His large shape blotted out sight.

As if a lever had been thrown, the Graygual turned and fled. One dashed right by Sonson. Sonson grabbed him, ripping him back and shoving a knife in his armpit as he flailed. He tossed him away and lurched for another, but before he could grab him, a cat sprang, knocking the man down.

The beast roared again before cutting off a loud scream.

Sonson looked around him, not seeing any more shapes running. Not that he would be able to see more than a few feet.

"Did any get through?" It was Denessa's voice from four paces away. She knew better than to get too close in the darkness without announcing her presence.

"I don't know. The cats will probably get them if they did."

"I questioned keeping those animals alive. I didn't think they could be domesticated. Looks like it's good that they can't."

Sonson started picking his way back to the fire. "They were meant to be. Now we know why. They'll serve us well."

"They'll serve the Chosen well, you mean. I get the feeling they'd rather not be in our presence."

"*Your* presence, maybe," Tunston said before he came closer. "Anyone who gives them a good scratch behind the ears becomes an immediate favorite."

"But for how long?" Denessa snorted. "They are too moody for my taste."

"You prefer the beasts, I take it?" Tunston asked.

"Yes. The beasts can be trained. Those cats do whatever they want."

They walked into the sphere of light. Those gathered around the fire looked up at their entrance.

"Graygual. I'd doubt they were higher level." Sonson looked down at himself. He had splatters of blood across his chest and down his legs. "Another tunic gone. I hope we come across a stream. I need to wash some of these or I'll end up naked."

"In that case, we *all* hope we come to a stream." Boas entered the light looking similarly stained. "They weren't great at stalking in the night. They weren't top stock. Boring."

Sonson stripped off his shirt. "The Graygual are scrambling. They don't have anyone in the area that can stop us."

"Probably because they are massing somewhere else, aiming for the real threat." Denessa took a swig from her water skin. "We've made it through. We're not worth them losing more life."

"What do you mean?" Boas asked.

"Just that, we've made it into the land. We've made it past the flimsy defenses. Xandre won't waste any more good resources on us, because that means he'd have less to send to the Chosen. We cut down a lot of his elite forces in the Shadow Land. It takes time to train. Years. He no longer has years. He needs to save them to take down the Chosen."

Sonson nodded thoughtfully. The threat wouldn't be the siege on the Captain's city. That was too soon. Whatever Xandre was planning, it would be on a grand scale, Sonson had no doubt. And it would wipe them out if they didn't act first. The battle to end all battles was coming.

CHAPTER 16

SHANTI SAUNTERED BESIDE Alena, noticing each Graygual, his positioning, and level within the army. Near the orphan house, most of the Graygual were lower rung, and bore surly expressions. Their movements were jerky and their focus fleeting. They would be easy to take down.

Near the prison things became a lot dicier. One and two slashes turned into three and four. Movements turned graceful and stances balanced. The Graygual there had hard expressions, watchful and focused.

"Do new fighters ever enter the city?" Shanti asked as they neared the prison. She lowered her eyes as they passed a Graygual. He eyed them for a moment before his gaze moved on. Here, unlike the Hunter's camp, the women weren't invisible, they were just not considered a threat. That was a very big difference.

"No. He is cut off from getting any more soldiers, I think." Alena started to chuckle. Her hand touched her breast before gliding through the air to land on Shanti's shoulder. "Smile as if you just told a joke."

Shanti's smile probably looked like a grimace.

A Graygual across the street glanced at them. His gaze lingered on Alena for a moment but stuck a little longer to Shanti. Sweat beaded on her brow. Her knives felt hot against her leg. Her back felt cold without the weight of her sword. This was a terrible idea.

"If he keeps staring I'll cut his eye out," Shanti muttered, her smile slipping. She forced out a laugh.

As if hearing her thought, Alena said, "This is a bad idea. You don't move like us. You look…dangerous. Like you're about to kill someone."

"I might be if he keeps staring." Shanti forced her gaze to the ground.

"Lower your head a little more. You look defiant."

Shanti gritted her teeth and tried to push away the intense urge to run at that Graygual and stick a knife in his gut. "With my eyes on the ground I can't check anyone out."

They ambled a little further up the road. The prison loomed off to the right, a Graygual and an Inkna standing in front. Two more Graygual walked up from the side, their faces grim as they both went inside.

"I wonder why there are so many guards…" Alena looped her arm in Shanti's, pulling her close. She leaned in with a smile. "There aren't usually so many."

"You are very good at pretending to be happy while being terrified." Shanti drew her *Gift* in and slammed her shields home. "We shouldn't go close to that Inkna. If he gets curious, he'll figure out what I am."

"We can't very well turn back. The Graygual you silently threatened is now following us."

Shanti risked a glance behind them. The Graygual was still on the opposite side of the street, but he'd started walking after them.

"*Flak,*" Shanti quietly swore. Another Inkna had shown up at the prison, not far from them now. "Why are they so heavily guarding men behind bars?"

"Unless Lucius took the elixir…"

"The what?"

"I gave Lucius… What's wrong?"

Shanti went rigid, feeling the poke of power against her shields. Alena staggered a moment later, letting out a whimper of pain.

"This situation just got worse." Another poke pushed against her shield. The Inkna was now looking right at her. "Get us out of here!" Shanti hissed.

"There's nowhere to go. We can't just turn around! That'll be obvious. And for God's sake, *smile* or you'll get us both killed."

Shanti let a grin twist her mouth while gazing vaguely ahead, catching the Inkna still staring in her peripheral vision. Alena gave her arm a tug, leading her across the street. They'd be closer to the other Graygual, still keeping pace, but it would be infinitely better than that Inkna getting more curious.

Alena grunted as another poke hit Shanti's shields. The woman sucked in a ragged breath, her face turning white. Shanti let her smile fade and gave an exaggerated stumble, pretending to feel the pain just as acutely.

"He must be relatively weak if he can't tell I have shields up," Shanti said softly as Alena put her head down. She was lagging behind now, clutching Shanti's arm in a claw-like grip.

"Can't you feel it?"

"I can feel him poking me. Look at him. He's just trying to make us suffer." Shanti felt her ire rise. "He has no idea what suffering is. I could give him a lesson…"

"Look *down*!" Alena wheezed. "You look like you're about to go on a killing spree."

"I *feel* like I'm about to go on a killing spree. He has it coming." Shanti risked a glance behind. The Graygual was still back there, keeping pace, his face intent. His scowl was aimed at her.

"If he only has a little power, I'd hate to see what a lot of power is like."

"Yes, you would. C'mon. It's not permanent. Push through the pain."

"Easy for you to say," Alena said through a stiff jaw. "You're not the one in pain."

"Yep. Supportive, though, aren't I?"

“No, not really.”

They passed the prison, having no more information now than they had before they started this hazardous stroll. Shanti felt the mental pokes lighten before they disappeared altogether. Alena straightened up with a sigh.

“Not out of the woods yet,” Shanti said quietly, opening up her *Gift.* She kept it tightly around her, having no idea who she might meet around the next corner. Behind her, the Graygual kept pace.

Shanti felt fear spike in Alena. “He’ll want to question us. That might mean a trip to the Hunter…”

Adrenaline coursed through Shanti. She considered their options.

She could easily lie in wait and then kill the Graygual. He was only one man, with three slashes, and he wouldn’t expect much from her. She was acting suspiciously, but she was still a woman in a big frilly dress. The women here had given the Graygual no reason to suspect them of being able to fight. The problem was that trying to hide him in broad daylight, in a populated area, wouldn’t be easy. Besides, she’d probably get blood on the dress. That would attract all sorts of attention.

“Why didn’t I wear black or red?” Shanti muttered.

The other option was the one that made the most sense.

"C'mon!" Shanti grabbed Alena and started to run. "Let's lose him."

"But…these shoes…"

They clattered around a corner in heeled shoes and then ducked into an alley. Shanti had been this way before, knowing where it emerged. Unfortunately, that excursion had been in pants. The dress climbed the walls, stuffed into the small space. Behind her, Alena waded through her shiny purple fabric, pushing through like she was walking through mud.

"We can go to Fabienne's house," Alena huffed out. "She's close by."

The Graygual had paused when Shanti and Alena turned the corner. Shanti felt his indecision about leaving his post, but he was suspicious. He knew something wasn't right.

Halfway down the alley, Shanti held her breath. He was on the verge of turning back.

And then he followed them. His determination spiked. He wanted to cure his curiosity.

"Faster," Shanti urged, battling the material as the dress dragged along the dirty alley walls.

"I can't…" Alena stalled, trying to turn sideways. She forced down the billowing fabric in panicked, jerky movements. "The corset…is making it hard…to maneuver."

Shanti grabbed her by the arm and started pulling.

"Push through it, Alena. That corset will feel like a lover's embrace compared to what the Hunter will do."

Shanti yanked Alena the rest of the way. She felt the Graygual approaching the alley. He'd probably pass by with a glance. Then he'd see them.

"Hurry!" She popped out of the alley and turned to pull Alena with her. The wall scraped the woman's arm as she was dragged around it. They flattened against the stone, panting.

The Graygual did pass, but then stalled. Shanti's breath became shallow as she felt his indecision once again. And then acute focus. He was tracking them.

"Shit." Shanti leaned forward so she could see around Alena to the mouth of the alley. As she'd suspected, the walls had lines where the dresses had scraped away dust and dirt. "C'mon, we have to go."

At a fast but noisy pace thanks to their shoes, they turned down a deserted lane. Toward the end, Alena pointed out another small alleyway. "We should go down there."

Shanti glanced at the ground. Their heels were scraping away bits of filth. Nicely dressed women didn't take to the alleys. Obviously only those up to no good in soft-soled shoes passed this way. Like she would have done in a normal situation.

This was anything but normal.

Shanti glanced at the alley. Then their dresses.

"Bloody hell." Shanti grabbed the other woman by the shoulders, and wrenched her around. A hem ripped. Alena gasped.

"It's just a dress," Shanti said, exasperated. She undid the back, exposing the laces of the corset. Without wasting any time, she started yanking, unlacing it.

"What are you *doing*?" Alena demanded in a loud whisper. She reached back to stop the progress.

Shanti slapped the woman's hands away and hooked her finger in the string and pulled. As she worked, the thing popped open, then caught in the dress. With rough but quick hands, Shanti ripped the dress open and down to Alena's waist.

"Oh my God," Alena gushed, covering her chest.

"What is *with* you people? You still have a garment on." Shanti slapped her elbows up and out of the way. With some finagling, she got the stiff corset off and tossed it to the ground. She did the dress back up as quickly as possible and then yanked the woman around again. "Let's go."

"But my—" Alena reached down to scoop up the discarded item. "These are expensive."

"Stop wearing them. See? I just saved you money." Shanti grabbed the woman's arm and started pulling, intent on dragging her through the second alley.

"He's going to wonder why we are traipsing through alleyways," Alena said, panting once again.

"I think I've shown that I don't fit in here. One suspicious Graygual is better than a city full of suspicious Graygual. Besides, he has to catch us to be able to ask."

"This could raise their suspicions, though!"

"The men we killed not turning up for their duties will do that anyway."

"No one ever mentioned you were a know-it-all," Alena grumbled.

Shanti couldn't help a bark of laughter.

They came out of the confined space and paused, Shanti scanning with both her eyes and *Gift*. Someone she knew waited a short distance away to the right. Keeping Alena to the side so as not to be seen, she inched along the wall until they had to cross the street. A few citizens ambled along, but none of the enemy lingered.

"Quick." Shanti jerked off her shoes now that the way was clear of debris and ran, crossing the open space. On the other side, she led them around a bend before stepping into an alcove partially covered by a large, bushy plant. "Leilius."

Leilius jumped. His arm flew out, a knife at the end jabbing at her chest. Shanti batted it away and gave him a shove, knocking him back against the wall.

"Oh, S'am, it's you!" Leilius slumped and clutched at his chest. "I thought I was a goner."

"Good reaction, though the chest would be hard to

pierce. You should aim for a more vulnerable area. Listen—"

"S'am, you look a mess! Your dress isn't on right, and your hair looks like you got caught in a whirlwind. You should've let them try to make Rohnan fit in that dress. He would've pulled this off better than you."

"When people judge me, Leilius, I kick them somewhere soft that hurts an awful lot..."

Leilius shut his mouth.

"I need you to tell Rohnan to watch that prison if he can get close enough. We need to know who has the key and when we can force our way in. If at all possible, I'd love to know how strong the various Inkna are that pass him by. If he can feel it."

"He's already doing all that, S'am." Leilius stowed his knife. "He's got a good hiding place. He said to tell you that he can't feel the Inkna from where he is, and he can't get any closer. Then he sent me to wait in a quieter part of the city until you found me. Which is here. I've only seen one Graygual walk by, and he didn't seem particularly observant."

Shanti felt a rush of gratitude that she had Rohnan by her side. They had always been a good team. "We're being followed, so we're going to go into hiding for a few hours. I need to think of what we need to do next. Sneaking around seems like a better plan than dressing like a party favor."

"It would probably work better if you looked like a lady."

"And you'd probably get punched less if you stopped voicing observations."

"Yes, S'am. Please don't punch me."

Alena ducked her head around the bushy plant. "Hurry! Someone just looked down the other end of the alley."

Shanti sighed. "Nothing is going well in this venture." She gestured Leilius out of the alcove. "You'd best move on. That man is annoyingly tenacious. He'll probably walk by here looking for me."

"That's okay, S'am. I need to check in with the orphans, anyway. See if I can help."

This time Shanti did punch him. Why couldn't these guys keep their mouths shut? She jerked her head at Alena. "Let's go."

"What did he mean about the orphans? That's the second time someone has brought them up."

"Nothing. They just wanted to help, is all."

"You're having the orphans help? Through here."

They cut through a yard, closing the wooden gate behind them. Shanti directed Alena to the little brick path that cut through the garden. It was a lovely little spot, even better to have this cultivated nature in one's backyard. Shanti had to remember to tell Cayan she wanted something like this.

"Why'd you grimace? What's wrong?" Alena looked behind them in a panic.

"Nothing. Sorry. My thoughts get away from reality sometimes. Here, this way."

"I can't climb a fence in a dress!"

"Yes you can. Probably." Shanti pointed at the small path and then the border of flowers. "Careful to keep your feet out of the dirt, and make sure you don't knock any flowers off with that horrible excuse for fashion."

"You just wish you knew fashion," Alena mumbled, keeping hers eyes on her feet as she hiked up her dress.

"My people have fashion sense, believe me. And you can run and fight in it. Here—" Shanti pulled Alena up to the fence and then took fistfuls of her dress.

"What are you doing?"

"You should just stop asking. I can't explain when I'm in a hurry." Shanti pulled the dress around Alena's middle and tried to tie it in a knot. With the stiff fabric underneath, there was no way that was going to work. Instead, she settled for two knots—one in front and one behind.

"It'll have to do." Shanti tucked the extra pieces into the giant, pant-like undergarments. "Okay, up you go." She bent down and threaded her fingers together, ready to give Alena a boost.

To Shanti's surprise, Alena didn't take it. She grabbed the top of the fence, bounced, and hoisted herself up. A leg went over, then the other, before the woman dropped down to the other side with the slide of fabric on wood. Shanti threw the corset over after her.

After a quick glance behind her, noticing a couple of areas that a more experienced tracker could follow, which she hoped ruled out this Graygual, she tucked her dress up and easily scaled the fence behind Alena. Dropping down to the other side, she let her dress back out, smoothing it down.

"We've ruined these dresses," Alena said with a sigh. "I don't usually get ones this nice."

"There's that one Rohnan wouldn't wear. Take that one."

"It'll be way too big. He's...built. Um...muscular. Well built, I mean." The woman's face colored with embarrassment.

"He's handsome, yes. And popular with the ladies. I've never heard a complaint from his prowess in bed. You should spend a night with him."

Alena coughed as she stopped next to a walkway leading up to the red door of a quaint little house. "I don't... That's not what I meant."

Shanti glanced behind her. She couldn't feel the guard within the limited scope of her *Gift*. If they ducked into this house, they might have a shot at disappearing. "Shall we?"

"Oh. Yes." Alena turned and made her way to the

door. Once there, she did a series of knocks, tapping out a code, and waited. Impatience radiated from her as she glanced behind her, scanning the lane.

"There's no one around," Shanti said.

The door swung open. Fabienne, the outspoken woman from the night before, stood in the doorway with a severe expression. "What are you doing here? You're—" She noticed Shanti, waiting quietly off to the side. "Come in."

Alena entered with a swish of her dress, walking erect with her shoulders back. She looked like she was still wearing the corset, apart from her natural, free-swinging breasts. Something Fabienne noticed immediately. The scowl deepened.

Shanti walked through next, tossing the corset on the ground like trash. In the living area sat three women, one of them Tabby. Their dresses weren't as puffy, nor as shiny, but the same impression of frill flowed over their laps and brushed the floor. Each held a threaded needle and an open-weave canvas.

"Needlepoint." Shanti deflated. She hated needlepoint.

"Would you like a cuppa?" Fabienne's question sounded more like a command. "You will, won't you? You will." She nodded decisively and stalked off toward the kitchen.

"A cuppa?" Shanti asked Alena quietly.

"Tea." Alena picked through some boards of needlepoint until apparently finding one she liked. After delicately setting it on the couch, she moved with a slow grace that completely contradicted their harried plight from a moment before, then she organized a new piece of canvas.

"No, thank you." Shanti stepped toward the kitchen. "I'd much rather do something useful. Do you have any knives to sharpen?"

"This *is* useful." Tabby used a convincing tone. "Look at the beautiful patterns you can make."

Shanti's smile froze. She couldn't think of anything uglier.

Alena lifted her brow. "Your hands are probably much too calloused. You'd do a terrible job."

Shanti was about to smile thankfully but instead indignation took over. "A needle thrown just right can kill someone."

Alena smiled in a placating sort of way. "That's okay. Not everyone can do it."

A surge of stubbornness rose up. If they wanted a stupid flower stitched into a coarse white sheet, fine. They could chop with dull knives.

As Shanti sat down in her uncomfortable dress to waste her time, Tabby said, "This is Maggie and Gabrielle. They are members of the Circle. They'd already left by the time you got there last night. I was just filling them in on what they missed."

Maggie, a woman with pockmarks on her face and a bad scar on her jaw, nodded in greeting. The other, Gabrielle, a petite woman with a prim set to her countenance and stature, said "hello" demurely. In appearance, the women couldn't be any more different.

"How did your walk go?" Fabienne asked as she came out of the kitchen with two cups of a steaming liquid. She set those on the low table in the middle of the chairs and couch before checking the level of milk in a little canister on a tray.

"One, please, and a splash of milk," Alena said to Fabienne as she started to stitch into her project. "Not well. An Inkna blasted me with his power and a Graygual started following us."

"A Graygual followed you?" Tabby dropped her project to her lap. The other women let theirs hover in midair as they homed in on Alena and Shanti.

Alena told them the story as Shanti concentrated on the pattern of a tree, a rabbit, and a bit of grass. Why someone would want this tableau on a pillow or a wall was anyone's guess. As Alena was finishing, Shanti made her first stitch.

"Did you tell her what we were thinking?" Fabienne said, delivering the cups into the girls' hands.

"No." Alena sipped her tea delicately. Shanti took a sip, burnt her mouth, and then put hers on the little table next to the couch.

"Maggie?" Fabienne said.

"I think I can rig up an exploding device," the pockmarked woman said, placing a stitch into her canvas. She raised her eyebrows and glanced up at Shanti. "You would throw it into the Graygual and it would explode, killing those near it. If you need something like that."

Shanti dropped the canvas. "Come again?"

"I'm sure you've noticed the state of my face." With the needle tip, she pointed to a pockmark, then the scar. "This wasn't the result of disease or puberty. I accidentally came across a chemical mix that explodes. A few, actually. After discovering the first, making me look like this, I experimented with others. I can delay it long enough to throw it. It'll explode enough to harm, and maybe take off a limb. I might be able to make it more violent..."

"This city just keeps getting better," Shanti said in a breathy whisper. A smile drifted up her face. "Does Cayan know about this?"

The women glanced at each other. "No," Tabby said. "We thought it best that this knowledge stayed with us. There has been no need for it before now. Men can be careless, and if this information got into the hands of children..."

"Plus," Gabrielle added, "the men haven't discovered it, which means they'd question that we have. Many of them think we're as soft as kittens. The Captain knows about our art, but exploding poison…well, that might ruffle even his feathers."

"This would be an act of war," Fabienne announced boldly. "But if you think it's a good idea, we'll give it a debut."

"Can you control it?" Shanti asked.

"Now, see? She asks good questions." Fabienne nodded in approval.

"She's just using logic," Gabrielle said.

"My late husband would've asked how much he could blow up." Fabienne sniffed.

Maggie ignored the women. "After a fashion." She threaded another needle. Pride drifted out from her. Pride, and passion. She clearly had a love for mixing chemicals, and using her creation pleased her. Shanti could understand that mentality. "I would only trust a select few with both the knowledge, and the use. If mixed incorrectly, or timed badly, it would have devastating results."

"I understand." Shanti let the seriousness of the situation sink in. "I think you should use it if you can control it. The enemy would greatly love the knowledge, I can guarantee you. And they would take it if they could. We can't risk them having any more of an edge."

"We could use the help of men, though…" Tabby's

face was bright red. Her head was bent farther than normal to her task. "They're stronger. They could throw farther."

"A catapult would be better, don't you think?" Shanti asked. "A catapult might counteract the reach of some of the Inkna. If you can work at the edge of their range, and fling these at them, I wouldn't be so outnumbered."

"Why didn't we think of that?" Maggie scowled at the others. "Yes, I could time that. We'd still need the army men, though. They have the knowledge of that machine."

"I doubt they'd go along with the plan of a woman..." Gabrielle said in a dry tone. Her lips pursed.

"They'd do what Shanti said," Alena said with fierce determination that didn't match her graceful movements.

"How?" Fabienne arched an eyebrow.

"Your people need to blur this divide between sexes. There's no point in it." Shanti chanced another sip of her brew. "In this, it's as simple as giving them the plan, then showing them the execution. Besides obeying their superior officer, they respond to skill, or violence. Often, I use both to make my point."

"Well, whatever works." Maggie shrugged. "We just need someone that can help us rig something up. *Help,* though. Not try to take over."

Frantic knocking sounded at the door. All the women in the living area went rigid, except for Shanti, who stood and backed toward Alena. "Get ready to get me out of this dress."

"Who is it?" Fabienne yelled through the door.

"Rohnan. I need Shanti."

"Let him in," Shanti said, moving toward the door.

The door swung open, revealing Rohnan with tight green eyes. Alarm rolled from him and into the room. "*Chulan,* three things. First, three people were carried out of the prison. Dead, it seemed. There was a big stir, so it must've been someone important."

"You don't know who?" Shanti asked, unease clawing at her.

"No." His glance went beyond her and into the room. "But they don't seem worried, so they might."

Before Shanti could glance back to get more information, Rohnan continued, "There is a Graygual working his way in this direction. He's not a great tracker, but he's good enough to follow the many clues you left thanks to those dresses. I do not think that was a great idea, *Chulan.* Even if you managed to pull it off, it was hindering you."

"Next?" Shanti asked.

The alarm intensified. "Three Graygual have been sent to collect someone. They plan to make an example of them to force the Captain's hand."

Shanti's mind raced. The Hunter collecting someone meant he or she would be tortured or killed. As the Hunter would easily have picked up on this people's affinity for protecting the female sex, he would be grabbing a woman.

There was no situation where Cayan would let the Graygual kill one of his people, especially a woman. He would either kill the Graygual and then give himself up to stop the killing of anyone else, or he'd just go quietly, thinking he could get himself out of the situation somewhere down the line. Either way, he'd shake the hourglass, draining what little time they had.

"*Flak.*" She turned, showing him her back. "Have you heard who it was?"

She felt Rohnan's deft fingers working at the dress. "Sanders' wife, Junice."

The color bled from Shanti's vision for just a moment, intense fear flashing through her. Sanders would go ballistic. Cayan wouldn't even have a chance to give himself up. Sanders would tear through the Graygual without a second thought.

In the end, he'd join the pile of bodies. They all would.

All of that was assuming Shanti didn't step in. Which was, of course, preposterous.

"What can we do?" Alena asked, at her elbow. The other women had stood up, too, needlepoint discarded.

Shanti stepped out of her dress and flung it to the side. "Nothing. Stay here. Stay out of the way. If I get caught, get those explosives working. Free as many men from the jail as possible. It won't be long before this whole city is caught up in warfare. You will need to work with the men to save yourselves. They won't want you to, but I'd bet seeing one explosive work will change their minds."

"They'll work," Maggie said with complete confidence. "But what about Junice? We can't stand aside while one of our sisters is taken."

"She won't be." Shanti turned to Rohnan. "I need to get my sword."

CHAPTER 17

REFLECTING ON THEIR situation, Sanders walked his horse through the trees. The sun had passed its zenith and was slipping down toward the horizon. He probably had no more than four hours of solid daylight left before twilight snuck in and played with his vision. Tobias moved out ahead of him, bow in hand, staring up into the trees.

They had been walking around the perimeter for the last few hours. He'd told the Captain it was to scout out the area and see if there were any holes in the defense, but he suspected the Captain saw through him. What he'd really needed was to get moving. Sitting and waiting for their fate from the Hunter wasn't his style.

"This one has been vacant for a while, sir." Tobias pointed up at the wooden platform built into the branches of the tree like a tree house. "They aren't putting much effort into the areas away from the gates."

"Not that they would. They can sense with their minds. Relaying information is a lot easier."

"How?"

Sanders thought about it for a moment. "Hell, I don't know. But it must be, right, or else why aren't they spread out around the city?"

"Maybe they don't have enough men."

"Hopefully, yes." Sanders walked in toward the city a little, to see if a flash of pain would have him retreating again. So far, he'd mapped out how far they could veer in before the Inkna blasted them with their mental power. Around the gates, it wasn't far at all. Out here in no man's land, they could just about see the stone wall surrounding the city. Not that that would help much. Shanti might be able to scale the wall and drop in undetected, but that was because someone was running interference. With all their men and no distraction, someone would notice, then they could just stroll on over and knock the Captain and everyone down with a few Inkna.

Sanders balled his fists and turned his horse around. There was no point in mapping this out anymore. He had all the information he needed. His conclusion was the same as before he even started: they needed more warriors.

"All right, let's head around the far side and then head back in," he called to Tobias, who was inspecting another crow's nest.

"This one has a little blood on it, sir," Tobias said, getting off his horse.

Sanders stomach lurched with implications. "Someone didn't want to come down peacefully."

Tobias climbed up into the crow's nest, looking around. He peered over the side and down at the ground. "Nah. Doesn't look too bad. Not much up here. If it was an arrow, it probably wasn't a mortal shot."

Sanders refused to look around to get their exact location. He didn't want to know who, specifically, had been in that tree when the Graygual came calling. Ten names were already scrolling through his head with the general area—he didn't want to narrow it down. Not before he could do something about it.

"C'mon. Let's move on," Sanders grudgingly called. "I'm sure the Hunter could have a surprise for us at any time."

"I'd rather miss it." Tobias gave one more glance out.

Me too. Sanders looked out to the side, not focusing on anything. As usual, the image of Junice invaded his thoughts. Her smell. Her beautiful smile. He missed her something awful. He'd never wanted to settle down. As soon as he had enrolled into the army, he had known that that was his life. That was what he wanted to do forever. It was his one great love, and he could think of nothing better than protecting his people with the strongest Captain to ever grace that city.

She'd blindsided him. Completely turned his world

upside down. She'd been walking down the street, all done up for some occasion or other, and she'd noticed him across the way. One smile. That was all it had taken.

From then on, all he could think about was her. Her witty comments, her funny jokes, and the way she bent and twisted him until he didn't know which way was up. He'd been wrapped around her little finger from the word "go," and it had never bothered him a bit. If his friends made fun of him, all he had to do was point at her. That was it. If they were any kind of man, they'd know that a girl like her was worth any kind of personality adjustment.

"Good to go, sir?" Tobias asked quietly.

Sanders hadn't even heard him walk up.

He pretended not to see the look of pity in Tobias' look. "Yeah. Let's head back."

"Sure."

They walked slowly, Sanders' thoughts constantly returning to his wife and what she might be going through. Ten minutes later, without warning, a stab of pain crashed into Sanders. He jerked his horse away from the city to get out of the danger zone. This time, the pain cut off instead of bled away.

"Shit."

He looked over at Tobias' exclamation, expecting the other man to be shaking out the pain. Instead, he had his bow in his hand and was looking at the ground about ten yards away.

An Inkna lay facedown with half an arrow sticking out of him. "Crap, Tobias, now look what you've done!"

"Sorry, sir! I saw him, and just when it registered what he was, the pain hit. I reacted."

"Ordinarily, that would be a good thing." Sanders looked around. Seeing no one, he kicked his horse toward the Inkna. A crimson pool inched out from under the body, shining in the speckled sun. "Damn it. You killed him. That makes things a little more complicated."

"In all fairness, sir, they shouldn't be this far out. I really don't think I can take the blame for this, sir. It's definitely his fault I killed him. Maybe we can just hide the body and claim ignorance."

Sanders huffed out a laugh. There really wasn't much else to do, really. They couldn't very well give him back with an "oops, sorry" and expect it to go away.

Rhythmic shuffling and crushed leaves had Sanders jerking his head toward the city. Black shapes moved within the trees, lurching and labored, as though toiling with something. Tobias noticed it a second later, bringing up his bow again.

"Think they were following that Inkna?" Tobias asked quietly.

Sanders looked around for somewhere to hide.

"They're on foot, and they don't seem to be rushing out here. Looks like they're carrying a load."

"What are we going to do, sir?"

Sanders thought about it.

If they left quickly and quietly, the Graygual might not notice their dead countryman. Sanders could kick a few leaves over the dead body, cover it up a little. The longer it took to find the Inkna, the longer until the Hunter *really* punished them.

They'd figure out that the Inkna was dead eventually. With one already dead, what was the harm in killing a few more? The result would be the same. Especially if Sanders kicked leaves on all of them.

"Fuck it. Let's just kill them." Sanders kicked his horse forward.

"What if they have more Inkna?" Tobias asked, kicking his horse to start moving, too.

"Get that bow ready. Let's hope we get him before he gets us." The black-clad men halted. Someone shouted. It sounded like a name.

"Nope, he's dead," Sanders mumbled, ripping out his sword.

Thuds sounded, something large hitting the ground. Footsteps pounded, but no steel slid against leather.

"They're running away!" Tobias shouted, kicking his horse faster.

"That's mighty cowardly." Sanders steered his horse

around a large tree until he had some space, and then kicked its flanks, urging it to keep up. He passed the things they had been carrying, three large shapes decked in blue—

Dawning froze Sanders' insides. Bile rose in his throat. "No."

He didn't look any closer as he passed. He couldn't right now. But he knew what they were.

"Haw!" He kicked the sides of his horse again, leaning forward. Men ran in front of him, terrified. They were too stupid to realize they should head into the dense foliage so the horses would have a hard time following.

Tobias shot. The arrow stuck in the center of the closest Graygual's back. The Graygual went down, screaming. Tobias nocked another arrow, sighted, and then shot. The arrow hit a shoulder this time, making the man stagger away from the others.

Sanders was on them. He slashed down, chopping into the neck of a running Graygual. The man twisted and fell, leaving one more on his own, running blindly. Sanders swung his sword, cleaving into the last. The man grunted, stumbling. Sanders slowed his horse to get in a final swing that cleaved the man's head from his shoulders. The body tumbled into the dirt.

Pulling back on the reins, Sanders slowed his horse, scanning the area in front of them. He could barely see the wall through the tree trunks. No one else had made their way out. He bent down, looking right and left, wondering if they had come from a different direction. He still didn't see anyone.

Making his way back, he did little more than check to make sure the Graygual were dead. He didn't bother turning the first over to check for slashes on the chest. Sanders didn't care. The other was groaning, on his side. Sanders finished him off. No lines marred his chest.

Throwaways, Shanti would say.

"Sir."

Sanders knew that tone. Bracing himself, he walked his horse up to Tobias. And finally looked down at the shapes that had been abandoned.

Lucius lay, sprawled out. His complexion was pale and ghostly, his mouth slightly open, and his limbs at awkward angles. It didn't look like his body was broken, just uncomfortable. If he were alive, he would've moved. Sterling lay next to him, alongside Galen, a newer officer who had shown a lot of promise.

"Maybe he's just knocked out," Tobias said in a quiet voice. Sanders could hear both the hope and concern in those words. If that had been the case, though, the Graygual wouldn't have brought them all the way out here to kill them. Unless they planned to leave them after…

"Do you think this is the Hunter's response?" Sanders asked, getting off his horse. "Because if so, he would've wanted to kill them in front of us."

"Why would they bring them out here, though?"

Sanders bent, placing two fingers on Lucius' neck. His pulse didn't push back. Sanders moved to the other two men, checking each in turn. His heart dropped as he looked down on a couple of his oldest friends. Both dead.

"They brought them out here to leave them. Somewhere where the stink wouldn't bother anyone." Sanders hung his head, the pain of loss consuming him. "Let's get them back to the Captain. They shouldn't be left out here alone. We'll bury them the right way."

Tobias climbed off his horse slowly, his movements stiff, his face filled with grief. "If this is where they bring the dead..."

"I know." Sanders waited for Tobias, and together they hoisted Lucius up, struggling to get the muscle-laden man over the horse's saddle. "Let's get these back, and we can search for any others."

"Yes, sir."

As Sanders started back, the sorrow of losing his comrades, and the fear of possibly losing Junice, started to burn. Anger flared up to cover the pain. Higher and higher it fanned, becoming its own entity.

The Graygual would pay for this, starting with whoever came out of that gate to deliver the Hunter's message.

CHAPTER 18

"YOUR SWORD IS here." Rohnan backed away from Fabienne's door and held up the sword. "I got it for you before I came."

Shanti grabbed it, letting her *Gift* spread a little further as she slipped out of the house. An empty lane greeted her, this area quiet. Mostly homes, so there was probably little worth the Graygual patrolling.

Taking advantage, she ran as fast as she could. At the end, she slowed and drifted to the side, feeling minds around the bend. Breathing heavily, she pictured in her mind where Junice's house was from where she stood. Thankfully it wasn't far, with a mostly clear area between her and it.

"Where is Leilius?" Shanti asked, peering around the corner to identify the minds.

"He's waiting for us there."

City people, mostly men, worked in their yards on their various crafts. One was building something out of wood, completely out of place among the trimmed bushes and grasses of his front yard. A Graygual with five stripes stood in the middle of the lane, surveying the goings-on. Shanti couldn't see his eyes from the distance, but she would bet they were hard and focused, missing nothing.

"Only one Graygual," she said, scanning the way. She'd have to go around this area. Trying to get past that Graygual without arousing suspicion would take longer than running around.

"They'd only need one of that caliber against a ragtag crew of craftsmen."

"I should kill him. That would be a significant loss for the Hunter."

Rohnan paused before answering, thinking it through. He gave the answer she was expecting: "He'd be missed. And while all these deaths will eventually bring down his wrath anyway, this one would speed things up. Every minute of peace is precious."

"You forgot to point out that it would take too long." Shanti waited until the Graygual's back was turned before sprinting across the lane, sheltered again by a house on the other side.

Rohnan dashed behind the house right beside her, panting as he said, "If you knew the answer, why ask the question?"

"Just making sure you're paying attention. Sometimes you can be really dumb."

"Pot calling the kettle. Do you know the way?"

After feeling the way with her *Gift,* Shanti started to jog. "Vaguely. I know the city enough to get around, but not enough to plot the most direct route."

They cut through a yard and crossed another sleepy lane, trying to pick the fastest possible route to Junice's house. Shanti's map of the city was hazier than she thought, though. Her time in the city hadn't been spent in these outskirts and within the quieter areas. She kept leading Rohnan into fences and dead ends, having to backtrack or waste time scaling the blockage.

After fifteen minutes, many of those lost in wasted efforts, they came upon one of the larger streets. Shanti sensed the people walking or standing around; many of them were clearly cunning and alert. Probably Graygual. She touched off one mind that had her collapsing her *Gift* in a hurry, pulling it back behind a shield.

"Inkna." She took deep breaths as she leaned back against the wooden fence sheltering her from roving eyes. Rohnan crouched next to her, waiting for her decision. "We have to find another way," she whispered.

"How close are we?"

"Not much closer than when we started. I just don't know the little out-of-the-way paths."

"I was not accusing, *Chulan.*"

Shanti's stomach twisted just a little bit more, time starting to weigh heavily on her. "I know, I know.

C'mon, let's find another way."

She darted away from the wall, taking a right through an alley. Scraps of trash littered the sides, no one taking care of the city with the Graygual keeping a watchful eye on activities. A barrel lay on its side up ahead. A discarded scrap of paper danced in the mouth of the alley.

Without her *Gift* to guide her, Shanti put faith in her survival instinct as she slowed near the end of the alley. She scanned what lay beyond their shelter, then peered around the corner, but didn't find anything to cause her alarm. The lane was small and bare, more trash littering the walk.

"This one isn't used much. Let's—" Something niggled at her awareness. She paused for a moment, trying to place it. It wasn't an alarm, but…

"Someone's coming." Rohnan looked behind them.

It took Shanti a moment to see it. A small body, perfectly still, stood in a shadow halfway along the alley. The little boy stared at them.

"Arsen!" Shanti jogged to the boy, time draining with each step she took in the wrong direction. "What are you doing here? This isn't the place for you!"

"I delivered my poison." He blinked up at her with those trusting brown eyes. "I didn't see Gracas, so I just dumped it into the stew. No one noticed me. I'm really quiet."

"You went into the prison camp?" Shanti put her hand on his frail shoulder, her heart thumping with fear for what could've happened. "Why did they send you there? That is way too dangerous."

"I told you," Rohnan muttered, looking around the corner.

"Shut up, Rohnan," Shanti spat, pulling Arsen in for a quick hug. "I'm sorry. I thought they'd have you kids doing easy deliveries and then getting out. I didn't think there would be any danger."

"I did what they assigned me at first, which was take a box to Miss Molly. That was easy. Her guard just stared at nothing the whole time. But then I heard that Gracas was having trouble getting close to the stew. And that was a big deal. So I just went to see if I could. It was really easy, Miss Shanti. No one ever notices me. Even my father never did."

A surge of emotion welled up. With such a problem procreating, her people protected and cherished children, coveting the little creatures. Ignoring them, or not noticing them, was unthinkable. That idea was as foreign as it was atrocious to Shanti. Putting them in harm's way was unthinkable. If she wasn't desperate, she would never have consented to them even leaving their house. Not that they'd given her a choice.

"Wait until we leave, then get on home." Shanti gave his shoulder a light squeeze.

"He won't," Rohnan said with equal parts impatience and uneasiness. "He'll continue to follow us. We'd have to personally take him home, and even then, he'd probably just leave again. He's as willful as you ever were."

"I can take you where you want to go," Arsen chirped, eagerness in his face. "Please. I can take you."

Shanti shook her head. "Not a chance—"

"*Please.* Miss Junice was always nice to me. She gave me cookies. And you keep getting lost. If I don't help, you won't get there in time."

Shanti's logic warred with her heart. He was right, but he was so small. If any harm came to him, she would die inside.

But then, with the way these people were worming their way into her heart, any of them dying would have the same effect. Her desire to keep others at a distance after losing her people was being eroded with each new person she grew close to. Each new stranger who became an acquaintance…and then a friend. This city had become her home, and these people were becoming family. If it could be prevented, she couldn't sacrifice any of them. It just wasn't in her.

Taking a deep breath, she said, "Okay, but only because I have no other choice if I want to keep Junice alive. Listen to me, though. If something happens, I want you to *run*. Do you hear me? Run!"

"Okay," he squeaked.

"Promise me."

He looked up at her solemnly, holding out his pinky finger. "I promise."

"He's telling the truth," Rohnan said.

Shanti held out her pinky, as well, though she wasn't sure why. "Lead the way."

Confusion crossed his face as he glanced at her finger before her words must've registered, because he quickly dropped his hand and said, "Yes, ma'am." A smile lit up his face. He scampered toward Rohnan. "This way."

His little legs moving, he burst out of the alley and across the path.

"Wait!" Rohnan sprinted after him.

"There's no one around here," Arsen said, scurrying along a leaning fence and then crawling under a hole in the dirt.

Rohnan pulled the top of the fence. A crack announced its destruction. Rohnan finished it off with his foot, bending it toward the ground as the rest of the barrier fell.

"Someone is going to be pissed about that," Shanti said, jogging into the unkempt yard after him. Weeds tangled her feet, tall and wild.

"It's abandoned." Arsen waved them on. "This whole row is."

"Why?" Shanti wondered quietly as she followed behind him to the next yard, then the next, jumping over or helping fences finish their fall to the ground.

"There are a few others like this in the city. One was mine. No one lives in it now." Arsen got to the end of the row and crouched in the shadow of a decaying wooden structure. "Sometimes there's a bad guy out there."

Rohnan closed in on the bent and slightly swaying fence, then squatted. He glanced over the side, paused for a moment, and lowered back down. To Arsen, he said, "How close are we?"

"Three streets away."

Rohnan looked at Shanti. "It's an Inkna on horseback. No one else is on the street."

Frowning, she moved to the fence and glanced over. There he was, in the middle of a medium-sized thoroughfare, a solitary figure sitting atop his mount. He seemed to be waiting for something.

She noticed the area around him, placing the wild batch of shrubs on the corner. She vaguely realized where she was, never having viewed the area from this vantage point, but recognizing the layout of that intersection. "Produce carts and horses often use that way, don't they?"

"Before the bad guys." Arsen stayed where he was, hunkered down. "Now only bad guys' horses come and go."

Shanti rolled her eyes. "The gate. This leads out to the side gate."

Rohnan's eyes collided with hers. "This is where they will take Junice out of the city. I've seen this done before. They'll tie her behind the horse and drag her—" He cut off, glancing at Arsen.

Shanti didn't need him to finish the sentence. The Graygual wanted to create a spectacle. They must've told Cayan to come quietly, Cayan would've refused, and now they intended to weaken him. The Hunter had taken note of what crippled the men of this city. He would strike by brutalizing one of the wives. The Inkna was guarding the starting point and then probably the procession. Him being there now meant their fun was about to begin.

"We don't have any time." Shanti threw off her shields and let her *Gift* flower out. It brushed the mind of the Inkna immediately, the power of the other fairly substantial. The Inkna's head turned her way.

She *stabbed*. But not the man.

The horse screamed, rearing. The Inkna, taken by surprise, gripped the reins but didn't brace for it. His body flew. The horse bolted forward, the reins ripped out of the Inkna's hands, jolting his shoulders midair. He hit the ground with a crack.

Rohnan was on him as Shanti stifled his *Gift*, beating down into his head and crushing his ability. Rohnan grabbed the man by the hair, pulled, and then slid his knife across the throat. A gurgle sounded the end of the Inkna's life.

Shanti turned to Arsen, who was peeping over the fence. "You don't go beyond this point. I know where I am, and I'm going to cause trouble."

"Yes, Miss Shanti."

"Okay." Then, because it felt right, she said to him what she, and the other fighters, often said to the children from her village when they left their sight, even for a moment. "I'll miss you."

She almost missed his shy but delighted smile as she turned and met up with Rohnan. Grabbing the Inkna's ankles, she helped carry him out of plain sight. "We're leaving a huge trail of blood."

"His absence will be noticed. I figured I might as well get rid of a little aggression."

"Cracking a neck doesn't do it for you anymore? My, my, Rohnan." Shanti dropped her half and dusted off her hands, waiting for Rohnan to fling his half so the body was hidden behind a heap of garbage. "You're getting pretty violent…"

"They've created a smoldering hatred inside of me, *Chulan.* Killing in this way won't cure that, but it does make me feel better. For now."

"Well, then. Continue to slit throats. We may only

have a small amount of time in which to do so." Shanti started to jog down the street, keeping to the sides and somewhat out of sight.

"Yes. We've just sounded the alarm. He was one of the stronger Inkna."

"And now he is a dead Inkna." Nearing the next intersection, she felt the touch of power. It was only a glance at first, but it became a pressure. Someone didn't recognize her mind and wanted a better look.

The joke was on him.

She *grabbed* his mind with her substantial strength and *yanked,* sucking him in. She held on like gripping a rope, sapping him of energy as they ran. When they reached him, Rohnan pulled him down off his horse, making quick work with his knife. Blood soon pooled under the various holes in the Inkna's body.

"Now you're just showing off." Shanti helped him carry the Inkna out of sight, and then tethered the horse off to the side and out of plain view. Hopefully no one would come close enough to see the blood. With no time to spare, they started running again, soon reaching Junice's house.

The shriek from inside froze Shanti's insides.

She burst through the door. A woman lay on the floor, eyes closed. No blood. A thump and another shriek sounded off to the left. The kitchen.

"No you don't!" someone shouted.

A slap of skin on skin rang out, following by a woman's gasp of pain. A clatter rang through the house.

With her *Gift*, Shanti identified three men and two women, one single-minded and the other terrified. Shanti *squeezed* the three male minds to render them immobile, not sure if they were all Graygual, so reluctant to kill just yet.

"Run, Junice!" a woman shouted.

Shanti sped between the homely furniture, arriving at the kitchen just as Valencia jabbed one of the Graygual in the kidney with a carving knife, a grim look on her face. He called out, staggering into the stove and slipping, dragging a pot down with him.

Valencia stepped over him toward the next Graygual, her brow furrowed with concentration.

Shanti's knife got there first, the hilt hitting his neck. He reached for it as his body slammed back into the third Graygual. There was not enough room for everyone in that kitchen. Blood gushed between his fingers and down his front. He sank to his knees.

The last Graygual stood rigid, his face screwed up in agony. His hand clutched Junice's front, having yanked her to him as his fellow fighter fell against him. He staggered, ramming her hip against the edge of the table. Her hand came away from her face to catch herself. Blood oozed from a cut on her temple, trickling down her cheek and dripping from her chin. Her palm slid against the table surface, smearing blood.

Valencia stepped over the dying bodies on the floor. With two hands on the raised hilt of her knife, brow furrowed in concentration, she drove her blade into the Graygual. The point pierced his chest, forcing a groan from the man's mouth. His fist tightened on Junice's dress front, wrenching her to him again as he staggered backward into the wall. A framed picture tumbled down, rattling to the floor in its cheap wooden frame. Valencia yanked her knife free as Shanti applied more force, finally driving the Graygual to his knees.

Valencia stabbed down a second time. He clearly wasn't dying fast enough for her taste.

His grip finally released. Junice stumbled to the side, trying to regain her bearing on wobbly knees. Rohnan waded in, grabbing Junice and whisking her up into his arms. With the balance of a natural fighter, he threaded through the bodies and blood on the ground and rushed her into the outer room. Her wound was not life threatening, but would require aid.

"Well then." Valencia snatched a little towel off the stove. Without haste, standing next to a man sounding his death rattle, she ran the blade against the towel, cleaning off the blood. She slipped it into the sheath, all safe again. That done, she looked up with a nonchalant expression. "Not exactly like killing a pig, but close enough." She dropped the knife into her apron pocket and made her way out of the kitchen.

As Shanti blinked after her for a moment, one thing became clear: they had more fighters than she'd originally thought. These women might not be trained, but they would help take back their city. Shanti had just guaranteed that that would happen sooner rather than later.

CHAPTER 19

AS THE LIGHT crawled across the expansive floor, Qadir sat before his dinner. He inhaled deeply, enjoying the savory aroma of a dinner prepared by a skilled artisan. In front of him, swirling with colors, sat a hand-blown glass of the finest quality. True craftsmen, these people. Their goods could fetch a handsome price at market.

He would make a note to pass on this information, but it was hardly his discovery. After all, the Inkna's botched attempt at a takeover had made these people infamous. The Inkna salivated with the desire to torture and kill, desiring vengeance for their dead kinsmen.

The hatred was cyclical. After all, the Inkna had started it.

He paused in his efforts of readying a bite as the sounds of his Battle Commander's footsteps echoed down the hall. Qadir waited until the man came into view, his shoulders back and his six stripes worn proudly on his breast. Something haunted his eyes, though. He didn't have his usual air of confidence and superiority.

That meant something had gone wrong.

Qadir lowered his fork slowly, watching his Battle Commander come to a precise stop. His body poised and hands at his sides, his man waited for Qadir to speak first, as he should.

Scenarios flashed through Qadir's head. He loved to anticipate his enemy. This one especially. The woman was such an enigma. She seemed to defy him at every turn, presenting him with problems he hadn't thought possible, let alone likely.

Of course, this was just the raven-haired man in question. The Captain. Judging by the setup of the city, its organization and prosperity, and the love of his people, he was at the upper tier of adversaries. He would present a challenge, Qadir had no doubt. But divine? Assuredly not. There couldn't be more than one Fate-touched. Whatever had gone wrong was most probably easily remedied.

"Yes?" Qadir finally asked.

"Sir, we've had a problem. It seems as though the men sent to deliver the message to the Captain have disappeared."

Qadir reached for his wine. "Surely they were just destroyed. I expected that."

"No, sir. They didn't leave the city."

Perplexed, Qadir paused, his wine hovering above

the table. Scenarios shifted.

"There is more," the Battle Commander went on. "Two guards have vanished as well. And those that carried out three of the dead men have not returned."

Qadir's hand in the air stopped the babble. "Those are separate situations. The last is as I expected. They left the city, were discovered by the enemy, and killed. Has a head been sent by the enemy?"

"No, sir. We have heard nothing from them. I sent a small team to check out the disappearance. They found a few kill sites, but no bodies. There were hoofprints around the area and the dead men have been carried away. In addition, their men have been scouting the perimeter, but not engaging."

"They saw their men dead and claimed vengeance." Qadir waved the issue away. The loss would barely be felt. "What of this other occurrence?"

"Two guards have not been seen since their shift last night. There has been a report of neglect about a third guard as well—he left his post early—but that has happened before. As of my report, they haven't seen him, so it is probable he is also gone."

Qadir sat forward. "Are all the prisoners accounted for?"

"Yes, sir. There have been no uprisings that we are aware of."

New scenarios filtered through Qadir's mind. He

replayed the report from the Captain's first landing. The men they took, the power used, the retreat...

They could have tried harder to gain entry. Without knowing what awaited them in their city, they *should* have tried harder, needing to know what had become of their people.

And then there was this day of waiting. Endless waiting, it would seem to the Captain, while Qadir held their people under the knife. That would drive a good commander stir crazy. They wandered the walls, yes, but they didn't engage except for the little incident with their own men. If anything, that incident showed that they wanted to fight, but were being held on a leash.

The question was, whose leash?

"Do you suppose the Captain is the type of warrior to remain under orders while his men are under attack?" Qadir asked his Battle Commander.

"That man has been described as coiled and ready, sir. From what my men have seen, he is excellent with a sword, incredibly strong in power, has a skilled force under him, and seemed intelligent. My men were reasonably assured he would prove extremely difficult to defeat in a fight."

Qadir's lips curled in a smile. "The violet-eyed girl has breached the walls. Find her."

CHAPTER 20

SHANTI STOOD BY the door to Eloise's living room, her mind made up. Rohnan waited beside her, his ire rising. He knew what Shanti had planned, and she would have to go through him to accomplish it.

So be it. She'd assumed that would be the case, anyway.

Alena paced the floor. The Women's Circle gathered around. Inky night coated the windows, temporarily hiding the pile of Graygual and Inkna bodies stashed in the refuse area. There were too many, though. They'd be missed, if they weren't already. Shanti had ensured that they'd run out of time. Worse, she knew for certain that there was no way they could beat the Hunter with their limited resources. Without the Shadow, Shanti would get taken, Cayan with her, and the rest would almost certainly be killed.

What was the point in putting off the inevitable if it cost lives to do so? It didn't make sense. She'd made a mess of this whole situation. It was time to make it right.

"I realize you don't like it, but I have to turn myself in. It's the best course of action." Shanti wiped the hair from her sweaty face. "I am what he wants. Cayan with me. We can go with him now and escape somewhere along the way. The Hunter will treat us like royalty."

"He'll treat you like livestock," Rohnan corrected.

"Royalty among prisoners, then. Same thing."

"Absolutely not!" Valencia uttered.

"No!" Alena stopped and faced Shanti, her eyes pleading.

"It wouldn't help, would it?" Tabby asked, wringing her apron.

"Of course it would help." Shanti kept her voice soft but firm. "He will take me and leave this place, his men with him. I'll be protected. The Hunter needs me in one piece for Xandre. And he'll need to travel. I will have plenty of time to escape, and I'll have a lot of help to do so. By then the Shadow will have shown up—"

"I forbid it!" Fabienne said. "Forbid it!"

The other women voiced their agreement. Shanti half turned to look toward the door. They were speaking with their emotions, not with logic, and Shanti would be lying if she said it didn't affect her. These people only had her to blame for all of this. *All* of this. From day one, she'd been a bane to this city, protected, sheltered, and all at their peril. For them to object to her making things right touched a place deep inside her.

It didn't change her duty. She owed this to them, if nothing else. "This is for the best."

"Don't be daft." Eloise took a sip from her teacup. "Besides, one person making decisions that will affect the whole Circle will not be tolerated. One person making decisions that will affect the whole city is a gross misuse of power. You are one of us now. You will follow our rules. And our rules dictate that we discuss this and agree on the best course of action. Now. Who would like to speak?"

"Cayan has the power to rule this city alone…" Shanti quirked a brow.

"We had no say in that." Eloise sniffed. It was clearly a sore point. "And we've been trying to get him a wife to even that out. The city should be run by two, at the very least."

"With you giving your say to one of them, no doubt," Shanti muttered.

Eloise sniffed again. That was a yes.

"The Captain asks for support from his men, his officers most of all," Junice said. She sat on the couch with a wrapped head. Thankfully, though it had bled a lot, her wound had been fairly superficial. "When a large decision will affect them, or the city, he takes counsel. In the past, the city has been ruined by unfit leaders. It doesn't happen often, and hasn't for generations on generations, but no ruler of this land can be left unchecked."

"There. See? Now, as I was saying, who would like to speak?" Eloise looked around.

"She protected me," Junice said. "If it wasn't for me, we wouldn't be discussing this."

"Those weren't the first we killed," Shanti argued.

"I was the first person she protected," Ruisa said in a loud, sure voice. "If anything, this is my fault. Maybe I should be the one to turn myself in."

Shanti crinkled her brow. "How could that possibly help?"

"How could you doing it?" Ruisa shot back.

"S'am, if they took you, we'd be left defenseless again." Leilius withered as the women's eyes turned toward him.

"Listen," Shanti said, moving further into the room, quieting the backlash. "Here are the facts. If I turn myself in, the Hunter will take me, and all the men he needs to secure me, and leave the city. That's it. He will no longer have need of any of you. He doesn't care about you or this city. You'll be safe. If I *don't* turn myself in, he will kill everyone in his path to get to me. Once he has me, then what do you think he'll do?"

Shanti eyed everyone with a hard look. It was her battle gaze. No one spoke. She answered the question. "He will leave the city with his men. Do you see? The outcome is the same. It's the way we reach the conclusion that changes. Death versus no death. My goal is to save lives. *Your* lives."

Silence descended on the room. The women looked at her, or each other, with wide eyes. A tear dripped down Tabby's face.

"I call bullshit."

A few people gasped. Eyes found Gracas, who had stepped forward. Hands balled into a fist, he stared at Shanti with simmering anger. "If not for you, we would already be dead, S'am. That first invasion with the Mugdock would've been a shitstorm. You are the reason we pulled out of that."

Murmurs sounded among the women. Gracas nodded at them. "Yes, exactly. Didn't tell you that, did she? Then she was the reason we were able to rescue Sanders. Without her he'd be dead, the Inkna would've moved in here to get our stuff, and we'd all be dead or slaves or who knows what. And if you get taken, guess what'll happen? That's right, the Inkna will finally get to move in again. They want our city, I'm as sure as I'm standing here. The Hunter will take off with our strongest protection, and then those others will take what's left. Only this time, they'll kill all of the army because they hate us. So if you leave, S'am, you'll be *killing* us, not *saving* us. You're full of shit."

Leilius cleared his throat.

"Yeah, I know I'll get punched in the head for saying that, but I don't care." Gracas looked around at the women before back at Shanti. "I'd rather get punched in the head and have you stay than say nothing and lose you again."

Warmth spread through Shanti's middle. She didn't know what to say.

"Well then. It's time for a vote." Eloise looked around at the women. "Who votes that Shanti should stay and defend the city, even though it will mean fighting and possibly death, raise your hand…"

All the hands shot up. The warmth within Shanti spread to fill her up. Tears glistened in Rohnan's eyes.

"And who would rather she sacrifices herself at our peril?" Eloise's eyebrows rose. "Yes, that is what I thought."

"I think we should also discuss, at a later date, what language we will, and will not, tolerate within these meetings…" Fabienne gave Gracas a poignant stare.

"I think we'll allow him an exception just this once." Eloise took another sip of her tea before setting it down on the table. "Now that we've gotten that out of the way, we need to discuss how to get our city back. Bring out the map."

CHAPTER 21

THE NEXT DAY, Sanders walked through their tiny camp with an impatient air. The sun was just coming up over the mountains, blazing through the sky in a burst of color. The men sat around the fire, quietly watching the flames dance. A pot sat among the rocks just within the fire pit, only a little water bubbling in the bottom. The rest had boiled away. No one seemed to have noticed.

Without a word, Sanders took the pot out, dropping it to the ground to cool. He continued on to the Captain's tent, amazed the man was still asleep, let alone had slept at all. As he pushed open the canvas flap, he changed his tune.

The Captain sat cross-legged, his elbows resting on his knees with his head in his hands. He glanced up when Sanders came in. "Close the flap behind you."

Sanders dropped the canvas and walked to the corner, bending. "Sir, reporting for orders."

The Captain straightened up. His eyes were red and puffy, proof of very little sleep for the last couple days.

Haunted, too. In front of him lay Lucius' body, stretched out and lifeless.

"Something is happening in the city," the Captain said in a firm voice that didn't match those sorrow-filled eyes. "Shanti's emotions are all over the place. She killed a few times yesterday, I'd bet my life on it. I know what those shocks of adrenaline and the flashes of remorse feel like."

"Flashes of remorse?"

The Captain rubbed his eyes and then reached back, tying his hair at the nape of his neck. "She doesn't show it, but every time she kills, she has a flash of remorse. She was trained for destruction, but I get the feeling she is more like Rohnan than she lets on."

"I can't imagine she'd feel remorse for killing the Graygual, sir."

"Even the Graygual. She has never had the choice of whether or not to kill. She was pushed to it as a young girl. And then it became her mantle, and perhaps her burden." The Captain sighed, looking at Lucius again. "That's neither here nor there. I probably shouldn't have told you that."

"I bet she wouldn't get a flash of remorse when trying to beat that little tidbit out of my brain, sir. So I'd just as soon we keep that knowledge between ourselves."

A ghost of a smile graced the Captain's lips. "Wise."

"You wouldn't have been able to stop them coming in," Sanders said lightly. "They would've taken you and Shanti, and fucked off, killing everyone in their wake. Lucius died to protect his people. I would've done the same. Still will, in fact. Ready for it."

"You will not be able to reason this out, Sanders." The Captain's voice was low, his body bowed in slightly. The cracks of grief and guilt were starting to show. "Whatever *might* have happened, this is what *did.* And I take it upon myself."

Sanders hardened his voice. "Well, sir, with all due respect, but we've still got people in there depending on us. My *wife* is in there. If Shanti is killing people, that means the time has come. Time to take back our city, sir."

The Captain stared at Lucius for another long moment, his gaze locked on his lifelong friend's closed eyes. Finally, he straightened up again. "Yes. I have a plan, but it will take synchronization."

CAYAN STOOD, GRIEF pulling him down and filling his stomach with acid. Sleeplessness clouded his mind and sullied his judgment. He needed to get moving. To dull the ache with action.

He reached for Shanti's emotions, feeling her *Gift* surging along their shared plane of power. His *Gift* danced and played, eager to join it.

Cayan stepped over the lifeless body of his friend.

I will properly grieve for you, he promised. *I will bury you the right way when this is all done.*

"Ready, sir?" Sanders prodded.

Cayan left the tent. The blast of frigid air hit his face, clearing a little of the haze. The trees of his land waited for him, hiding the enemy within their fold. Leaves shook and danced in the breeze.

His men looked up when he walked among them. The younger men stood, staring at him eagerly. The veterans remained where they were, their eyes echoing what Cayan felt.

They'd lost damn fine soldiers already. Three of the best. Sterling and Lucius were extremely hard to kill—excellent with their weapons, great with tactics, and unable to say die. They wouldn't have gone down without a fight, and should have been smart enough to get themselves out of trouble. Galen, the third officer down, was also a good man. He was a step down from the other two, perhaps, but younger, too. He was working his way toward greatness.

The Graygual had claimed them all and God knew how many more. That was what Cayan and his men were up against.

"We've taken a severe blow," he said, looking at the faces all pointing in his direction. "I won't deny it.

We've already lost some of the best. But we have to remember that Lucius, Sterling, and Galen didn't have mental warfare. They couldn't protect against the Inkna. I can. Shanti can. We are the strongest this land as ever seen, especially paired. We are what Inkna want to be. And you are what the Graygual want to be. We have enough force between us to take them down, as long as we work together."

The men, one by one, started to straighten their spines.

"Shanti is already in the thick of it. She's still alive, and from what I can tell, she's fighting in the dirty, underhanded way only she could make glamorous. We need to give them hell out here so we can gut them from inside the walls."

The men's eyes sparked, fire starting to kindle.

"We work together better than the Graygual and Inkna. I've come up with a plan to make the most of that. I'll hit them hard with my mind, while you cut their legs out from under them. Together, we can kill every last one of them."

Cayan only hoped it would be enough.

SHANTI WAITED BY the window and looked out. Another mind touched hers then fled. Checking in. "That's three."

"There can no longer be any doubt. They know." Rohnan paced in the living area of the orphan house, his hands clasped behind his back. Molly sat on the couch with a few of the other women, watching Shanti silently. Molly's newest night guard decorated the garden. They had been unable to dispose of him like the others.

"Yes. They think they are being sly."

"They know where you are?" Molly asked. She fidgeted, afraid of what might come next.

"They know my location, yes. They're preparing." Shanti glanced at the streaks painting the sky. "The longer we give them, the more time they have to box us in..."

"We need to all go at one time, *Chulan.* We've talked about this." Rohnan flexed and re-clenched his fingers. Impatience rolled through the room.

"When are Lucius and Sterling supposed to wake up?" Shanti looked at Molly.

It was Eloise who answered, "It depends when he took the concoction."

"Excellent. Extremely helpful," Shanti said dryly.

"Using that tone is not helping anyone, young lady." Eloise lifted her eyebrows in disapproval.

"Sorry." Shanti's tone hadn't improved. It was her little stand against female tyranny, of which this city apparently had plenty. If Eloise didn't remind her so much of her grandfather, she would've shrugged off any niceties. That was what she told herself, anyway.

In truth, she still couldn't believe these women had elected to keep her with them even though it meant they'd have to fight. Their courage was remarkable, easily equaling their good nature. It gave Shanti an insight into why Cayan was so strong and capable while still so balanced and just. He was bred that way by the strong men and women before him, no matter what role they'd had within the city. He was the best of them, and that was truly inspirational.

"What is the Captain's current emotional state?" Rohnan asked softly.

Shanti turned back to the window. Another mind touched hers. If they kept at it, she was going to retaliate. "He's grief-stricken, obviously. Hence my asking when Lucius would wake up…"

Eloise tsked. If she was waiting for an apology for that one, she'd have to keep waiting.

"Any word on the Graygual in the prisoner camp?" Shanti asked.

Gracas said, "A few of the smaller-built Graygual were walking around like drunks last night, S'am. I couldn't find any drinking parties, though, and they were all spread out. I'd bet it's working."

"It is. We made that dose particularly strong. More than a few won't be getting up this morning." Eloise pursed her lips, glancing toward the stairs leading up to the rooms where all the kids were supposed to be staying out of the way.

"And the prison itself?" Shanti asked. She already knew all this. All of them knew. They'd been over it several times during the night. But hearing it again settled her a little. It kept her from rushing out of the house and killing every Graygual she saw.

"We didn't know which officer held the key last night, but we know which one holds the key now. Today, I mean. We *knew,* I should say." Rohnan's hands flexed and clenched again. "If the Hunter knows you are here, he will change his defenses. Nothing will be done the same way twice."

"That's confusing, S'am," Leilius said, near the window with Shanti.

"He just means the Hunter will keep changing things." Shanti felt another mind touch hers lightly. It was the same that had done it an hour ago.

"No, I mean…always changing things would confuse people. Even without a battle, it's hard to keep that straight. They'll mess up. Maybe even hand the key back to the Graygual that is normally supposed to have it…" Leilius rubbed the bridge of his nose. Then unconsciously patted the knives at his belt. Shanti could feel his nervousness. Just another unpleasant emotion filling the room like soup.

She couldn't stand this waiting.

She got up as the front door opened and closed. "So the officers are cut off from us," she muttered. "The men with the most experience will be cooped up, out of reach." She scratched her head as another mind touched hers.

Without thinking, she snapped.

She grabbed that mind and *wrenched.* A shock of pain colored the connection, spiking Shanti's adrenaline. She amped her power and *stabbed.* The mind winked out. "That'll stop them from touching my mind for a while…"

"*Chulan…*" Rohnan gave her a warning glance.

Maggie came into the room, face flushed. "I'm ready."

The door opened and closed again. Alena, breathing heavily as she jogged in, held a heap of clothing. Ruisa came in right behind and said, "We barely made it. If I didn't know a secret way, we wouldn't have. They're massing."

"Shit." Little bursts of fire jolted though Shanti. Her fingers tingled. "Are the other women ready?"

"Yes." Ruisa dolled out pants and binding to the women in the room. "The men who aren't cowards, or condescending, are with them. We're ready, S'am."

Shanti took a deep breath. She looked at Gracas, then Leilius. Both boys had their jaws set and a glimmer in their eyes. Fear, adrenaline, and pride glowed out from them. Time for battle. "We're counting on you two."

Gracas gave a nod, more mature now than she'd ever seen him. "Yes, S'am. I can do it."

Leilius didn't move at all. Just patted his knives again.

"Aim for the vital points and move on," Shanti told Leilius. "Retch after the kill strike, not before."

"Yes, S'am," Leilius said. "I'm getting better about that."

"It's okay. Keep your humanity. Just make sure you stay alive to do it."

"Yes, S'am," Leilius whispered.

Eloise tsked as she took the clothing offered her. "Wearing pants. Unsightly!"

Ruisa hid a smile as she picked out a size that might fit Molly.

"Well, I won't be exposing myself, if that's what you think!" Eloise lifted her chin and headed to another room to change. They heard a "harrumph" as she disappeared out of sight. The other women quickly followed.

The women wouldn't be doing much in the way of fighting, Maggie's explosives aside. While some said they would take to the streets with knives, none of them were trained fighters. Even the worst Graygual fighters would have an easy time dispatching the women. What the women could do, however, was help the wounded. That, and make sure any wounded Graygual stayed down.

Another Inkna was stupid enough to touch her mind. She *yanked,* to get him off balance, and *stabbed.* A shield came up to block her, ready for her assault. She added more power, splintering his defense and piercing his fragile mind. His consciousness split, like a knife to the brain. His lights blinked out.

"We can't wait for Lucius to wake up. We have to go." Shanti checked her weapons and adjusted her binding. She rolled her head to loosen her neck, and then her shoulders. "Gracas, Leilius, get moving."

Maggie turned to go with them.

"Wait." They all turned back at Shanti's voice. She looked at Maggie. "Where are you going?"

"I have some explosives set to go off. To provide distraction."

"No." Shanti glanced out the window. The sleeve of a black uniform melted behind the house across the street as someone stepped behind it. "You'll draw attention."

"Excuse me!" Maggie put her fist to her hip with an indignant expression. "This is *my* city. When I was a girl I ran through these streets, just like all the boys. You ask the Captain if he could ever catch me. Just because I wear a dress and was assigned domestic duties, doesn't mean I'm useless outside of the house!"

Shanti looked at the woman for a moment. She had touches of fear, just like everyone else, but her fierce determination showed through. Inexperienced though she was, she had just as much of a glimmer in her eyes as Gracas or Leilius. Maybe more so. She wanted to defend her home, and if she'd been born a man, or to Shanti's culture, she'd be the fighter she longed to be.

"Forgive me." Shanti gave her a slight bow. "Just don't get caught and killed. I'd hate for you to be wrong."

Maggie scowled even as a grin threatened her serious expression. She turned to leave with the boys.

"Okay. Time to get to work. Molly." Shanti waited for Molly to finish adjusting her pants and look up. "Make sure the kids don't leave this house. Some will want to. I heard them muttering. Keep them out of danger."

"Okay, S'am."

Shanti huffed out a sarcastic chuckle with the name. Molly was not like Maggie. She wasn't born a fighter; she was born a caregiver, like Rohnan. She was sweet and soft and deserved to be in a warm home with a fire and cookies in the oven. Why she had never mated and had children, Shanti didn't know, but seeing her like this, holding a knife in a shaking hand, eyes tight with consternation, broke Shanti's heart.

There was nothing for it, though. Freedom came at a price. Shanti just hoped none of them would have to pay with their life.

"Ruisa, stealth." Shanti pinned the young woman with a hard stare. "Like I taught you. Do not try for the officers. Anyone below three slashes is fair game. Stay away from the all black. Inkna will feel you coming."

"I know, S'am."

"Good."

"I'm going with her." Alena left the room for a brief moment, and came back with a bow. "I can hit the Inkna while she gets the Graygual."

After Maggie, Shanti knew better than to say no. "Can you shoot that?"

"Yes." Alena's gaze was hard. Her slight frame was flexed in defiance.

"With any accuracy?"

"Yes. I have two brothers—they're locked away in the prison camp. My father taught me just as he taught them. Lucius got me practicing again, way back when. I like it. It's calming. I'm an excellent shot, though I don't have a great range. I've always been better than my brothers."

"You have singular focus, that's why." Shanti glanced at Rohnan.

"She will do it, anyway," he said. "She's not asking

your permission."

"How does Cayan keep people in line, that's what I want to know," Shanti muttered. To Alena and Ruisa she said, "I hope to see you when this is all done. Keep your risks small. Your only mistake will be getting caught."

"Or getting dead." Ruisa flashed the other woman a tight grin. "C'mon. We'll have to keep moving."

Finally Shanti met Rohnan's solemn gaze. They, more than anyone, knew what they were up against. With odds this great, there wasn't much hope they'd make it out alive.

CHAPTER 22

"WHAT IS THIS place?" Kallon bent, running his fingers through the hard, brittle brush. Charred trees, bent and twisted, hunkered low to the scarred, burnt ground.

"Dead, by the looks of it," Sayas said, glancing around. He took out his water skin and gulped down a mouthful.

"Why would the Chosen stay in land like this, I wonder?" Mela wiped her brow then glanced at the sky. The frigid weather didn't match the blaring sun. "Summer must cook the skin in this region."

"She's always had terrible jokes..." Sayas kicked a stump. Charred debris flaked off and drifted to the ground like snow. "And living in a region like this would certainly be a terrible joke."

"She wouldn't have settled in a land like this." Kallon straightened up, taking a swig of his own skin. He couldn't imagine living with no natural life around him. It would stunt his *Gift* and crush his spirit. Chosen had always been one of a kind, feeling and doing things differently from others, but she had a heart like the rest of them. At the core, she needed the same things. "Maybe it's a defense mechanism. This is a large region mostly left to itself. Possibly this is a barrier to keep people from venturing onward."

"Are you sure we're going the right way?" Sayas looked at Dannon.

"I'm sure." Dannon reached for his map. He traced their route with his finger. "The map indicates that there should be woodland here. She probably swerved so far north because she needed to replenish her *Gift*. That's what I would do. And stay out of sight. Traveling through the plains to the east would surely get her snatched up. It would've been smart if this land was as we expected."

Kallon closed his eyes and let his *Gift* spread out, covering the ground. Even pushing, all he felt were those around him, fighters he knew better than most people knew their own siblings.

"Anything?" Tulous asked quietly.

Opening his eyes, Kallon scanned the devastated lands. "Nothing. My *Gift* isn't like Chosen's, though. She might've found something different when she came through."

"Just…to make absolutely sure…" Sayas walked up next to them, his eyes serious despite the half-smile on his face. "We are *positive* she came this way?"

"Yes." Dannon took out the letter they'd received from Chosen. "She mentioned the burnt lands, though she didn't go into detail. This is the right way. She must've come through here."

"Or she was told which directions to put in the letter," Mela said, cleaning some dirt from underneath her nail. Her nonchalant tone was misleading. Kallon could feel her uncertainty matching his own.

Kallon's gut pinched. "That letter came from her. She put in the right words."

"If she was being tortured…" Mela's brow crinkled.

"She wouldn't have summoned us if it wasn't safe." Sayas crossed his arms over his chest. "That woman was as hard as could be. She won't break. If she was under pressure, she'd take the pain and wait for death rather than putting us in danger."

"Sayas is right. She wouldn't have broken," Kallon said.

Mela dropped her hands to her sides in defeat. "I know. I just…it's been so long."

Kallon turned toward his horse, their conversation eating away at his guts. The letter had definitely sounded like Chosen, with the same clear outlines and firm tone that he remembered of her instructions when training. But toward the end, her tone seemed…whimsical, almost. Lighter than the duty-ridden woman he remembered. If he had to guess, that letter didn't feel like she was under duress.

He glanced around the desecrated lands again.

So what, then, was the gnawing in his gut that said they were too late? It was like the expectant vibration of battle ahead. He didn't have the *sight,* but every fiber of his being said something was coming. Something was *off.* He didn't know how, but he knew that if they didn't hurry, they might never see the Chosen again.

CHAPTER 23

"IT'S TIME. SHE'S getting ready," the Captain said as he stood beside the freshly doused fire.

Sanders checked his weapons, and then took a long look at each of his men. Eyes tight, but expectant all around. Ready. Eager, he'd say, in most of their cases. They were like him—he'd rather be in the thick of it, no matter what the situation was. He wasn't the type to let a girl get all the glory. Ridiculous.

"Let's do it." Sanders clapped Xavier on the back. "You ready for this, boy?"

"Yes, sir." Xavier put his hand on the hilt of his sword.

"This is your first command, aye, Xavier?" Tobias asked, his smile not reaching his eyes.

"Yes."

Sanders pretended not to notice the kid gulp. He had a helluva job in front of him, so he was right to be close to shitting his pants. While Sanders, the Captain, and all the experienced men cut down as many Graygual as they could, Xavier and the other members of the Honor Guard would move from tree to tree, trying to sneak up on the Inkna to put a knife, sword, or arrow in their backs. The hope was that the boys could free the Captain up, and as a unit, they'd make it to the city.

Sanders clapped the boy on the back again, drowning out the doubt with an action. They owed it to the city to attempt the impossible. Sanders owed it to his wife to make the impossible become a reality.

"Check your weapons one last time, men," Sanders ordered while the Captain took two steps away. His eyes were glowing faintly. Checking his mental weapons, by the look of it.

"Okay, I'll—"

A ghost staggered toward the fire from the Captain's tent. His hair mussed, his eyes bloodshot, and his face white, he lurched and fell to his knees at the Captain's feet.

"What the fuck, sir?" Sanders yelled. Scared as hell, he jumped back and yanked out his sword.

The Captain took a step back as well, staring down at his oldest friend with wide, shocked eyes.

"Another one!" Rachie pointed at another lumbering shape. Sterling stumbled to the side, throwing out a hand to brace himself on the tree. A moan sounded from the tent where Galen lay.

"What in holy hell is going on?" Sanders asked. His

stomach was flip-flopping all over the place.

"Lucius?" the Captain said in a hoarse whisper, stepping forward and helping the man up.

"Is this witchcraft?" Tobias asked with terrified eyes. "Because I checked for his pulse. He was definitely dead."

Lucius coughed out a laugh. "You guys will strap on a smile to charge toward an enemy that is sure to overwhelm you, but a ghost wanders through and you piss your pants?"

"Yes. That's about right." Tobias took a step backward.

"I was given a concoction to make me appear dead for a day. The women got us out of prison," Sterling said with a scratchy voice. "I need some water."

"And here I was going to blame this on the foreign woman," Daniels said. "We live among witches."

"Thankfully." Tobias stepped forward with a gratified smile and shook Sterling's hand. "Good to have you back. Thought you were a goner."

"How did we get out here?" Lucius asked, shaking his head in what looked like an effort to clear it. "We were supposed to go to the hospital where they prepare the bodies for burial."

"The Graygual aren't in the habit of preparing bodies for burial, it seems," the Captain said gravely.

Lucius gave him a hard look, then glanced at Sterling. Something was being communicated there. Sanders didn't think he'd like what it was.

From the look around, the other guys had the same thought. If Lucius had thought he would have gone to the morgue, it meant someone else probably had. For him not to…it probably meant their stores were already full.

Sanders refused to think more heavily about that. It wasn't something they needed to hear right now.

"Well, damn glad to have you. When do you think you'll be able to fight?" Sanders said.

Sterling shook his arms out, swaying. "I'm going to need some time. I've been dead for a day."

Galen staggered from the nearest tent.

"We don't have time," the Captain said.

SHANTI FLUNG OPEN the door with bow in hand. It was a little too small, being a boy's size, but it was better than the ones that were used by the strong men in this land, like the one Rohnan would be forced to use. The street was bare and quiet, no one in sight.

Shanti laughed. "They are hiding their bodies, but they can't hide their minds. The Hunter, in all his wisdom, doesn't understand the *Gift.*"

"And he's too egotistical to properly learn," Rohnan said. "How many?"

Shanti took off down the street toward Cayan's mansion, where the Hunter would be. "Ten. Shall I kill them now, or do you want to run around and get as many as you can first?"

"Kill them. If it won't hinder you too much in the long run."

Shanti gripped their minds and *stabbed* with one sharp point of power, drawing on the substantial combined force that was hers and Cayan's. She felt the minds wink out as Cayan's *Gift* surged within her, hearing its mate's call and wanting to answer.

"He'll know we've begun." Shanti increased her pace. "Let's hope he's ready to go."

"I think he's been ready since you left. That man doesn't relax much."

"He does, you just have to be in the right setting."

"Since I won't be bedding him, I'll take your word for it."

Shanti snorted as a blast of mental power assaulted her. "Woke up the Inkna." She slammed up her shields, trying to block out the barrage. "I liked it better when I fought against people without mental power. I got so much more done."

They turned down the larger street, running into armed Graygual stretched out in a line, their swords drawn. Inkna stood behind the line, three of them with grim expressions and plenty of power ready to be unleashed.

"They're going to be too much for me," Shanti said, gritting her teeth at the pain spreading across her skull and making her hair stand on end.

"Then I'd better kill them." Rohnan put down his sword before nocking his bow. He sighted and released. An arrow flew in a shallow arch, hitting an Inkna in the shoulder.

"You're going to need to shoot better than that…" Shanti sighted as the line of Graygual started jogging toward them. She loosed.

The arrow flew in a similarly shallow arch. The Inkna, inexperienced in battle, put his hands in front of him, trying to defend with the flesh and bone of his arms. The arrow stuck in his center. He hadn't even had his arms in the right place.

"Well, this weapon didn't last long." Shanti's words were not much more than a string of grunts as she took out her sword and looped the bow around her for safekeeping. The first Graygual reached her as the pain started to prickle, burning down into her head. Scouring her shields.

The sword was a blur through the air. The man screamed and fell. Rohnan jerked his sword, dislodging the blade. He turned to another Graygual. "Push through the pain, *Chulan*!"

"Easy…for you…to say," Shanti grated as she

swung her body to the side, barely escaping a sword strike. She lunged, her tip parting flesh before another was on her. A quick step and she kicked, catching the man in the jaw, as she dipped and struck. Her sword sliced through his center. She whirled back, cutting through the first Graygual's throat, ending him.

A stab of pain in her head made her wince. They were working through.

"Hurry, Rohnan," she said, but her words wouldn't be heard over the din.

The next Graygual was on her, his sword moving so fast she could barely focus. Another point of agony stabbed through her shields, prying its way into her brain.

A gleaming sword tip approached. Her sword came up in a numbing hand and blocked, completely muscle memory. Another hot knife of power drove through her, searing down her spine.

Shanti stumbled, her sword clattering away. Her legs were becoming numb now. They were attacking her nervous system.

"Excellently trained, these Inkna," Shanti slurred.

An explosion rocked the street. A body flew to the side like a piece of rubble. Rock rained down. People staggered.

The pain cleared from Shanti's head as a net fell over her.

CAYAN FELT ANOTHER surge of power. Shanti wasn't just killing one or two now, she was battling. "We don't have any more time to wait. Let's get going!"

"Let's go, let's go, let's go!" Sanders urged, pushing his men, as few as there were, toward the trees.

"I'll work a bow," Sterling said.

"Me too." Lucius staggered toward the tents. They weren't much good, but they'd have to do.

Cayan waited for the two commanders, back from the dead, to get armed.

The small force started out toward the main gate. As they approached the line, the closest they could get without the Inkna reaching them, he turned to Xavier and his remaining Honor Guard.

The younger man looked at him solemnly, his face set, his shoulders squared. He was no longer a novice. "Remember all Shanti's teaching. She's prepared you for this. Don't let her down. I'm counting on you."

"Yes, sir," Xavier said, his bearing becoming a little straighter.

Cayan spared a glance for Rachie, and then the terrified but resolved Marc. The doctor had seen more battle than most of Cayan's army. He hated every second of it, but still he prepared, and executed his orders, then healed when it was all done. He was one of a kind.

"Hate to lose you," Cayan said with a wink.

"Yes, sir!" Rachie said. "I won't let you down, sir."

"Yes, sir," Marc said, looking at the ground.

Cayan gave everyone else a glance before mounting his horse, and then kicking its sides. He launched past the line as a huge boom sounded from somewhere in the city.

"What the hell was that?" Sanders asked from behind.

Hooves battered the ground as they got up to speed. Another boom sounded.

Leaves slapped Cayan's face. He ducked under a branch. A slap of pain accosted him. He squinted, releasing his power on instinct. His *Gift* pushed out from his body, spreading out in front of him. More pain came at him, working through his attack and still reaching him.

His sight dimmed. Agony flared, jabbing his body and squeezing his mind. Panting, labored, he flexed, *roaring* with his power in the direction of those Inkna.

The torment lightened a little. One by one the claws scratched through his offense, though, piercing him. His vision started to blacken. He couldn't feel the saddle beneath him.

He forced down his shield, grabbed the reins, closed his eyes, and focused all his strength on his defense. He had to hang on. All he had to do was hang on.

MARC'S HEART THUMPED as he spurred S'am's horse toward the first tree. He was the only one, besides S'am, the animal would allow on its back.

Following Xavier, he passed the Captain, who was slumped in his saddle. The Inkna would be focusing all their attack on him. Sanders and the others came into view. Swords rang out. Sanders was on his horse, swinging down at a Graygual. The Hunter must've sent out more warriors. The sword sliced into a neck. The enemy fell away.

Xavier turned away right. This wasn't their fight.

Marc yanked at the reins. The horse, bullheaded as it was, refused to turn.

"No, you blasted thing!" he yelled, tugging. "We have to get the Inkna!" He yanked with everything he had.

The horse did a small zigzag. "Turn, you bastard!" Marc hollered.

He almost wasn't prepared for the quick change of course. Clutching the reins, he sideswiped a Graygual horse, making the other animal buck wildly. The Graygual flew off, his arms windmilling. Tomous, the man they'd picked up from their journey to the Shadow Lands, was on him in an instant, swinging his sword down for a kill strike.

The horse galloped, hot after Xavier's horse. Marc

leaned forward, not in control. Trying to hold on. His teeth chattered with each hoof thump. Alarm had his eyes wide, going so fast through trees and branches the leaves became a blur.

Xavier's horse came into view, slowing down. Xavier jumped off, about to sneak up on the first Inkna in the crow's nest.

Marc's horse blew past him.

"No," Marc begged.

The horse didn't respond.

They weaved in and out of trees toward the gate. The horse slowed, stepping more cautiously in the lush area.

Seeing his chance, Marc swung his leg over the saddle and jumped off, aiming for a cluster of large ferns. He misjudged his speed, though, hitting the ground with his feet, but then unable to stop the forward motion. He rolled, tumbling over a rock and crashing to a halt in a briar.

He groaned, yanking his limbs and crawling out, the thorns scratching along his cheeks and forehead and snagging his clothes. Out of breath, and seeing the horse continuing on without him, Marc shook his head and glanced around, trying to get his bearings.

The horse was fast, and it was excellent in battle, but the thing was wild. Sanders thought it would follow the horse in front of it. Nope. It just did what it wanted all the time. Marc was no match for the animal.

He took out his knife and tried to picture the area in his head. Southeastern side of the city. If he wasn't mistaken, there was a crow's next not too far away.

Staying silent, hearing the distant clang of swords and shouts of battle, Marc snuck through the trees, careful not to disturb leaves or snap twigs. Exactly where he expected, he saw wooden boards nailed to a large trunk. At the top he could just make out the edge of a platform within the leafy green.

The wood planking groaned as someone above shifted. It was definitely occupied.

Sweat dripping down his back, his breathing rapid no matter how he tried to calm down, he climbed the tree with his knife in his teeth. Putting it back in its sheath might've been wiser, but if he needed to grab it quickly, this would probably work out better.

The small board at the top of the trunk squeaked as he gripped it. He paused, staring up at the platform with wide eyes.

Nothing peered over the edge at him.

He pulled himself up slowly until his eyes were just over the lip of the platform to see black boots rooted to the wood. The Inkna was braced against the railing, staring out to the south. No doubt attacking the Captain with his mind.

Marc climbed up as slowly as possible, careful not to

make a sound. The Captain had been right: this Inkna was so focused with his mind power that he wasn't paying attention to anything else, including the guy with a knife crawling onto the platform.

Thank God.

Marc pulled himself up the rest of the way, straightening slowly. Knife held out and shaking dramatically, Marc took a step. His breathing turned shallow. Pressure pulsed in his ears. With a quick movement, he grabbed the Inkna's shoulder with one hand as he stabbed with the other. The knife stuck in the man's neck.

The Inkna yelled out in surprise and pain. Blaring agony tore through Marc's head and blistered his body, so intense his teeth clicked shut and his eyes rolled back in his head. Before he knew it, he was tumbling backward, running out of wood to hold him up. The ground pulled at him, tugging his body away from the rest of the wood.

The pain bled away. Marc's body stopped convulsing just as his torso went over the edge. He gave a panicked cry, his hands scrabbling for purchase. He was barely able to close his grip around a step.

His weight wrenched his shoulder, but he held on, dangling from the tree.

Marc gave an inarticulate sound and glanced down. The ground seemed to smile up at him, promising pain.

Feet scratching at the trunk, looking for purchase, he managed to get his other hand on the step. A moment later he was secure, clinging to the tree with his eyes closed, breathing a sigh of relief.

Why can't I just doctor? That's all I've ever wanted to do is just doctor. I shouldn't be killing people. I should be saving them.

He rose up just a little, knowing the job wasn't done. His gaze barely reached over the ledge where the limp body in a black uniform greeted him. The Inkna was definitely dead.

Rising up just a bit more, he snatched his knife off the ledge. He moved it to his teeth before he stopped himself. Deep crimson shone in the light. And it wasn't his own blood.

He threw the knife to the ground. He'd clean it and tuck it back in his holster with the others.

Then he'd try and find the next Inkna before the Captain succumbed to the mental bombardment.

CHAPTER 24

SHANTI PUT UP her hands, pushing at the net. The heavy material resisted, confining her. She bent to the ground. Finding the end, she gripped it with both hands and flung it over her. She crawled out, looking up.

Rohnan drove his blade into a Graygual. The man fell, his body next to one of four ropes connected to the net. Another Graygual lay dead near her, an arrow through his middle.

"You are not pulling your weight, *Chulan,*" Rohnan said, moving to another Graygual running at them. He bore four slashes and was the last on the street.

"I am overseeing. I hate getting my hands dirty." Shanti picked up her sword as Rohnan jogged into position. The Graygual slowed on balanced feet, his knees bent, his eyes wary. He thrust in a smooth, practiced movement. Rohnan, using his *Gift,* was already in position to block. He knocked the blade to the side and stabbed, finding a shoulder as the Graygual twisted at the last moment.

The Graygual lunged, his movements precise. Rohnan was already stepping to the side, out of the way. He kicked out, connecting with the Graygual's hand and knocking the sword free. Then Rohnan leaned forward, digging his blade into the other's ribs.

"Quit wasting time, Rohnan. We have a lot of ground to cover."

Rohnan danced to the side as the Graygual grunted, feeling the pain from that strike but not succumbing to it. He put out his hands, ready to grapple, knowing that if he went for his blade, Rohnan would stab him easily.

"You could end it quickly with your *Gift*," Rohnan said, rushing forward and cleaving a forearm. The Graygual jerked it toward his body, a defensive reaction that left his side open. Rohnan took advantage, and ended the fight.

"I need to save my strength. It's a lot against one. They are bullying me."

"Challenging, *Chulan.* There's a difference."

"You'd better hope I hold out. Once they kill me, they'll turn their *Gift* on you." Shanti started jogging, stepping over the fallen bodies. Two more had arrows stuck in them, the shots well placed. It spoke of technique and practice. Alena wasn't lying when she said she knew her way around a bow.

"I wonder if Cayan knows these women are practicing with weapons when no one is looking." Shanti turned the corner, her *Gift* sensing no one in the area. Up ahead, though, bodies dotted the way, blocking her path. If she took a right or left now, she could travel along empty streets, but once she turned toward the mansion again, Graygual would be in the way.

"I wonder the same thing," Rohnan said, slowing with her. There was no point in just running around the city, not when all the paths would end in the same fight. "He must. Yet he's never mentioned it?"

"No. No one has." Shanti cleaned her sword in an effort to stall. She felt Ruisa and Alena moving slowly in the direction she was heading, already way in front of her. They were probably getting into position. Other women dotted the way as well, mostly staying still. They were hiding with their explosives.

"What are we waiting for, *Chulan*? Are the others not in position?"

Shanti took a deep breath and looked around, enjoying the beauty of the city. Usually it was spotless—these people took great pride in clean streets. They lived at a slower pace than other cities of this size, ambling along the street instead of hurrying. Friendlier, too. With the lush surroundings and the breeze blowing in the sweet smell of nature, this place couldn't be beat. It was a little paradise tucked away in the north of the land. Perfection.

"I could've been really happy here, Rohnan."

"Something you never mentioned to the Captain, I'd wager."

"That man loves to chase. Who am I to make things easy for him?" Shanti inhaled, taking it all in.

"It is a lovely place, I agree."

Alena and Ruisa stopped near the first line of Graygual. Shanti wondered how many Inkna were in that group; how strong they were.

"I don't think I like the net technique." Gracas and Leilius were moving slowly. Hardly at all. Not fighting, either. Shanti could feel their impatience and trepidation. They probably had too many blocking their way. The poison could not have taken down as many as it should have.

"This is a fool's errand," Shanti said in sudden exasperation. "Fuck it. Let's just start killing people and see what happens."

Shanti felt a piercing of intense pain from Cayan. It overtook her thoughts for a moment, begging her to climb the wall and toward him. He was probably overcome with Inkna, just as she was about to be.

Definitely a fool's errand, all of this. But what choice did they have?

LEILIUS STABBED A Graygual in the back. Right in the middle of the shoulder blades. Some people called that cowardly. Leilius didn't care.

He slapped his hand over the man's mouth, muffling the "arrgh." His stomach churned and exploded, Leilius unable to help a dry heave. Killing hadn't gotten any easier.

At least he'd stopped eating before battles. That helped.

He dragged the man a few steps and then dropped him, stashing him behind a tent. A scuffle sounded to the right. A leg covered in black pants kicked out. It disappeared for a moment, kicking out a second time, this time with the other one. The legs convulsed on the ground, kicking up dust, before going still.

Leilius looked out, through the gap in the line of tents. Prisoners sat on the ground in a cluster, herded together like cattle, looking all around them. Dirty, wild-haired, and unshaven, these guys had had a rough time of it for however long they'd been here. The ropes securing their arms had chafed, many with skin that had been rubbed raw. They were squished together, with very little room between them.

Graygual surrounded them, more than Gracas had said there'd be. Many more. It seemed like the Hunter was trying to fortify these ranks. It was smart. Without more men, there was really no point in fighting today. Especially not with all the Inkna running around, blasting people with their mental magic.

"What do you—"

Leilius jumped and turned, sticking out his knife before he realized it was Gracas. He swung the knife wide as Gracas reacted, slapping his hand away.

"You need to pay more attention," Gracas whispered with a scowl. "If I was as slow as you, I'd probably be dying right now!"

"Sorry. I'm jumpy."

They looked out through the gap again.

"What do you think?" Gracas asked.

"I don't know what we're going to do. I think Maggie only has a few of those chemical things, but everyone is all huddled together. The Hunter knew we'd come here."

"Of course he knew. I've seen a bunch of dead Graygual in the tents, but there's plenty out there, too."

Leilius gripped his knife so hard his hand hurt. "They just seem like a bunch because we have no one to fight them."

"Should we just charge, or should we head back to S'am and help her?"

"I'm not the leader!" The pressure of command weighed down Leilius' shoulders and clouded his judgment. He was used to ghosting around, listening and reporting. Strategy and battle eluded him. He'd never been good at it. S'am *knew* that.

"Boys, what are you doing?" Maggie asked from behind them. She held one of her contraptions. Blood spattered her shirt front. A few drops were on her cheek.

For a novice, she sure learned in a hurry.

"There are a lot of them," Leilius admitted, feeling sheepish. He was in the army and she was a woman. He should have a plan.

"We might just go back to S'am," Gracas said, probably thinking the same thing.

Maggie's brow furrowed. She looked beyond them, through the gap. "We need those men. They'll be stiff and weak, but Shanti didn't seem to have much hope. I don't think this will end well without them."

"Yeah, but they're surrounded by Graygual..." Gracas said. "And Leilius can't fight for shit. And you don't know what you're doing. So what does that leave us?"

"Same as what you started—idiots." Maggie was still staring out beyond them. "Well, we have to try. The ones at the far end are a little removed. Not much, but enough that I can set off one of these explosives. The explosion should toss them toward the prisoners without actually hurting the prisoners. Maybe a few will be a little...uncomfortable, but we don't have much choice. Those men will make short work of any Graygual, I think. Stomp on them or something. It'll be a distraction, at least. We'll dash in and cut as many hands free as we can. Then, hopefully, we can work on the other Graygual together."

Leilius was nodding before she stopped talking. Gracas just stared.

Her look grazed each of them, her brow furrowing a bit harder. "This is the best Shanti had to work with, huh? You might as well have drool running out of your mouth, kid. Cripes. C'mon, we're wasting time."

Leilius followed her around the perimeter of the tents, moving toward the area she wanted to hit with the explosives. They passed a dead Graygual lying facedown. Then another. A few more. All of them looked like they'd been trying to go somewhere, and then died. Just…keeled over and died. There were no wounds that Leilius could see, and no blood.

"Nasty poison, that," Maggie whispered, pointing at one of the bodies as she jogged by it. "Someone must've slipped it into water or food or something. It's a really fast-acting poison that's clear and odorless. It could kill within an hour. The body doesn't even have time to properly evacuate its stomach or bowels before it starts shutting down."

"An hour?" Leilius asked as Gracas said, "You made that?"

"We're not allowed to use it," Maggie said, slowing. Her words were barely a whisper now, hard to hear. "It was a mixture passed down the Captain's line, actually.

Sonya, the Captain's mother, put it into Eloise's care until the Captain marries again. It is supposed to stay with that line until times of war. Thank God she had the foresight to pass it on. It's helped."

"But…who used it here?" Leilius asked.

"One of the women, I imagine. We distributed it to everyone we could for just such a situation." She took a few more steps and then crouched down, putting her finger to her lips to signal silence.

Leilius held up his knife and crouched beside her, watching as she mixed some powered substance with another in a clear container. She shook it, and then paused. Her forehead beaded with sweat.

Leilius' stomach clenched, a sign danger was near. What she was about to do made her nervous, and a woman who looked like she did, with scars all over her face, knew when something could work out badly.

"Which one of you can throw the farthest *with the most accuracy*?" Maggie asked, very clear about that last part. Her eyes had the sort of intensity Sanders might, and while she might not be able to fight really well, she seemed to be able to kill just fine. Leilius was not very comfortable in her proximity.

He pointed at Gracas. Gracas' finger was aimed at Leilius.

Maggie rolled her eyes. "Is there a purpose in your existence?" She took a deep breath and held the liquid over the powdered mixture with a steady hand. "If I say run, go to your left, is that clear?"

"Yes, ma'am," they chorused.

She poured the liquid slowly, the slightly yellowed mixture running down the small powder hill in rivulets. When done, she put a lid on the container and twisted. Rising, she cocked her hand, sighted with bent knees, and then threw.

Leilius watched the flimsy material turn end over end. It barely cleared the top of the last tent. Maggie exhaled. "Okay. Get ready to—"

The explosion drowned her out. The tents in the front line flapped violently. The air compressed around them, knocking them to their butts.

Maggie was up first, a large knife in hand. "Hurry!"

Leilius scrambled to his feet, scooping his own knife up amid a handful of dirt. He jumped over an upturned bench and burst through the tents into the open space crowded with bodies. Three Graygual were among the prisoners, fighting for their lives as the prisoners, army men all, did exactly what Maggie had said they'd do. The other Graygual didn't bother wading in after them. They stood their ground around the outside, most facing the explosion, some still looking away, expecting an attack.

Leilius dodged the divot in the ground from the blast and made it to the first few prisoners as the nearest

Graygual ran at him. Wasting no time, he slit the ropes of three pairs of wrists and two pairs of legs. As he was reaching for the third, one of the newly freed men jumped over him, tackling the Graygual aiming a sword at Leilius' back.

"Do you have weapons?" one of the army men asked. He looked vaguely familiar but his name wasn't coming to mind.

"No. Take them off the dead men." Leilius kept cutting, freeing as many and as fast as he could.

The men waiting did so without moving, holding out legs or twisting around to make it more efficient for Leilius. His arms started to grow tight, and then started to burn, as he repeated the same action over and over without rest. He kept on, though—these men were vital to S'am's survival. To *all* of their survival.

"Staff Sergeant Jenkins, take a few men and go get weapons," someone shouted.

"Yes, sir," Jenkins called.

Leilius glanced up at the men they still had to free. Maggie and Gracas were both working their way through the crowd, over a hundred strong. It would take them forever to get through everyone, especially as the bodies became more condensed.

A blast sounded in the distance.

"Hurry!" Maggie shouted.

"Where is the fighting?" one of the freed men asked.

It was the same one who had ordered Jenkins around.

"In Green Fields Square. Shanti is going to try and get through there," Maggie said, out of breath.

"Alous, get some knives and start cutting people free," the man ordered.

Out of the corner of Leilius' eye, he saw a little body dart between the tents. He glanced up, about to sound the alarm, when a kid ran toward the crowd. He had a bunch of knives and dirt all over his face. Another orphan ran out between the tents, three knives held at the ready.

"She got *kids* to help out?" someone asked incredulously.

That little kid, Arsen, ran out next, holding two more knives. He passed them to the officer.

"Where did you get these, son?" the officer asked, passing the knives to one of the other men.

"From the bad men. Sir." Arsen pointed out through the tents.

More kids came out from the sea of canvas, these the larger of the orphans, holding swords and other weapons. All recovered from the Graygual dead.

They hadn't stayed put like Shanti had told them. And they were probably the only kids in the whole city who would rush into danger like this. It was madness.

"Hurry up!" Maggie yelled as another explosion went off. "Shanti needs our help!"

CHAPTER 25

SHANTI BRACED HERSELF against the fire scouring her body, grimacing. She had her shields up, figuring out how to get around this pounding so she could mentally fight back.

A mass of Graygual waited in front of her, weapons out, looking supremely confident. She was still half the city away from Cayan's house. The Hunter had given himself plenty of space to work in, and he'd crowded all of his men into this city. He had planned for the worst, a scenario she wasn't even close to delivering.

A sword came at her, clumsy but fast. She batted it away with her own sword, stepped in, and stabbed her attacker in the throat. She kicked out, crushing a nose with the sole of her boot before swinging her hips, kicking forward to break a jaw. One tendril of fire stabbed through her body, sending her stumbling into a Graygual. His knife came down, aiming for her shoulder. She stabbed him through the gut and then head-butted him, cracking his nose. She danced away from the knife strike in time to slice a chest with her sword.

"There…are…so…many!" she yelled at Rohnan as she cut through a cheek, slashed down a stomach, and came back to pierce the first man. He fell backward, into the men behind him, giving Shanti a little room.

She twirled and kicked. Her foot hit someone in the solar plexus. Rohnan stabbed him through, yanking his sword free a moment later and sending him to the ground.

"I wish I had my staff," he said, taking on two others.

"I wish…you did…too." Shanti ripped her shields off and sent a wave of power at the Inkna cowering in the back. Her mind *raked* the minds of the Graygual in front of her, slowing them down, before reaching the Inkna. Their attack stopped for a moment, as they shielded themselves as a unit from her huge rush of power.

Unfortunately, when they worked together, they were superior, and they had much more energy between them.

A blast came back, punching her mind so hard she staggered back. A Graygual batted her sword away as though she were a child. His face a twisted mask of hate and rage, he lunged in for the kill shot.

An arrow parted the air, landing in his chest.

Shock smacked into his expression. His attack lost strength, giving her enough time to slam up her shields, to ignore the pain, and fall on her ass. His blade ruffled her hair as she fell.

Bows sang. Arrows rained down, coming from the sides. Alena clearly wasn't the only one that kept up target practice! Many in the Graygual crowd staggered, the fletchings of arrows sticking from their bodies.

"Stop sleeping through the battle!" Rohnan yelled, working through the Graygual with speed and precision, his movements graceful. Almost delicate. The result brutal.

"My head hurts." She gritted her teeth against the constant drum of pain working through her shield.

Three men ran up, a net held between them.

"Oh for fuck's sakes!" she groaned.

"They think you are a fish," Rohnan called.

She jumped up, trying to think around that thump of agony. She ran toward Rohnan, leading the Graygual in a chase. They had no stripes on their breasts, which made them probably stupid or naive. Either could be true.

They stepped forward and then to the side, ready to throw their net. Rohnan moved forward too, until he was right at their sides. He stabbed the first, stepping in to grab the man's collar and pulling him onto his blade. Letting go, and stepping to the side as the man painfully stumbled out of the way, Rohnan pierced the back of the next.

Shanti covered him from two Graygual. She swept the ground with her foot, knocking the first to the ground. She jumped over him, her sword coming down on the other. She threw her knife, hitting someone on the far side of Rohnan as he finished dealing with the net holders, and then stabbed down, taking out the one on the ground.

"There are still too damn many!" She huffed, growing tired. The pain grew more intense, starting to saturate her mind.

A roar of men's voices echoed up the street behind her, bouncing off the buildings and working a shiver up her spine.

"I wondered if the Hunter would send people to box us in. Clever." Shanti looked off to the sides, wondering which way she should run.

SANDERS GROWLED, STABBING through a Graygual and then stepping in to punch another. He backtracked before taking two quick steps and barreling into two more. He ripped a knife from its holster and brought it down on one of their faces before jumping up and stabbing the other with his sword.

Tomous careened backward, barely missed by an enemy sword. Sanders bent for his knife, straightened and threw it, its blade sticking in the side of the

Graygual neck. Not exactly on target, but it would do. Tomous finished the job.

Sanders glanced back. The Captain had fallen from his horse, and lay on the ground in a ball. Whatever was attacking him was not visible, and it was a hell of a lot more painful than the slash on Sanders' side. From the look of it, the Captain would not be able to hold on for much longer.

"What is taking those boys so long?" Sanders yelled, more out of frustration than anything else. He hacked into a Graygual, no style in the effort, just pure rage. He then ran forward, attacking with everything he had.

"One was too much for us, sir," Tobias yelled. Blood coated the side of his face and a cut marred his forearm. "He's probably got a few or more. It's a wonder the Inkna aren't killing him."

"Which is what the boys were for."

"Those Inkna probably know we only have one mental fighter, apart from Shanti, who is tied up in the city." Tobias' words dried up as two more Graygual came at him at once.

That was the thing. They could've cut through the first bunch of Graygual, but more kept coming. Some of them were poor swordsmen, too, but there were just too many of them.

Sanders growled, hacking into someone else. He stepped back and turned. A sword tip swiped past him, tugging at his shirt. The fabric parted. Thankfully his flesh didn't.

"Fall back! Regroup!" Sanders called desperately, cut off from Tomous by black shirts.

Tobias jogged closer, but someone stepped in the way, the sword work fast and perfect. An officer.

The tide was turning. Sanders couldn't keep up. Hopefully Shanti would save the day, because he was all out of miracles.

CHAPTER 26

EXCRUCIATING PAIN VIBRATED through Cayan's body, searing his skin and scraping his bones. It felt like needles stabbed his eyes and sharpened sticks jabbed his inner ears. Everything in him wanted to let go. To let them beat him into unconsciousness so the unyielding pain would end.

Breathing as deeply as possible, not letting the pain turn his breath shallow and have him blacking out, he held on to the thread of consciousness. If he gave in, the Inkna would turn their efforts onto Sanders and the others. The battle would be over nearly as fast as it had begun.

One stream of agony winked out, relieving the pressure on the back of his head. One of the boys must've killed an Inkna attacker.

Cayan sucked in air as the throb of the other attacks continued. Constant.

Without warning, fire burnt down his throat and blistered the roof of his mouth.

His eyes snapped open. He thought that someone

had lit a flame. Through his watering eyes, he saw Sanders hacking at someone, brutal but slower than usual. He was tiring. Next to him fought Tobias, his feet dragging with fatigue. They were closer than they should've been, pushed back by a crowd of Graygual.

No fire licked at their toes. Or his face.

Another Inkna must've joined the fray. The boys were few and the Inkna many. The Hunter was obviously waiting for this attack, and he had planned well. The other side of the city was probably vulnerable. It was too bad Cayan didn't have enough people to take advantage of that.

The fire dumped into his stomach, churning. He curled into a tighter ball, trying to block out the soul-crushing pain. Trying to think of anything else.

Shanti's face swam into view. He couldn't feel her through the *Joining*—he couldn't feel anything but the attack—so he focused on his memory of her. He pictured her shining violet eyes, so expressive, as she assured him they'd make it through this. An image of her body swam into view as it lay before him, nude and glistening in the morning sun as they lay among the flowers in the Shadow Lands. Her thighs parted for him as a slow smile curled her lips. He could almost feel her soft thighs rubbing up his sides, and smell her scent, lilac and mysterious femininity. He wanted nothing more than to see her in that moment. To fight this battle with her, side by side. It was how it was meant to be. Them together, battling, felt as natural as breathing.

A body-consuming throb added to the stew of pain right before a generalized sort of agony blinked off. The boys must've taken another one out of the conflict, which meant at least one of the Honor Guard was still alive. That was something.

He noticed bodies drifting out of the trees like phantoms. In unison, their movements perfect and in sync, the men and women stepped forward without a sound. Swords held up in stances relaxed and graceful, their eyes swept the battle in front of them.

Cayan blinked a few times through the searing pain. They looked like Shanti.

Hallucinations—they had to be. He had pictured her so completely that now he saw her in life.

"Should I kill them, sir?" Lucius' voice drifted through Cayan's consciousness. He had trouble making sense of it. "Sir?"

Cayan focused on his breathing. He tried to push away the pain. Tried to think as he looked up at the blond man moving gracefully toward him. The man's weapon was even like Shanti's, delicate and well made, created by a master craftsman. Cayan could make a fortune with work like that, as unique and exotic as it was useful. Nobles all over the north and east would pay dearly for sword wrought in the style of the violet-eyed girl.

"Captain." Lucius' face swam into view as the phantoms drifted closer, so perfect in their movements. So deadly.

"Westwood Lands." The man was close now, his eyes hard and gray, like the skies as a storm blew in.

Cayan blinked up in confusion. The man could've been Shanti's brother, with the high cheekbones and strong jaw. Her face was more delicate; beautiful where this man was ruggedly handsome. But then, Cayan had thought that about Rohnan, too. They all bore a similarity.

"He is taking the Inkna attack," Lucius said, his arrow pointed at the man's chest. Only three steps separated them. It would be an instant death. The man didn't seem to notice.

"Where is the *Chulan*?" the man asked, eyes beating down onto Cayan.

Cayan tried to answer as tears of agony dripped from his eyes. His couldn't get his jaw loose. Couldn't take a deep enough breath to do anything but hold on and hope the boys worked faster. He didn't have much left.

"She's in the city with Rohnan. We need to get to her," Lucius answered.

The man's eyes widened a fraction. "Rohnan is alive?"

"Yes. Are you from her land?" The plea in Lucius' voice was evident. Or else Cayan was projecting his own plea. It was hard to say.

The man glanced to the side where his countrymen spread out in a semicircle. As he turned back, Cayan could swear his eyes unfocused for a moment.

The fire scorching his insides subsided. The bone-crushing agony slackened. Cayan sucked in a full, sweet breath as the pain reduced to a simmer, easily ignorable after what he'd just endured.

He blinked up at the man, who was looking down at him with calculating eyes. The man said, "Only one in all the land could've endured power that strong by herself…"

Shaky, Cayan uncurled. He flexed his fingers, working some blood into them. "Now there is two. If you mean to help, then help." Cayan felt his *Gift* boil. He ripped down his shields and sent a pulse of power at the Inkna still breathing. The next second he was running, sword in hand.

KALLON STOOD IN awe for a single beat, his *Gift* still tangled with one of the more powerful of the Inkna. He could feel the others in his merge shifting then *slashing*, trying to take out the remaining enemy fighting with their minds. The amount of power was…unreal. He wasn't even sure if the Chosen could've stayed cognizant in the face of that.

"Rumors are true. Chosen is a lucky girl. I wonder if she has learned to share..." Mela laughed, her sword in hand.

"Are we going to drool, or are we going to fight?" Sayas asked, his anticipation coloring the merge.

Kallon glanced at the others, relaying his intentions without needing words. As expected, everyone started jogging, falling into the fighting pattern most suited for this area and the layout of the enemy ahead. He and Mela lead the charge, intending to slice right through.

An Inkna *slashed* at his mind. Kallon retaliated, grabbing the other mind and attempting to beat at it. More Inkna joined in, their enemy merge competing with Kallon's.

A peal of thunder rocked their mental battle, making Kallon stumble. It rolled and boiled, pounding into the Inkna minds. The Inkna wrestling with Kallon's merge winked out, a silent scream announcing its defeat. Another man, off to the other side, let out a physical scream. His mind went silent a moment later.

"That makes our job easier," Sayas said as they gained speed.

What must be the Captain of these men joined his fighters, running into the Graygual like a battering ram. His sword moved almost too fast to keep track of, his movements precise and powerful. He took on two immediately, freeing up a shorter man with harsh and brutal strokes.

"Very lucky," Kallon heard Mela yell as she sprinted at the Graygual.

"Now we're cooking!" the shorter man yelled, tearing into a Graygual in front of him with redoubled effort.

Kallon lost track of their fight as he approached a Graygual, also running at the fight, coming from the city. The Graygual attacked using a straightforward style and rapid feet. Classic Graygual teaching, unlike the many Kallon had encountered across the land recently.

With almost lazy efforts, Kallon met the sword strike, moved his blade in a circle, carrying the Graygual blade with it, and flicked. The Graygual struggled to hold on to his sword. He stepped forward, putting him off balance. Kallon lunged, sword puncturing the other man before yanking it free.

He kicked the Graygual, knocking him out of the way, before engaging with another. With lesser skill, this Graygual couldn't keep up. He swung his sword at Kallon, who blocked and struck. Another kick and Kallon was moving forward again.

"What is your plan?" Kallon yelled at the Captain.

The Captain blocked the thrust of one man, stabbed

another with a knife, and then stuck his sword through the first's neck. He was already moving to another man, the Graygual half stumbling backward, not wanting to go up against an obviously superior fighter.

"We must get to Shanti," the Captain shouted, on to the next.

"They're bringing men around," the shorter man yelled. "Did you kill those Inkna?"

"Yes." The Captain downed two more men as though they were unarmed. The fight was no contest. But then, these men had few or no slashes. They had been sent out there to die.

"Who holds the city?" Kallon asked as they ran toward the looming walls. Solid and stone, the barrier was built with defense in mind, except for one thing. Individuals climbing. The stone was coarse, with cracks not smoothed over, leaving plenty of pockmarks and crevices a skilled climber could navigate.

"The Hunter," the Captain panted, veering left. "Where are the horses?"

"They fucked off," the shorter man yelled in something like a growl.

The Captain whistled, a shrill sound.

"Here's more!" someone shouted as a group of Graygual emerged from a large gate in the distance.

Made up of two large wooden doors, this gate was open on one side. But as they approached, it was already starting to close.

The whistle sounded again. A horse whinnied somewhere to the right. The thundering of hooves announced a large black stallion. The Captain darted to the great horse, climbing on with an innate athleticism. Another horse came running up with it. Shiny and sleek, this animal looked like a fine specimen. The shorter man reached out to it, but it chomped down at his hand and pranced away.

"Damn horse!" the man yelled. The man ran forward. No one else reached out to the animal. "We need to get to that gate."

"I got it." The Captain leaned forward with a "Haw!" The horse lurched forward, running straight at the group of approaching Graygual. Thunder rolled, the Captain's *Gift* sending the enemy staggering and falling, clutching their body or heads.

"Cut 'em down!" the shorter man yelled.

"Very vocal, these men," Sayas said as he ran with his sword at the ready.

Kallon stabbed a man writhing on the ground as he ran by, seeing the Captain nearly at the gate. The others did the same—not much to do with a *Gift* that strong clearing the way.

"He was not foretold!" Dannon said. He kicked a Graygual's head, knocking the man out.

"I love surprises." Mela laughed, running beside

them.

The sound of more hooves announced two younger men, one as large as any of Kallon's despite his age. Both with spatters of blood and pale faces, they reined in to join the larger group.

"Help the Captain," the shorter man yelled, pointing at the gate.

The larger of the two new arrivals kicked his horse before the command was completed. The other was on the way a moment later.

The Captain reached the gate. He urged his horse forward, probably trying to batter his way through. The horse reared, unwilling. The sleek horse whinnied, battering the black horse out of the way. It reared as well, but for a different reason. Its front hooves clattered at the wood, stopping the closing movement. It turned and kicked out with both feet, clattering at it again.

Someone stood over the wall, arrow at the ready. Kallon *struck,* tearing through the mind like a knife through melon. The man fell away. Another took his place, before succumbing to the same fate.

Another clatter as the horse attempted to force its way in.

"That horse is a strange sort of wild," Sayas said, out of breath. "I want one."

"We were foolish to leave ours behind!" Dannon yelled.

The Captain jumped from his horse, dodging the crazed animal, and sprinted at the crack in the gate. He made it through, disappearing inside.

"Follow him!" the shorter man urged.

The younger boys reached the gate right after the Captain, jumping from their horses and slipping inside. Another bout of thunder rolled, the sign of the Captain's *Gift*. The gate started to open as more men appeared over the wall. Kallon shot out with his mind, killing them as he finally reached the gate.

The wild horse barreled through, followed by the other horses. Kallon charged in behind them. An explosion sounded from somewhere to the right. A spray of rocks flew through the air. The Captain was in front of him, battling a line of disposable Graygual as his *Gift* boomed out.

"Shanti is on the other side of the city," he yelled, stabbing one of the Graygual through before turning to another. "We have to hurry. She's getting bombarded by Inkna!"

Kallon ran at the surging Graygual, not seeing one officer among them. He attacked, blocking a thrust and stabbing before moving on. A blade caught the sunlight, glinting, before swinging down at Kallon. He knocked it aside, slashing. Dannon appeared to his right and Mela to his left. The others arrived, forming a sort of hollow diamond, cutting through the inexperienced and altogether useless Graygual with ease. With his mind, Kallon reached farther still, cutting those down in front of them, clearing the way.

"Holy shit, you guys make me feel lazy," the shorter man growled as he ran into their formation. "And bored." With a great show of strength, he hacked and battered his way through with skill Kallon wouldn't have thought possible with the coarse and often brutal fighting style.

"Where are the officers?" the Captain asked, taking out two Graygual. He ran back for his horse.

"They will be fighting the *Chulan,*" Kallon said, feeling that urgency tug at him. "They will be trying to capture her."

LUCIUS GRABBED ONE of the loose and rider-less horses. His body felt stiff and weak. He shook when he moved and felt like an old door with rusty hinges. Whatever those women had given him, it wasn't natural.

"Ready?" Sterling rode closer, looking bedraggled and in pain.

Lucius glanced ahead to where Shanti's people were slipping through the gate. They were some fearsome fighters; that was for sure. They were greatly needed.

"Yes." Lucius climbed on, ignoring the groaning Graygual at his feet.

They rode toward the gate, every movement misery. "I think we were supposed to rest for longer," Lucius said in a dry tone, raising his voice over the sound of hooves and the distant roar of battle.

Sterling didn't respond, but he surely felt the same way.

As they came to the gate, Lucius caught movement out of the corner of his eye. He turned with a wince and raised his bow, fighting the fatigue in his limbs.

"Don't shoot!" Marc, spattered with blood and wide-eyed, threw his hands in the air. "It's me!"

"What are you doing out here still?" Sterling demanded. "Why weren't you with Xavier?"

"That damn horse went crazy. I was working on the Inkna, but the one I was sneaking up on dropped dead. There might be some more to the back..."

"I doubt it," Lucius said, gesturing Marc forward. "The Hunter will have called them around. It sounds like Shanti is giving the city hell."

As if to punctuate his words, an explosion sounded within the city.

"Come on." Lucius motioned at Marc again. "Get on. You aren't any good on foot."

Marc climbed on the back of the horse, the weight of two riders slowing the animal considerably. They wouldn't be able to fight like this. Although Lucius could barely lift a bow—he wouldn't be able to fight anyway.

As if hearing his thoughts, Sterling said, "Let's check to make sure all the men are free. We're no good for anything else."

"If they aren't free, you still won't be any good, right?" Marc asked. "You can barely move…"

"No wonder Shanti beats on you so much," Lucius said, slowing at the gate's entrance.

Bodies littered the ground, some of them with no signs of violence. Having mental warfare was excellent against those who didn't. Unfortunately, it wasn't so good when his people were the ones without it.

Fighting raged down the street, as the Captain led everyone toward Shanti. Lucius went right, speeding up his horse. They would go around the fighting to the jail cell, making sure the officers were freed.

Horses hooves sounded loudly. Every step sounded like a blast, echoing against the buildings and announcing their presence. But no one came out after them. No Inkna guarded the way. No Graygual came running.

They continued, winding through the outskirts of the city. As they neared the prison, movement caught Lucius' eye. He stopped, Sterling stopping beside him.

"What is it?" Marc asked, his knife in his hand. It was shaking slightly. He must've known that if danger came at them, he'd be largely on his own.

"Don't know." A flash of black drew Lucius' eye. A

swish of long hair and rustle of dress disappeared into a house up the road. The door closed quietly. "Let's keep moving."

They slowed again as they neared the prison, stopping across the road in the shadow of a house. Nothing moved. Apart from the sound of the distant battle, all was quiet.

"Should we chance it?" Sterling whispered, eyes sweeping the road.

"What choice do we have?" Marc asked. "Either we do this, or we go toward the battle. We can't do *nothing.*"

"Fast or slow?" Lucius asked.

Sterling raised his bow, at the ready. "Slow. I'll need to be still to aim. My arms are jelly."

"They'll hit us easier, though," Marc said, throwing his leg over the horse and sliding to the ground. "I think I'll stay on my feet, if that's okay. I like having the option of being able to run."

They walked out into the street. The stillness pressed on them, hinting at dangers lying in wait. The horse's clomp blasted out, but nothing stirred.

"Maybe they just abandoned them," Marc said as they neared the open prison door.

"The Hunter wouldn't have left officers on their own." Lucius threw his own leg over the horse. His knee gave out, dumping him to the ground. Marc helped him up. "He suspected we had an extra key."

"Of course there is an extra key." Marc reached up to help Sterling. "What city would only have one?"

"We gave him four keys. He suspected there were more. I had to let Alena take a few hits before giving him what was supposed to be the last key. He had to believe I was sincere. She suffered for it." Bile rose in Lucius' throat. He would never forgive himself for it. To see her face, blotched red on both sides, tears in her eyes—it was a disgusting thing he'd done, but he had to for the sake of the city.

They walked closer to the prison, silent. Sterling had his bow up, the arrow waving. Lucius took out his sword. Marc did as well.

"I'll go first," Marc whispered with a quivering voice. He jogged up, throwing himself to the side of the door and pausing.

"He has much more courage than I ever gave him credit for," Sterling whispered, aiming at the door.

Lucius nodded, remaining silent, as Marc moved to peer in the door. He yanked his head back, and then looked in again, leaving it for a moment longer this time. His body followed.

Sterling started forward. Lucius gave a glance behind, in case this was a trap of some sort, and slipped in after him. At the mouth of the door, though, it became clear.

Three guards lay on the ground, two in a puddle of their own vomit, their bowels evacuated, the third in a pool of blood.

"Hurry!" Barus waved at them through the bars.

The other men crowded the front, grasping the metal with white knuckles. Lucius could see their impatience and desperation to get out and help with the battle.

"Who killed the guards?" Lucius asked as Sterling left the prison with jerky movements. He'd get the hidden key they hadn't turned over.

"A couple of kids," Timken said while shaking his head. "A tiny one, too. Jerkin's kid."

Lucius thought for a moment, vaguely remembering the name Jerkin. It was the man who had run off, leaving a small child behind. "The orphan kid?"

"Yeah, him and another one. Threw poison at the guards and took off. I think they are trying to find the guard with the key."

Lucius shook his head, glancing out toward the door. Before he could comment further, or even think about how insane it was that small kids had the courage to take on an enemy like the Graygual when grown men had shied away, Sterling was walking back in. He held up a dirt-crusted key before fitting it into the lock with a smile.

"What about weapons?" Barus asked with fire in his

eyes.

"I'm just back in the city. Check the stores." Lucius stepped out of the way as the men poured from the cells. Once freed, they ran, going to collect their weapons and help take back the city.

"Now what?" Sterling asked, grabbing his horse.

"Now you two help me doctor any of ours that we find alive," Marc said, his expression one of confidence and purpose. "C'mon. We have work to do."

CHAPTER 27

THE ROAR GREW louder as a wall of men ran at Shanti and Rohnan. Their ripped and frayed clothing waved in the wind. Facial hair and bedraggled appearances contrasted with their gleaming swords and knives.

"Thank the Elders!" Cayan's army had been freed.

Shanti turned toward the Graygual with renewed determination. She hefted a knife and threw, hitting an enemy in the face. She tapped a blade to the side before grabbing another knife and bringing it down, stabbing the next Graygual in the chest. An arrow whistled by, sticking a man in the stomach. Staggering, he clutched at his stomach.

The wall of army hit them, ramming into the line of Graygual with a wave of pent-up rage.

"They are weak," Rohnan said, slicing across a thigh. He stepped in and elbowed someone in the face, cracking his nose. He lunged to the side, getting another Graygual in the side.

"Their anger will make up for it," Shanti said. Her

power boiled and built. The spicy quality of Cayan's *Gift* invaded her senses. She smiled. "Cayan is in the city somewhere. He's close. I can feel him."

"Where?" Rohnan jumped to the side, a blade narrowly missing him. "I nearly lost a cheek."

"Pay attention!" Shanti said, her heart in her throat. She *blasted* out with her *Gift* before dropping her shields again. Graygual in front of her clutched their heads and sank to the ground. Pain battered her head. Energy leaked from her body.

"I don't have much left," Shanti called to Rohnan. "Give me a miracle."

Arrows rained down in front of them, fewer now than a few minutes ago. The women were running out of supplies.

Rohnan grunted, turning with a limp and taking out someone to his right.

They pushed on, Shanti using sword then *Gift,* cutting people down. The class of fighter was decent, though. Each step was grueling.

Something flew into the crowd up ahead. An explosion tossed three bodies into the air. Shanti flinched from the concussion of air as debris rained down. Another object flew, sounding another explosion a moment later.

The untrained panicked.

A Graygual ran at Shanti, his eyes wild, his sword

tip down. She ran him through as arrows rained, turning the Graygual into pincushions. Another sprinted by, screaming in fear.

An explosion shook the ground, much too close.

"Their aim leaves something to be desired," Rohnan said. He turned a sword away before stabbing forward. A Graygual sword clattered to the ground.

Shanti tore away her shields before sending a pulse of *fire* into the minds before her. Shrieks filled the air right before her power surged. A wave of deep, intense power rumbled toward them from the other direction.

"Cayan!" Shanti *searched,* letting the army push ahead of her, giving her a moment to concentrate on something other than the battle. She felt him, angry and focused, making his way toward her. And then she felt another. Sharp and intense, she felt someone she grew up with. Trained with. Learned with and fought beside. Then she felt the rest of them. Mela, Sayas, Dannon, Tanna...*they were here!*

"Rohnan!" she said, her voice high-pitched and filled with excitement. Her heart pounded and flashes of joy raced through her body. "They're here, Rohnan! They live!"

Shanti reached out to them mentally and sucked them into a merge as natural as breathing. Joy and bliss burst from each as they felt her. Their minds fit together like pieces of a puzzle. Except now there was one more.

She felt confused and out of sorts. Cayan's deep well of power was a strange new facet to an old way of working her power.

Shanti reorganized her thoughts as the minds in the group also changed. Instead of Kallon pushing up to link more firmly with her mind, the other minds backed away, making room for Cayan. The *Joined* power took precedence, with the lesser power bolstering them ever higher. Then Rohnan's *Gift* was sprinkled on top, giving them insight into their enemy's actions. It was only when they were together like this that each *Gift* could feed off the other. Shanti hadn't realized how lame she'd been without them, and how powerful they all were now.

"Kallon will not like being pushed further down in the ranking," Rohnan said with a delighted chuckle. "Their fight for dominance should be interesting."

"Not the time, Rohnan," Shanti called, feeling Cayan getting closer.

Renewed with power, she lashed out, *scoring* those in front of her with blistering mental power. Screams rent the day. Two rows of Graygual sank to their knees.

"More, *Chulan,*" Rohnan yelled, kicking through the writhing bodies to attack the next man standing. "Take out as many as possible."

Another explosion went off, flinging two people away right. A peal of thunder rolled up the street. Men fell or ran. Pandemonium and power scattered the less-experienced Graygual.

"There!" Shanti threw out her hand to point. Working together, as only her people could, came Kallon and the others, stomping the Graygual in their path. Sanders was stuck in the middle, harsh compared to the sleek killing going on around him, but just as effective. Their swords swung and dipped, their bodies glided, their enemy fell.

"Where's…?" The enemy shifted and moved before mostly clearing to the side. The Hunter was blocking himself off.

On the side of the street, riding his black horse, came Cayan. He chopped downward with elegant economy. Xavier and Rachie were behind him, also on horseback, running at the scattering enemy before them. And then Shanti's horse, the biggest bastard of them all, wasn't just running among them—he was biting down or kicking out, catching Graygual as they tried to run.

Cayan looked up. His gaze connected with hers.

A zing went through her. The spicy element of their *Joining* intensified before warming her whole body with that deep feeling that was becoming harder to ignore. Her gasp was feminine and the tightness in her core defied their present situation. All she wanted was him by her side.

"Not the time, *Chulan,*" Rohnan said.

"I wasn't planning on ripping off his clothes, Rohnan. Some things can't be helped."

"I will remember that for when you attempt to run after this is over."

"It is a rare talent to be annoying even in the heat of battle." Shanti jogged, following the scattering Graygual.

"And even with a painful leg."

"Even then. A rare treat, you are."

A wild-eyed Graygual sprinted right, his body bloodied, swordless. An officer ran straight ahead, aiming for the mansion. One of the army tackled him, the army man's sword skittering out across the ground. Both went down in a heap. Two more men were there in a moment, hacking at the officer before moving on.

"Things are getting out of control," Shanti said, glancing toward the women. Most were out of arrows, but they stayed with their sisters in arms, each holding a knife and a determined or terrified expression. "This is not a good situation for them. Things are turning into chaos. They don't have experience in hand-to-hand combat. They'll be trampled."

"He will unite us. Give us purpose and order. That is Cayan's role in all this."

Shanti followed Rohnan's point. Cayan rode through the emptying street, his shoulders squared and his stature supremely confident despite the mud caked down the side of his face and body.

"The Captain!" one of the army men shouted. A cheer went up, from the men as well as women, momentarily drowning out the clang of battle.

A Graygual ran straight for Shanti, his eyes hazed, his hands holding a net. He tripped once, hitting the ground in a confusion of limbs. Climbing to his feet, he looked around, confused. His attention once again found her. As if programmed, he started moving for her again.

An arrow struck his chest. A shout accompanied his hand as it flew to the wound. He looked out to the side, seeing nothing, before crumpling to his feet.

"The Hunter's plans have gone astray," Rohnan said as Cayan rode closer, his gaze hitting her again before sweeping those around her. When he noticed the women, still active with their dwindling supply of arrows, his expression didn't change. He looked as if he expected to see them. Shanti could feel his disbelief and confusion, though. And his fear. He didn't want those women so close to the battle.

He'd have to adjust. Some of those women would not let go of their bows after this. Freedom, once felt, was a hard thing to forget.

"*Mesasha.*" The word was a sigh. He jumped off his horse and reached her at a fast walk. He grabbed her face in both hands and kissed her hard, stealing her breath despite the situation. Another cheer went up, men excited to be celebrating anything to do with sex.

"Here they are!" Rohnan said.

Cayan released her. His eyes reached down into her for one moment, before he stepped away.

Then she saw them. Shanti could barely breathe as Kallon jogged up, his eyes just as intent as Cayan's. Reaching her, he ran a thumb down her forehead before putting it to the center of his chest. In the Shumas language, he said, "*It is good to see you again, Chosen. It has been too long.*"

"We're not done yet," Rohnan warned.

"*He still spoils a good time, huh?*" Sayas said, smiling at Shanti. "*Chosen…I missed you. Terribly.*"

"*Me too,*" Mela said with a tear in her eye.

Before Shanti could reply, a wave of pain scored them then fell away. The men and women groaned.

Inkna stepped out from the mansion, one by one. They spread out behind the Graygual, facing the street. There was now a crowd of black surrounding the house's entrance. Everyone else had fled or gone into the mansion. The sides were clearly drawn, and destination obvious.

This was the Hunter's last challenge.

"He has his best guarding the door," Kallon said, his accent near perfect.

Not all of them had learned the language, though. Dannon crinkled his brow and shook his head, looking at Sayas for help. He didn't get any.

Cayan glanced at the army men again, his eyes pausing on wounds, showing no emotion. Then he looked out at the women, his expression hard but otherwise still blank.

"You cannot tell them to go," Shanti said in a low tone, knowing what his turbulent emotions meant. "They are responsible for this. All of this. Without them, I would be dead, along with half of your city."

"That goes without saying," he answered, just as quietly. "I need to fit them into my usual system. I had not anticipated this."

"You were just as shocked, *Chulan,*" Rohnan said. Tattling, as always.

"What is the problem?" Kallon asked, glancing out at the women with an equally hard look on his face. He was hiding impatience and confusion with his battle mask. He had no idea that the women in this land didn't fight, despite them being here.

"Later." Shanti nodded at Maggie, who walked up with a sure step and a confidence some of the army men probably wished they had. "What is it, Maggie?"

She glanced at the Captain, hesitated, and then looked back at Shanti. "I can clear half of those Graygual, probably." She held up her explosive device.

"But…the Captain might need to make other sleeping arrangements."

"You are responsible for the explosions?" he asked in a level tone.

She hefted her contraption again. It was the size of a small melon. "Yes."

"Later," Shanti said again. She homed in on the power pulsing within her, coiled and ready. Cayan's power mingled and played with hers, dancing in the shared space of their *Joining.* Her people pushed them ever higher, spreading out the power like a living thing. It was like the wilds of the Shadow Lands, perfect and natural. All the merge needed was a *Joined* couple at their head. Amazing.

To Maggie, she said, "We won't need explosives."

She focused all the power, mentally checking in with Tulous, who would spin more complexity into the attack. She then took a moment to relearn the feel of the *Warring* power, a more vicious and one-sided attacking power that would make the assault more potent.

"This is—" Cayan cut himself off as he clamped down a surge of jealousy, feeling the other men within the merge and probably hating that they were so closely tied with her.

"You'll get used to it," Rohnan said.

Cayan's unease passed through the merge, his emotions bordering on violent. Kallon's nostrils flared. He probably sensed the challenge.

"What a time for learning," Shanti mumbled, ignoring the competing alpha personalities that hadn't yet had the chance to sort out a pecking order.

"*Men make everything more complicated,*" Mela said, eyeing Kallon with a grin.

"I'll speak in this language," Shanti said. "Rohnan, you translate to our people. Cayan, I will give the orders as it pertains to the *Gift.* You will need to coordinate with the army."

"You will need to give orders to the women," he said quietly. "I don't know what they are capable of." Unease spread through the merge again, followed by aggression. He probably didn't like that the others knew his emotions. Kallon stiffened.

Shanti gave Kallon a hard stare. "*Get along for now. Fight later.*"

"*She does not hold power over the Captain.*" Mela gave a delighted smile. "*How unusual.*"

"*What fun that will be to watch.*" Sayas laughed.

"When you clowns are done yakking, can we get to it?" Sanders growled, waiting directly behind them.

Shanti couldn't help a smile as she said, "Let's go."

"FAN OUT," CAYAN ordered the army. "Cover the entrances and exits. I don't want any Graygual in that mansion escaping this city."

"We should keep a few alive, sir," Daniels said, his bow in his hand.

"We'll keep an officer or two." Cayan looked at the women. His need to coordinate in battle overrode his earlier directive. "Stay within firing range. Bring down anyone who tries to get away. Look after each other. If anything goes wrong, get to safety."

"*I thought commanding the women was your job, Chosen,*" Kallon said in a low voice.

"*They are his people, and he is the battle lord. We each handle what we are best at, Kallon.*"

"*And what are you best at, Chosen?*"

Shanti flashed Kallon a warning look. "*I will help you remember when this is all done. For now, unite with the group, or leave.*"

"*He forgets what it's like to have to answer to another,*" Tulous said with a disapproving scowl.

"*The fun will be in reminding him.*" Shanti winked at a smiling Sayas.

"Let's go." Cayan started to jog, his sword in hand. Shanti stayed by his side, effortlessly reading the subtle cues both in his body language and with their *Joining*. Those in the merge gleaned what she knew, just as good at reading her body and cues despite the lapse in time since they had last been together.

Shanti's people fanned out as well, but in a tighter group, focused on the Graygual before them. They hit the mansion's entrance straight on, jogging toward the stationary army. A blast of pain hit them. Shanti felt the lead mind of the Inkna and attacked, using the *Warring Gifts* to lend brutality, imagining *bludgeoning* the collective mind.

The lead Inkna staggered backward as the others around him winced. She *slashed,* tearing at them. Weakening their defenses. Before they reached the line, she said, "Unleash the thunder, Cayan."

His *Gift,* bolstered by all the others, with the spice lent by the *Warring* minds, rumbled out, blazing before them. A low rumble of blistering power rolled over the Graygual and Inkna alike, shuddering their bodies before making them wither, unable to withstand the sheer strength. Inkna shrieked. Graygual officers went pale, trying to stand their ground in silence, but wavering.

Cayan pushed, *booming* before them. The first line, then the second, sank to their knees. Swords faltered. Eyes squeezed shut in agony.

Shanti reached them. She kicked the first man in the face as she reached over him and stabbed the one behind. Cayan slashed a Graygual before running his sword through another. Kallon, to her other side, made fast work of those in front of him, sweeping his sword left and right, cutting and slicing as he went.

Cayan urged them through, leaving the rest for the

army men and the women coming behind.

At the doorway, Cayan put out his arm, stopping her from entering first. He slowed as well, sword in front, pausing in front of the doorway.

Their *Gift* spread into the house, mapping out the officers covering the entrance, and those standing outside the living area. There were no others.

"He didn't expect us to get this far," Shanti said quietly, her hand on Cayan's large arm, letting his movements direct her.

"He's not at all afraid, can you feel that?" Cayan said in disbelief. "He must know this is the end."

"Would you be afraid?" Kallon asked.

"I would fear for those I loved," Cayan replied.

"He loves no one," Kallon spat. "He was bred, much like the Inkna. Much like their horses. He does not love; he does not feel. He's barely human."

"Let's make that bastard a dead human," Sanders rasped. "I have a wife to check on, and she had better not be among those women out there."

Shanti grimaced. Half of her people glanced at her with a grin.

"Not a damn card player's face among you," Sanders growled. "I am going to *kill* her."

Shanti felt the minds on the other side of the door, ignoring the yelling and clang of swords behind her. They were cunning and clever, focused and intent. She bet they were excellent with swords, which meant they had the potential to wound or kill some of her party.

What they didn't have, however, were any more Inkna.

She *cut* through the minds, fast and sharp, putting the substantial power at her disposal into the strike. The minds winked out. Though she couldn't hear it, their bodies would've thumped to the ground.

Cayan, having watched her, pushed through the door when she glanced his way. Sword out, he faced an empty room. Shanti glanced to the left, right behind him. Two Graygual lay on the ground, their bodily fluids spread across the floor.

"What caused that?" Kallon whispered.

"Later," Shanti said. There was so much she'd have to explain before the day was done.

They walked into the living area slowly where one lone mind lingered.

The Hunter sat peacefully on the couch, his sword sheathed, a small smile on his face. "Welcome."

"You are in my home," Cayan said in a level voice. "And in my city. You aren't the one who issues welcomes."

The Hunter tilted his head forward. "How right you are. Yet did I not keep good care of your city?"

"I suppose that is your way of asking for mercy?" Cayan asked.

"Oh no, not at all." The Hunter looked at Shanti, his dead eyes giving her the shivers. "The violet-eyed girl. I had hoped to present you to the Being Supreme. But you keep surprising me. It is miraculous."

"Not really." Shanti shook out her arms.

"Isn't it? First you make it into the city under the watchful eye of my Inkna. Then you wander around the city for over a day undetected, even after killing. You even managed to make the docile creatures of this city fight. *How,* Shanti Cu Hoi? *How?* I must know."

"I put faith in them."

"Faith in imbeciles. I would call that a weakness, and yet here you are." The Hunter tsked. "I expected you to give yourself up when you realized the city was in danger."

"I would've. I was talked out of it."

"Hmm." The Hunter crossed his ankle over his knee. "I snatched two women to hold for when you came in, did you know that?"

Cayan braced.

The Hunter smiled, seeing it. "Yes, you see? You would have stood down if you saw what I had planned. Unfortunately, they not only escaped, they killed my men to do it." He scratched his nose, an incredulous expression working at his features. "I am so very amazed by this city. By this whole affair."

"This ends here," Cayan said. "Now. I will give you

a fair fight, if you want it. Otherwise, I'll execute you. Your choice."

The Hunter laughed and reached over the arm of the couch. "Such a simpleton. What is the point in challenging? I do not have mind power. Even if I wasted my effort to best the violet-eyed girl, I would not make it out of this city alive. And if I did? My fate would be worse still." When his hand came back up, he was holding one of Maggie's contraptions. "I might have the timing wrong. Ingenious dev—"

"Run!" Shanti screamed, sprinting toward the door. She used her hands to shove and direct people out in front of her, getting everyone through the door, begging the Elders to give her enough time. Cayan was caught ahead, having been swept up with his men trying to get him out.

"*Chulan!*" Rohnan yelled as his blond head disappeared into the bright sunshine. Mela looked over her shoulder, pushed ahead by a frantic Rachie.

"Get S'am!" Xavier's shout was muffled.

"C'mon, Shanti, we need you alive!" Tobias hung back and then ripped her forward. He then filed in behind her, the last out of the door, pushing her ahead with his body.

Her foot hit the first step when her world turned white. Like a giant hand swatting her, pressure hit her back and sent her flying.

Shanti's head smacked against the ground. A body landed half on top of her before rolling off. A monotone ringing blocked out sound. In a daze, she lifted her head as debris rained down. Bodies lay all around her, some with limbs haphazardly stretched out to the side. A man had his leg broken, with bone sticking out.

A rushing sound filled her skull, louder and louder, before the crescendo of a small *pop.* Sound rushed in. People screaming. Yelling. Someone crying close by.

"S'am? S'am!" Shanti barely recognized Marc's voice. She felt a hand on her back. "That's the Captain," Marc yelled at someone. "No, don't move him. Wait for me. S'am, are you okay?"

She glanced to the side, unable to comprehend. Sightless brown eyes in a slack face stared at her. Blood ran down his cheek in rivulets from a partially crushed skull.

Tobias.

She knew one moment of intense, consuming pain before blackness consumed her.

CHAPTER 28

SHANTI AWOKE IN a sterile-looking room, all white except for the furniture, which was wood and metal. She shook her head, knowing instantly where she was. She'd woken up in a similar room a few times before, and each time couldn't help but reflect on how much metal these people had at their disposal. The Shumas would grin like children when they saw, not to mention the leather.

The Shumas.

Shanti's *Gift* exploded out, weak because of its extensive use in the battle, but enough to reach half the city. All she really needed was a glimpse in the hospital, however. They'd all be locked up in here just like she was.

She hoped they were, anyway.

Her mind touched on Kallon, awake and filled with wonder. He was only a few rooms away and probably checking out the riches. Mela and Sayas popped into her mental map, and then Rohnan, but no others.

The spicy feeling carrying relief bubbled up inside

of her. Cayan could feel her awake. She focused in on him through their *Joining.* Grief colored his thoughts, along with intense physical and mental strain. He seemed to be working, though, probably out in his city getting everything organized and helping everyone begin to patch together their lives.

"Ah. You're awake. Lovely. I've missed our chats." The city's doctor walked through the door and grabbed a wooden chair from the other side of the room. Fatigue lined his face. He sat down stiffly, looking at a sheet on his clipboard. "So—"

"Are my people okay?" she asked with a rush of panic.

His brown eyes flashed up, hitting hers. With a small sigh, he dropped his board to his lap. "I see your manners haven't improved. But I am rather glad you are asking about someone other than yourself. What a welcome change. I'm sure you have one or two more friends because of it."

"Doctor…" Shanti sat up, wincing. Her head throbbed. She touched it gingerly, feeling the bandage.

"It hurts to sit up, doesn't it? That is because you're injured. Or did you plan to self-diagnose, like usual?"

"I'm fine, but I won't ask you again. Are my people okay?"

He glanced at the board in his hand. "I don't know how many of your people are in the city, but I've treated fourteen and released eleven. As for the bullheaded boys trying to force their way in here, they are all fine. Minor cuts and scrapes, a knife wound—Marc looked at most of them."

At the mention of Marc's name, an image of dead brown eyes assaulted her memory. Her chest squeezed, the loss weighing on her. And he was only one. How many others?

"And the women?" Shanti asked.

"I really don't have time to pick through the records. I need to examine you, and then see to the others."

"No need. I'm fine." She pulled back the sheets as her door opened. Kallon walked in wearing nothing but a few bandages and a lot of scrapes.

"Ah yes, one of yours, I take it?" The doctor got up with a put-upon expression. "He doesn't like the bed gowns, either. Go figure."

"Are you well?" Shanti asked Kallon.

"He seems to think so." The doctor pursed his lips. "A people of nudists and doctors, hmm?" The doctor focused on Kallon. "And don't worry, the cold has that effect. I'm sure it won't stop you from getting dates."

Kallon's brow scrunched up in confusion.

"Did Cayan get admitted?" Shanti asked as she threw her legs over the edge of the bed and stood. A searing pain exploded up her leg. Reaching out to brace herself on Kallon's arm, she pulled up the end of the nightgown. A white bandage covered the side of her right thigh.

"A piece of wood lodged in your thigh," the doctor said, having stopped at the door. "If you women are going to play with explosives, you reap what you sow. And the Captain has been discharged. Not because he is well, mind you, but because he is apparently too important to listen to my advice. I don't know why I even bother."

The doctor's eyebrows settled over his eyes before he walked out.

"*He is put out by his profession?*" Kallon asked.

"*He is put out by people challenging his authority. Do you have any information?*"

Kallon shook his head, slipping his arm around her waist to help her stand. "*No. The healer wouldn't tell me anything. I was waiting for you to be ready before we left. Sayas and Mela recently woke up, and Rohnan has been resting. He has a back wound that is bothering him.*"

She glanced down at his body, and then surveyed the room. As expected, she had no clothes other than the silly drape that tangled her feet when in bed. "*You will need to cover up. These people don't like nudity.*"

"*Yes, I got that impression. I'd rather not wear a dress, however.*"

"*Me neither, but you don't see me complaining.*" Shanti failed to mention her previous stays. It would just confuse matters.

"*Have you heard from the others?*"

Shanti could hear the light plea in Kallon's voice. She felt a pang in her heart. Portolmous had said people with a similar description to her were spreading the rumors about the Wanderer, but locations had been vague. There was no telling if those rumors came from Kallon's journey, one of the other groups, or all three groups who had gone into hiding. "*No. I sent the messages at the same time. Your group was the closest. I'm sure they are coming.*"

Kallon's expression was troubled, but he nodded.

"*Come on,*" Shanti said. There was no point in worrying about it now. "*Let's get the others and see…where we stand.*"

"*You are close to these people,*" Kallon said as they left the room.

"*Yes. I don't want anything to harm them. They've helped me.*"

"*And the Captain.*"

"*Yes.*"

"*You've* Joined *with him…*"

Shanti opened Mela's room. She sat on the bed, her gown tucked up to her waist. Her eyes lit up when Shanti entered. "*Chosen!*" She hopped up, and then staggered, grunting in pain. Shanti stepped forward to grab her, stepping on her bad leg and teetering toward the wall. They hit with a thud.

"*I hope the Graygual give us a break. I could use a bath.*" Mela straightened up, hugging Shanti close.

"What the fuck is going on?" Sanders stopped outside the room. Angry red marks scored the side of his face and ripped the skin down his arm. "Why the hell is everyone naked?"

"Oh, I see you're releasing yourself, too," the doctor's voice drifted in. "Why does that not surprise me?"

"Because you're smart, doc, that's why," Sanders replied.

"Smart enough to be ignored, yes." The doctor walked by with a shaking head.

"*Put some clothes on,*" Shanti told the others.

"Shanti, a word?" Sanders said, glancing at Mela and then ripping his eyes skyward. He moved out of the line of sight.

Shanti glanced at Kallon, silently letting him know she was stepping out, and then left the room, closing the door behind her. Sanders stood in the hall, his body stiff, his mind uncomfortable. Shanti couldn't tell if it was physical or emotional. Whichever it was, Sanders was hiding it behind an impatient mask.

"I'm glad you're okay," Shanti said, stopping next to him.

Sanders' jaw clenched. "I told the Captain I wouldn't berate you for dragging all the women into your folly. I swore I wouldn't mention that you and I are going to have it out for involving Junice in those plots. And I planned not to let it slip, in a mushy sort of way, that I am eternally grateful to you for saving my wife's life. That is a debt I will never be able to repay, but I will keep trying for the rest of my life. I'll guard your back like family." He cleared his throat. "So I'll just keep all of that to myself."

Warmth and affection spread through Shanti, something that would probably make Sanders uncomfortable. She tried to clasp her hands behind her back, but her shoulder ached. Instead, she tightened her lips and said, "Mhm."

"What I did want to say is…I don't know what your deal is with Mister Striking in there, but if you play the Captain false, I will rip your limbs off and beat you with them. If I have to sneak up on you to do so, I will. I have no problem sucker-punching a woman if that woman is you, got it?"

Shanti laughed. "You will have your work cut out for you, guarding the back of someone with no limbs…"

"Don't make me have to accept that challenge." Sanders glanced down the hall and lowered his voice. When his gaze hit Shanti's again, it was serious. "Look, the Captain has been through a lot of shit in his life, and it's about to get worse. He hasn't really had a break.

Now, for whatever reason, he likes you. Don't ask me why—you're a huge pain the ass. But he does. So do the man a favor—if you aren't on his level, break it off. Don't drag him around by the nose while you shack up with some pretty foreign man, and don't make him look a fool. That's all I'm saying."

"Kallon and I have a tie similar to you and the Captain, we just touch more. All my people touch more, or haven't you noticed with Rohnan and I? I have no romantic ties."

Sanders made a sound like "Hmph." He took a step away. "Well, if you plan to get touchy-feely with a bunch of guys, you should expect the Captain to lose his shit. I'm just throwing that out there."

Shanti laughed and headed back into the room to grab the other two.

"And put some damn clothes on! You don't need to go flashing at the whole city!"

As Sanders strode down the hall, obviously trying to hide a limp, Shanti looked down at herself. "I'm covered." It was then she noticed the draft in the back. "Mostly covered, anyway."

AFTER SHE HAD bathed and dressed, Shanti walked across the city slowly, trying not to favor her right leg. The wound throbbed, her head pounded, and her body felt as weak as a water reed, but she refused to show weakness in a city that was mourning.

Kallon and Rohnan flanked her, quiet and somber. The rest of her people walked behind, knowing where they were headed, and giving their support.

"S'am." Valencia passed with a scrape down her face and wearing a plain brown dress. Her eyes were red and puffy from crying, but her face was determined. Both sorrow and pride emanated from her.

"Shoo-lan." A man with a bandage around his head touched his fist to his chest.

"Shoo-lan." Another man nodded slightly. Yet another touched his fist to his heart.

As she walked down the lane, people slowed, watching her. Those in her path veered to the side, saying her name and nodding or touching their chest.

"S'am." Marc jogged across the street, walking away from a woman with her arm in a sling. He glanced at Rohnan, gave a tick of his head in hello, and then flinched when he met Kallon's eyes.

Kallon dropped back with the others.

"Look, S'am," Marc said, walking close to her. "There's something you should know before you go over there." Marc lowered his voice. "The men aren't really pleased that the women put themselves in harm's way. I mean, most are grateful, of course. We all realize that without them, we wouldn't have been able to take back the city. But we do things a certain way here.

Change is hard."

"What's your point?"

"My point is, you might just...be a bit delicate where the women using weapons are concerned, you know? Let things come around gradually."

"War doesn't allow for gradual. You can't let a person spread their wings when you need them, and expect them to be content to let you clip their wings again when you're done with them. They were needed, they rose to the challenge, and now you will need to rise to the challenge as well."

"*Chulan* doesn't have subtlety, Marc." Rohnan's voice was colored with humor.

Sayas and Mela both chuckled.

"Okay, but if you go trying to train people's mothers and wives right in front of their faces, they're going to get pissed, S'am," Marc said, flustered. "You're going to get pushback. That's all I'm saying."

"Marc, some of those women are excellent archers. If they can stand on the wall and keep this city from being taken again, then I will make sure they are trained to do so. Ruisa has proven that women of this city can fight. Let some of the others prove their value as well."

"Please don't make me train with my mom, S'am," Marc whined. "She'd embarrass me."

Rohnan started to laugh, passing on what Marc had said to those who didn't speak the language. More chuckles sounded before her.

The smile drifted from Shanti's face when she saw the large expanse of park up ahead. A few trees were scarred and had been hacked into. The ground was torn up with clumps of mud and mounds of dirt. In the middle, laid out between the trees with their hands on their chests and daisies on their closed eyes, were the fallen.

Shanti took a deep breath, not allowing guilt to invade the moment. The fighters here didn't deserve that. She knew they wouldn't accept it.

Crying floated through the air. Many kneeled or stood between their friends and family, mourning with red eyes or tears streaming down their cheeks. A few just stood and stared out at nothing, eyes unfocused and faces utterly slack. Emotion and loss had dragged them under.

Rohnan faltered, grabbing on to Mela to stay upright. Shanti and the rest of her people closed down their shields, trying to muffle the intense grief that slapped them.

Shanti made her way through the dead slowly, looking on peaceful faces, many of which she'd never seen before. She stopped when she came to the first female, a woman in her later years with graying hair and a lined face. Tucked into her hands was a bow so worn and used it was obvious she'd been working with it for many years.

"She loved archery." Shanti looked up to find a man the same age as the woman. His eyes were red and swollen. Beside him stood a man of Shanti's age with a bandage wrapped around his upper arm. "She was the best shot in the family." The older man smiled fondly. "She'd always said she would be the best in the army if they had allowed her to fight."

The older man put his hand on the younger man's shoulder, looking down on his wife.

Shanti moved on, slowly, giving her respects. When she came to a middle-aged man, the woman standing with two children beside him said, "He felt helpless when they dragged him from the house. He tried to protect us. He was worried of what the Graygual would do." She sniffed. Her lip started to tremble. "They chained him in the park with the other army men. He got to defend his city in the end, though. He protected us in the end." She squeezed her children to her.

Shanti continued until she saw the Honor Guard gathered off to the right. They stood with miserable faces and bowed heads. Shanti felt Rohnan's hand on her shoulder. She'd been dreading this.

She stopped beside Daniels and Tomous. She looked down on Tobias' blank face.

"He fought hard," Tomous said in a grave voice. "He was always ready with a joke."

Shanti nodded slowly, memorizing his features. Tears came to her eyes, threatening to overcome her.

A low hum started behind her. And then around her, as her people spread out around the body. The humming grew louder as Shanti's emotion rose, before turning into a sorrowful melody. Her people's voices climbed, singing the song of the dead. The song of the lost. Singing to the Elders to take the fighter's soul and place him among the stars so that he might guide their feet in battle.

Kallon sang out the words, his voice deep and clear. A few others took up the harmony as her people pushed in close, wrapping their arms around each other. They pulled Daniels, Tomous, and the Honor Guard into their embrace, forming two tight circles around Tobias' body. Soon the entire field was quiet, listening to the solemn tune. When the song came to the end, Kallon sang it once more, this time for the other mourners.

Finally, with tears streaming down her face, Shanti said goodbye to Tobias for the last time. "I will miss you, my friend." She entwined her fingers in Rohnan's and moved on through the rest of the fallen.

CHAPTER 29

TWO DAYS AFTER the battle, Shanti saw Cayan standing quietly outside his mansion, looking up at the ruin. The front right had been blasted out, showing the scarred and blackened interior. The fire caused by the explosion had eaten through to the upper floor and damaged half the rooms on that side. The other end of the house was mostly intact, thankfully. The Hunter had kept good care of it while he had been there.

Shanti walked up beside him quietly and slipped her hand into his. He took his hand back and threw his big arm around her shoulders, hugging her close. Give the man a little…

"It could've been a lot worse," Cayan said in a somber tone. "We lost people, but we could've lost a whole city. I hate to say it, but we were lucky it was the Hunter and not someone else. He was after *us*. He was content to keep the city in order while he waited."

"What will you do now?" she asked quietly.

"Rebuild my house. Clean up our city."

Shanti felt the bubble of joy at *our city,* but just as quickly stiffened. She needed to talk to him about their plans. *Her* plans. She needed to tell him that she couldn't stay. Her duty wouldn't allow it. And she needed to do it now before it became any harder.

She'd opened her mouth to spill it out when they heard shouting.

Her people filed into the street a moment before she threw up her shields and clued in to the minds walking quietly into Cayan's lands. She glanced at Kallon, the one chosen to monitor their surroundings while everyone else got a needed break. "*You're getting slow. We should've known about intruders before the sentries.*"

"*He knew.*" Kallon pointed at Cayan. "*He is monitoring at all times. I did not want to...provoke him.*"

Kallon didn't want to speed up their penis-measuring contest before Cayan was totally healed, he meant. Shanti rolled her eyes.

"*He is trying to do too much,*" Mela said. "*You must scale him back for his health.*"

Shanti blew out a breath. That was easier said than done. Cayan wasn't a man to rest after his city had been taken by another. She should've known he wouldn't shut off. It was another thing she'd need to talk to him about.

"It's the Shadow," Cayan said in a monotone as he continued to look up at his house. He looked at her a moment later, and then turned toward the gate. His eyes and mind both warred with loss and exhaustion. "They made great time."

As they started away, Shanti's people, as one, moved behind them, fanned out, and completely synchronized.

"Not even the Shadow work together like your people," Cayan said in a low tone as Sanders came jogging into view.

"I just heard we have visitors, sir." Sanders glanced around them. "Looks like we don't need the sentries as much."

"It's the Shadow," Shanti said as they neared the gate. "Urgency rides their movements."

"The Shadow?" Sanders fell in beside them. "They shouldn't be here for another half-week."

"Sir! Sir!" A man jogged at them with a harried expression. "The intruders have huge animals with them! Should we take them down?"

"No." Cayan stopped just inside the gate. "They're friendly. The Shadow people come to aid us."

The news of who came spread quietly until the word "Shadow" was whispered within waiting crowds. A few women, including Maggie and Alena, showed up in pants and with bows, coming from practicing with their weapons.

Sanders mouth turned into a thin line. He was pretending he didn't notice. Cayan kept his face completely neutral. He'd already admitted that having more archers was a great thing, but including them in training would be tricky. A great many men had grudgingly accepted Shanti into their midst, but that was because she could easily kill them, and she wasn't their kind. They could ignore her. Having their wives training, or their daughters, made more than a few uncomfortable. They joined the army to keep their loved ones safe, not to fight beside them and possibly see them die.

Three black shapes came sprinting through the open gates.

"What the—" Men tripped as they back-pedaled, pulling out their swords. Maggie nocked her arrow as Alena dashed out of sight.

The three cats bounded up to Cayan and Shanti, playful. Midnight and Phaebus, Cayan's animals, gave their feline roars and nearly pushed him over. Shanti's, which still hadn't been named, if she didn't count calling it *nuisance*, rubbed its forehead against her legs and paused as she bent to scratch it.

A man with flaming red hair and a fatigued expression led the progression of Shadow warriors into the city. Three huge beasts lumbered in the back, the fur on their backs standing on end with the fear and worry they sensed in Cayan's people.

"Chosen," Sonson said as he greeted Cayan, a relieved smile gracing his face. He looked at Shanti.

"*Chulan.* You didn't wait for us?"

Cayan stepped forward and took his outstretched hand. Since there were two Chosen, they often called Cayan Captain or Chosen in his language, and Shanti Chosen in the Shumas language. "Welcome. We're still cleaning things up."

"We ran into some of the enemy," Sonson said, his expression turning grave. "The cats and beasts got most of them, but we took down a few with our bows."

"On the way?" Cayan asked as some of the stable hands jogged up, their eyes wary as they looked over the beasts.

"Yes, but also outside of your lands. None of them were officers, though. Looks like you didn't get everyone that invaded." Sonson's eyes sparkled with malice. "Xandre has something planned, I'm sure of it. He is trying to bar the Shadow from the land while locking you in. Our time is short."

Cayan's eyes turned hard. "We'll need to plan the next steps. But for now, let's get you settled, and a warm meal."

Sonson sighed gratefully. "I'm ashamed we weren't in time to help, but a meal would be just the thing."

After Shanti and Cayan left the Shadow to get settled, passing them off to Cayan's assistants and planning to meet up after they were fed and rested, Cayan walked Shanti toward the park slowly with the cats staying close. Once in the trees, and apparently ignoring her people who didn't plan to be separated, he stopped and turned to her. The failing light cast his handsome face in soft light, easing the lines of stress and fatigue.

"Things are changing now," Cayan said in a low tone. "Some of the Duke's men are going home to their families, but some are staying. They know that the war follows you. They want to be a part of it. So will others. Things will change even more in the future, but I want us to face it together, Shanti. I want us to deal with things as a team."

"We already do, Cayan."

"You've made this city yours," he went on, as if not hearing her. "You've earned the trust and respect of my people. More, the Women's Circle seems to think you are their voice. I've been told that they will talk to you from now on, not me." He paused for a moment, his gaze delving into hers. His *Gift* wound within her tightly. "That place is reserved for my wife."

Tingles went down her spine.

"I approve of their choice." A ghost of a smile graced his full lips. His dimples amplified the handsomeness of his face. "Marry me, Shanti, and lead this city with me. The Shadow view us as one entity, as do I. As do my people, after the battle. I would like to make that official, with your permission."

Shanti looked up with a dumb expression. That had completely come out of nowhere. Her mind raced. Flashes of war and pain crowded her memories; she felt the deaths of her parents, and then her people. What she'd told Rohnan in Clintos came back to her. Xandre was stripping everything from her that she held dear. If this city became partly hers, it would become an even bigger target.

She opened her mouth to answer, knowing what she should say, and what she was tempted to say. Before she could utter the words, though, she heard, "Captain!"

Cayan's assistant hastened up with a piece of paper. He held it out. "You and Shanti have received a message."

With a furrowed brow, Cayan took the slip of paper and unfolded it. He studied the contents for a second before handing it to her silently. His eyes were troubled.

Shanti felt her people drift closer, bursts of fear and curiosity emanating from them—they would have to get used to predators treated like pets. She read the note out loud: "The final stage has come. It is time for the Chosen to wander. You must fulfill your destiny. To fail in this will mean all of our deaths." It was signed *Burson.*

"No pressure, huh, Burson?" Shivers raced through Shanti's body. Her remaining people hadn't reached Cayan's city yet, not to mention the Shadow, and she had no idea how to get a message to anyone who was traveling. She needed all of them. She needed their *Gifts* and their fighting ability. The *Seers* had been adamant about the number and type of people who would need to be included in the last battle.

As a growing unease ate away at her gut, she looked up at Cayan.

His jaw was set and frustration raged through his emotions. Over that was steadfast confidence. He wouldn't want to leave his people so soon after an invasion, if ever. He'd want to merge with other armies and try to fight Xandre on his home turf. She didn't need him to confirm all that with words, she knew it as sure as she was standing there.

Shanti bit back an explosive urge to punch something.

"Burson was wrong about getting our city back," Cayan said, reading her as easily as she did him.

"He said it would be best to wait, not that it would be impossible if we didn't." Shanti was walking before she even knew where she was going. Feeling her emotions, her people filed in around her. "He isn't wrong, Cayan. We have to kill Xavier before he can get his army organized and more officers trained. Waiting here is as good as killing all of your people."

"Waiting here is death," Kallon agreed in a somber voice. "His army spans the land. Most aren't trained well, but they will act as the waves of the ocean, coming in force, one after the other, until they wash us all away."

"He's right," Shanti said. "Even with all of our allies in one place, it wouldn't be enough. Xandre is decades ahead of us, and he won't fail again. Our time is limited."

Cayan was quiet for a time, his emotions turbulent. Finally he said, "As soon as enough Shadow get here to secure the city with mental power, and we're sure the women archers can help bolster the ranks, we'll take the next step."

Shanti let out a breath. Her heart started to thump. The final leg of her long journey was about to begin. It was time to fulfill her duty and kill Xandre, or die trying.

THE END

Printed in Great Britain
by Amazon

15989882R00212